# STARFIRE

## THE ORION WAR – BOOK 10

### BY M. D. COOPER

M. D. COOPER

*Just in Time (JIT) & Beta Readers*

Lisa Richman
Scott Reid
Gene Bryan
Timothy Van Oosterwyk Bruyn
Steven Blevins
Randy Miller
Chad Burroughs
Gareth Banks
Constance Beebe

ISBN: 978-1-64365-033-3

Cover Art by Andrew Dobell
Editing by Jen McDonnell, Bird's Eye Books

# TABLE OF CONTENTS

# FOREWORD

As writers, we spend a lot of time thinking about what makes men and women different, about different personality types, and about how both sexes and all types of people interact with one another.

It's important for us to make our characters come alive and behave in ways that we feel real people would. And then, if you write science fiction, time needs to be spent considering how all the personality types and gender norms would be different if the societies were different, and advanced scientific knowledge made for a greater understanding of how we all came to be.

And so, (we like to think) we have a good understanding of what makes men and women different, as well as what traits we share and what values we hold in common. I'll give you a hint: we have far more in common than we have differences. In fact, there are few proven differences between men and women that transcend societal constructs and traits arising from the differences in our biology.

The biggest difference is that men prefer working with things, and women prefer working with people. This has been found in a number of studies, and you can find them by searching for "Men and things, women and people".

However, this is not a blanket statement. The study shows that it is roughly a 60/40 split both ways. That is to say that 60 percent of men are more interested in things than people, and 40 percent more interested in people than things. The same in reverse is the case for women.

In a future where many of the biological disparities and inequalities are no longer factors, we may find that men and women who like things have more in common with each other than men and women who have an interest in people.

In short, gender may become a minor factor in how society structures itself.

Even now, we are trending toward this, though it will take significant scientific and medical advances to fully level the playing field.

We're often told that women mature emotionally faster than men, and it is borne out by the evidence. Many psychologists believe that this is because women are 'on the clock'. That is to say that, beginning in their early teens, they get a monthly reminder that if they want to find a good partner, have a career, and start a family, they need to get things buttoned down in roughly twenty years. After that, options will start to fall off the table.

Men don't have that biological imperative. Men have roughly sixty years from the onset of puberty to achieve the major goals they've set out for themselves. They can dick around for longer, and they usually do.

But what happens when you change that? When both men and women have *centuries* to achieve the various goals they've set out for themselves? When they can become masters of multiple disciplines, including dicking around for a few decades?

When the biological pressures and societal constructs change, diminishing some of the core differences between men and women, what do we have in the end?

We're left with the question if what makes us special is just our particular collection of biological components. Are those things even that important? If we strip away our societal constructs, and the imperatives that come from our lifespans and biological realities, we find that we all share the same core attribute: we're human.

Now, what does that mean?

M. D. Cooper
Danvers 2019

# PREVIOUSLY...

A long time ago, before the *Intrepid* was even a twinkle in Terrance Enfield's eye, the FGT constructed a shipyard to rival any in the Sol System.

They undertook this project in the Lucida System (known as Beta Hydri), twenty-four light years from Sol. While there were many reasons for this, the simplest was that, after the Sentience Wars, the governments of the Sol System had turned their gaze inward and no longer funded the construction of new worldships.

In order to continue the spread of humanity across the stars, Jeffrey Tomlinson, the captain of FGT1, the *Starfarer*, brought the greatest minds from the eight worldships together, including his brother, Finaeus Tomlinson.

Though the FGT occupied the Lucida System for nearly a thousand years, they left little behind in the way of records, despite remains of their presence abounding in the system.

What is known is that the twelfth FGT ship, the *Perseus*, was constructed at Lucida, but it never arrived at its first assigned system. In fact, once it left its home system's heliopause, it was never heard from again.

Or so it was believed.

Nearly six thousand years later, Jessica and Cheeky found themselves in a star system far from home, named Serenity. There, they saw an ancient worldship later confirmed to be the *Perseus*. After being reunited with *Sabrina*, they found their way to a place known as Star City, where they learned the story behind the *Perseus* and how both Serenity and Star City came to be.

If you'd like to know more about that adventure, read *The Dance on the Moons of Serenity*, and *The Last Bastion of Star City*.

Star City, as it turned out, was a dyson sphere built around a neutron star. The sphere was built at a distance that allowed the outside surface to have 1 *g* of acceleration, thus creating a massive, planet-like surface. That was then covered in a protective shell.

The builders' idea was that, rather than terraforming hundreds of planets, the single sphere of Star City would have a greater surface area than over thirty-three thousand planets. It was a paradise that could house nearly every human alive at the time.

But the builders never even occupied a single percentage of Star City, because they began to ascend. When the people realized what was happening, they created an accelerated lifetime simulator, known as the Dream.

The Dream was different than regular simulators, as it was also capable of aging and evolving the mind of a Dreamer at an accelerated rate. Years inside the Dream were minutes without, and a person could live a lifetime in a year.

But Orion found Star City and attacked. To this end, the Bastions were created: powerful AIs capable of controlling the neutronium weapons that drew degenerate matter from the star within Star City and its sister neutron star nearby.

Neutron stars are the step between white dwarfs (what Sol will become someday) and black holes. The pressure in a neutron star is so great that electrons and protons merge to form neutrons. A teaspoon of neutronium weighs ten million tons, and the surface gravity is over 200 billion times that of Earth.

The neutron star that Star City is built around was made smaller via a mass transfer from one star in the system to another. This allowed for a more reasonably sized sphere to be built. It was this technology that was weaponized to keep the Orion Guard at bay, but it caused the Guard to desire Star City all the more.

When *Sabrina* arrived, they found that only one of the Bastions was still guarding the city, and the AI was unable to adequately defend the city on his own.

To that end, Jessica, Trevor, and Iris had sixteen AI children together, and raised them as a family in the Dream. Though they only spent a few days of normal time doing it, they were able to spend almost three decades with their children in the Dream before leaving Star City and continuing on their way back to New Canaan.

But Jessica, Iris, and Trevor have never forgotten their children, and long to return to them.

A return they tried to make in the previous book, but were stopped by the core AIs, who desperately want to keep them from learning the true secret of Star City.

Elsewhere in the galaxy, Cary, Saanvi, Faleena, and Priscilla are aboard the *Perilous Dream,* where Cary has fully taken on the persona of A1, leader of the Widows. She has also used an update Priscilla devised to place a compulsion upon all the Widows, including her sisters and Priscilla, forcing them to obey her.

Joe is still following after her, trying to get his daughter to stop with the plan that has consumed her, but that she has not shared with anyone.

In the Inner Praesepe Empire, Terrance and Earnest are still recovering from the harrowing attack on the core AIs' Command and Control center, which operated the drone sphere that is altering the orbit of the stars in the core of the Praesepe Cluster.

Learning how it works will be key to stopping the entire cluster from being destroyed and made uninhabitable in a few hundred years.

It has been some time since we've seen what Uriel, the self-styled Hegemon is up to. She controls the Hegemony of Worlds, the empire with Sol at its center. Though she is beset on all sides by the Allied Forces, Uriel has a plan to secure the Hegemony, and ensure that she will not be unseated.

Through all of this, Tangel is shepherding her people, working diligently to bring the war with Orion and in the Inner Stars to an end so that she can direct her attention to the true enemy, the core AIs….

### KEY CHARACTERS

**Amavia** – The result of Ylonda and Amanda's merger when they were attacked by Myriad aboard Ylonda's ship. The new entity occupies Amanda's body, but possesses an overlapped blend of their minds. Amavia has served aboard *Sabrina* since the ship left New Canaan after the Defense of Carthage, but is now the ambassador to the League of Sentients at Aldebaran.

**Beatrice** – Captain of the TSF Research & Recon vessel, the *Cora's Triumph,* currently deployed to the Inner Praesepe Empire, studying the methods the core AIs used to shift the cluster's central stars.

**Cary** – Tangel's biological daughter. Has a trait where she can deep-Link with other people, creating a temporary merger of minds, and is able to utilize extradimensional vision to see ascended beings. Currently aboard the *Perilous Dream*, having assumed the role of Widow A1.

**Cheeky** – Pilot of *Sabrina*, reconstituted by a neural dump Piya made of her mind before she died on Costa Station.

**Erin** – Engineer responsible for the construction of the New Canaan Gamma bases, in addition to a number of other projects.

**Eric** – An AI who once worked with Jason and Terrance in a covert ops team known as Phantom Blade.

**Faleena** – Tangel's AI daughter, born of a mind merge between Tanis, Angela, and Joe. Widow designation F11.

**Finaeus** – Brother of Jeffrey Tomlinson, and Chief Engineer aboard the *I2*.

**Iris** – The AI who was paired with Jessica during the hunt for Finaeus, who then took on a body (that was nearly identical to Jessica's) after they came back. She remained with Amavia at Aldebaran to continue diplomatic relations with the League of Sentients.

**Jen** – ISF AI paired with Sera.

**Jessica Keller** – ISF admiral who has returned to the *I2* after an operation deep in the Inner Stars to head off a new AI war. She also spent ten years traveling through Orion space before the Defense of Carthage—specifically the Perseus Arm, and Perseus Expansion Districts.

**Joe** – Admiral in the ISF, commandant of the ISF academy, and husband of Tangel.

**Kirkland (Praetor)** – The leader of the Orion Freedom Alliance (often referred to as Orion, or by its military's name, the Orion Guard). Kirkland was the captain of the second FGT worldship, and resides on Earth in the New Sol System

**Krissy Wrentham** – TSF admiral responsible for internal fleets fighting against Airtha in the Transcend civil war. She is also the daughter of Finaeus Tomlinson and Lisa Wrentham.

**Lisa Wrentham** – Former wife of Finaeus Tomlinson, she left the Transcend for the Orion Freedom Alliance when Krissy was young. Head of a clandestine group within the OFA known as the Widows, which hunts down advanced technology and destroys it. Former Widow designation A1.

**Misha** – Head (and only) cook aboard *Sabrina*.

**Nance** – Ship's engineer aboard *Sabrina*, recently transferred back there from the ISF academy.

**Priscilla** – One of Bob's two avatars, currently aboard the *Perilous Dream* with Cary, Saanvi, and Faleena. Widow designation R329.

**Prime** – An AI who went insane due to unethical experimentation in the 32nd century, Prime was thought to have been killed at Proxima by an AI named Eric, but a backup of the unstable AI escaped.

**Rachel** – Captain of the *I2*. Formerly, captain of the *Enterprise*.

**Saanvi** – Tangel's adopted daughter, found in a derelict ship that entered the New Canaan System. Widow designation E12.

**Sabrina** – Ship's AI and owner of the starship *Sabrina*.

**Sera** – Director of the Hand and former president of the Transcend. Daughter of Airtha and Jeffrey Tomlinson.

**LMC Sera (Seraphina)** – A copy of Sera made by Airtha containing all of Sera's desired traits and memories. Captured by Sera and the allies during their excursion into the Large Magellanic Cloud.

**Valkris Sera (Fina)** – A copy of Sera made by Airtha containing all of Sera's desired traits and memories. Captured by ISF response forces who came to the aid of the TSF defenders during the siege of Valkris.

**Tanis** – Not to be confused with Tangel's former human identity, Tanis is the oldest of Jessica, Trevor, and Iris's AI children. She resides at Star City.

**Tangel** – The entity that resulted from Tanis and Angela's merger into one being. Not only is Tangel a full merger of a human and AI, but she is also an ascended being.

**Terrance** – Terrance Enfield was the original backer for the *Intrepid*, though once the ship jumped forward in time, he took it as an opportunity to retire. Like Jason, he was pulled into active service by Tangel when New Canaan became embroiled in the Orion War.

**Tracey** – Captain of the ISS *Falconer*, currently deployed to the Karaske System in Orion space with Admiral Evans aboard.

**Trevor** – Husband of Iris and Jessica Keller. Originally from the Virginis System, Trevor is now a commander in the ISF and serves with his wives aboard the ISS *Lantzer*.

**Uriel** – Leader of the Hegemony of Worlds, Uriel has turned from an elected official to a dictator who styles herself the 'hegemon'. She rules from High Terra in the Sol System.

**Virgo** – An AI upgraded by Myrrdan to take over the *Intrepid*, Virgo was the rogue AI responsible for much of the sabotage on the *Intrepid* that led it to the near-disaster at Estrella de la Muerte. The corrupted node Virgo inhabited was too dangerous to attempt to purge or store, so Bob and Earnest ejected it from the *Intrepid* in interstellar space.

# MAPS

For more maps, visit www.aeon14.com/maps.

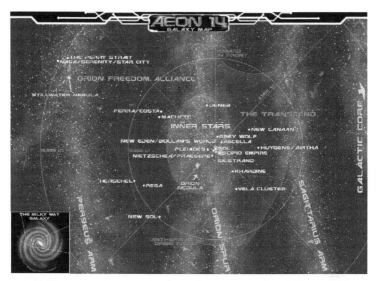

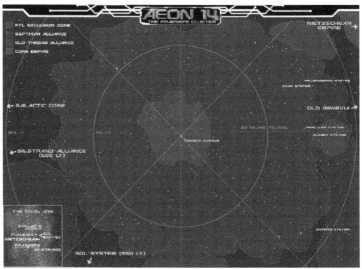

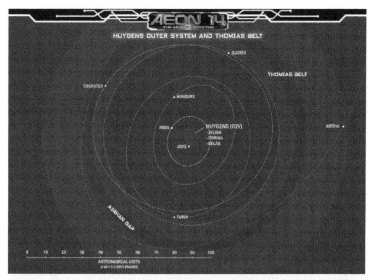

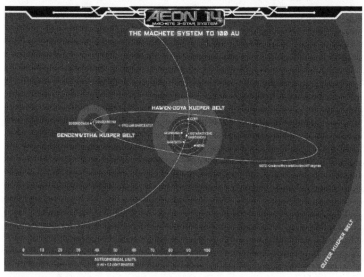

# PART 1 – HEGEMON

## BRILLIANCE STATION
**STELLAR DATE: 10.13.8949 (Adjusted Years)**
**LOCATION: Brilliance Station, Incandus**
**REGION: Lucent, Sirus, Hegemony of Worlds**

The hegemon strode through the airlock without a modicum of concern for what awaited her on the other side of the portal.

She supposed it might be prudent to show a little caution, but that wasn't why she was at Brilliance. Displaying weakness, fear, or even a hint of deference wasn't on the agenda. Her purpose was to set things straight with Sirius's governor, and ensure that he was fully prepared to do whatever was necessary to hold back—and ultimately defeat—the Hegemony's enemies.

The war had started off well, exemplified by the Hegemony seizing control of hundreds of systems, but Terran expansion had slowed over the past few months. Part of that was due to the continued incursions by the Scipian forces on the antispinward side of Sol, which were now exacerbated by the recent attacks launched by the League of Sentients. To make matters worse, the Hydeans had joined in as well, aiding the enemy in its fight against the Trisilieds, as well as launching attacks against Hegemony-controlled systems near their borders.

A lesser person would have been worried, would have considered capitulating or suing for peace. They would have sought a treatise—perhaps one where the Hegemony retreated to its prior borders, suffering once more in the resource-starved core of human worlds.

But Uriel was not such a person. She was the sort to put all her winnings into the pot and go for double or nothing.

Chief Operating Officer Leory, the governor of the Sirius System, on the other hand, was exactly the sort of person to give up before the fight was over.

Though Uriel had destroyed the Hegemony's senate in order to keep the member systems from using votes there to disrupt her actions, system leaders such as Leory now used less direct tactics against her: backroom deals, and encrypted missives suggesting it was time to bring about Uriel's overthrow made their way between the stars.

*No more*, Uriel thought as she swept past the guards who had taken up positions in the corridor outside the airlock. *I'll see this system's COO lick my foot before the day's done.*

Simply removing Leory from power would not be a great difficulty for her, should she so desire it. He was easily accessible, often in public with only a small detachment of guards; she had seven spies close to him, any one of whom could do the deed.

His downfall was not really what Uriel needed. It was the Sirian fleet.

The need for Leory's cooperation was driven by the

fact that the Sirians, despite their long-time membership in the Hegemony, still clung to their ancient—and rather ridiculous—form of government.

In short, they ran their system like it was a corporation. A corporation with an inordinate amount of red tape. Take out the COO, and there would follow an internal promotion review process that could take months. All company business would grind to a halt during that time, and there'd be no chance at all for Uriel to get access to the fleets.

The easiest way to gain that access was to convince the current Sirian COO that she could not only defeat their enemies, but crush them.

Only then would he put his full strength into the fight and bring his three million warships into the battle.

Once, Uriel would have thought three million ships to be a significant fleet, but it was not one that would win a war against a foe such as the Scipians. It would take more ships than that just to occupy each of their systems with a few dozen vessels. Before the war, the quintillion people of the Hegemony had boasted a much larger fleet, but the war had taken its toll.

True, their enemies had been diminished as well, but in her expansion, Uriel had spent her ships in battles against many independent systems. That had increased her resources, but it had also worn down her strength, so that when she finally butted up against the Scipians, she was weakened while they were fresh.

Not to mention, with their core fleets boasting stasis shields, the losses incurred to win clear victories were staggering.

So now, two years into hostilities with Scipio, a three-million-ship fleet could make the difference in halting their enemy's advances, or seeing Empress Diana fly one of her gaudy flagships into the Sol System, like the triumphant victor she had no right to be.

Of course, Diana wasn't the real problem. The Scipian empress was just a herald for Field Marshal Richards. That woman was the most odious example of an over-modded abomination that Uriel had ever seen.

*If only Admiral Sini had properly finished the job at Bollam's World. Then none of this would have happened.*

Uriel's thoughts had distracted her, and she reached the end of the concourse without remembering traversing it. She focused on her surroundings to see that a man stood waiting. It was not Leory, something that rankled Uriel further.

"Adjunct Hurom." Her words were not spoken in greeting. "Where is your COO?"

"He was attending to a matter down on Incandus," Hurom said, offering his hand to be clasped by hers. "He will be aboard Brilliance shortly. May I take you to his offices?"

"You may accompany me," Uriel said as she got into the dockcar that hovered behind the man. "I don't need you to take me anywhere."

Hurom coughed. "Of course, Hegemon."

Four of her guards also folded themselves into the car, and two other cars carried the rest. The Sirian was wedged between two heavily augmented soldiers, and spent the next ten minutes staring at his hands.

When the car finally arrived at the COO's offices, high

on one of the station's upper spires, Uriel gave the man a sour look. "You stay here."

For a moment, it appeared as though Hurom would object, but the two guards on either side of him didn't move, and so he remained put.

Uriel stepped out onto a wide boulevard lined with trees. The entrance to Leory's offices was a lift shaft set in a small grove on the right side of the road, and she strode toward it without hesitation. Two of her guards rode up ahead, and when they gave the all-clear, she proceeded up the lift with another pair of protectors.

While waiting for the lift to reach its destination, she checked over her external security detail. A smile settled on her lips as she counted the attack craft circling the spire, keeping regular traffic and even Sirian military vessels at bay.

The doors finally opened to a space Uriel had been in several times before. A crystal sphere surrounded on all sides—excepting the lift shaft—by the vacuum of space, the COO's office drew in the light from both Incandus and Sirius, refracting it in a thousand rainbows. So far as she was concerned, the effect was obnoxious, but she didn't care, as her vision filtered it out.

Visible below were the hundreds of kilometers of Brilliance Station, one of the oldest in human space. Though the Sirians liked to tout its venerable age, the structure had been altered and rebuilt so many times that Uriel doubted a single bolt from the original Brilliance still remained—unlike the ancient structures in Sol, such as High Terra and the Cho, which were both older, and contained much more of their original composition.

Uriel drew her gaze back into the office and gave a long-suffering sigh. Because Leory was an ass, something Uriel suspected was a job requirement for any Sirian COO, there was nowhere to sit in the room, barring the executive's chair.

*No way I'll stand while he sits,* she thought with a laugh, and walked around his desk to settle into the soft chair before lifting her legs and crossing her ankles atop his cool, stone desk.

The lift chimed, and Leory exited mere seconds later. Uriel found herself wondering if the act of placing her feet on his desk had summoned him like a mythological demon.

"Hegemon, I'm surprised you came in person," the man said in a tone that carried no deference as he approached.

Uriel shrugged without rising. "We have the jump gates between Sol and Sirius now, it would seem a shame not to use them. Though, it almost takes more time to get through Brilliance Station than it does to travel between our star systems."

The statement was raw hyperbole, and they both knew it; she often made disparaging comments regarding Brilliance's disorganized sprawl and garish illumination.

Though Sirius's ancient, class-based system that had been known as Luminescent Society was all but gone, that didn't stop the politicians from playing at being Lumins any chance they got. As a result, they relished in and touted Brilliance's 'character' and storied past.

Uriel considered such things to be foolishness, and gladly delivered derisive comments to get under Leory's skin and keep him off balance.

"So, should I expect to find you in my chair more often, then?" he asked, appearing entirely nonplussed.

"It wouldn't hurt for you to be prepared. Maybe I'll have an airlock put in over there." She gestured to her right without looking where she was pointing. "Coming in person seems to be necessary to get your full attention."

Leory stopped half a meter from his desk and folded his arms across his chest. "You always have my full attention, Hegemon."

"I don't think that's the case. If I did, your fleets would be defending the Hegemony, not holed up here at Sirius."

The COO's expression grew stony. "The Hegemony's constitution allows for all member systems to maintain a home fleet. That is all we are doing."

"Three million ships!" Uriel exclaimed. "That's not a 'home fleet', that's an invasion force."

"We like to think of it as the New Eden defense," he replied, referencing the stubbornly still-independent system with an unapologetic shrug. "We'll make it too costly to attack Sirius, just like we have for the past six thousand years."

Uriel rolled her eyes and sat up straight, settling her feet back on the floor. "Sol has conquered Sirius more than once."

"After we conquered you. After that, the conflicts were Sirians attacking Sirians. You even use our ancient

25

name, Hegemon."

She snorted in response. "The word 'hegemony' is far older than Sirius. Don't pretend to have invented it."

"Are we just going to trade barbs all day, Hegemon?" the COO asked in response. "This doesn't seem to be a good use of either of our time."

"You're holding the fleet in reserve because you expect us to lose." Her tone was blunt. "You're hedging your bets when the front is a hundred light years away."

"Jump gates remove that distinction. The entire Hegemony is the front—barring Sol, where you run interdictors…though you must shut them down to jump back in. How do the system operators know to do that? Or are there safe vectors?"

"Maybe if you'd shut up, you'd know."

The COO's eyes darkened, and his lips drew into a thin line, but he held his tongue.

Uriel gave a nod of satisfaction, and then launched into her explanation—which had been her intention all along.

"We've suspected for some time that our enemy has an advanced, faster than light message system. We'd heard rumors about something called FDL, which allows messages to travel through the dark layer at great speed, but our battles with the Scipians suggest that they have something even better: instantaneous communication between their ships."

"I've read the reports," Leory replied, his tone noncommittal.

"Good, then you'll not be surprised when I tell you that I can confirm our enemies possess quantum entanglement communication."

A snort slipped past the COO's lips. "It's not possible. People have been trying for seven thousand years, and it's been failure after failure."

"It *is* possible, and our allies have stolen the technology. They've replicated it and have it available for us to use."

"Allies? Do you mean Orion, or the Trissies?"

"Neither," Uriel glanced at the wall of the sphere.

Leory's gaze followed hers, and his eyes widened as he saw a luminous being hovering outside. It hung there for a moment before sliding through the crystal sphere and moving into the COO's office, a ball of light surrounded by sinuous tendrils of energy.

"Meet our new allies."

# PART 2 – KARASKE

## GATE WAR

**STELLAR DATE: 10.13.8949 (Adjusted Years)**
**LOCATION: ISS *Falconer*, near Durgen Station**
**REGION: Karaske System, Rimward of Orion Nebula, Orion Freedom Alliance**

"Tear them to shreds," Joe ordered. "Don't let those Orion bastards get to that gate segment before we do!"

"Aye, sir," Captain Tracey replied.

Joe listened as the captain doled out orders to the *Falconer*'s bridge crew, directing the weapons teams to unleash atom beams at the pair of Orion Guard cruisers that were closing on one of the jump gate segments left behind by his daughters' ship, the *Perilous Dream*.

*No, the Widows' ship. My daughters are **not** Widows.*

Joe turned his attention from that conflict to the tug that was maneuvering one of the other gate segments into the ship's aft starboard docking bay. The moment it was secure, technicians would pore over its logs, looking for the destination of his daughters' jump. The worry that they could have scrubbed its logs hung in the back of his mind, but he pushed that concern away, hoping that Cary did actually want him to follow after and that she'd left a trail of breadcrumbs.

*If not her, then Faleena, Saanvi, or Priscilla. One of them would have had the forethought to leave me a clue.*

The Orion fleet in the Durgen System appeared to have the same idea. That told him that at least Cary was acting in opposition to the enemy. It was a small comfort.

"Admiral!" the woman heading the scan team called out. "I have a trio of stealthed destroyers closing on Durgen."

"Good job," Joe replied as he strode toward her station. "How'd they give themselves away?"

"They didn't," the scan officer said, pulling up a holo over her station. "But there are four military shuttles headed from Durgen toward what appeared to be empty space, and I figured that was on the suspicious side. I fired off a set of drones and they were able to spot the destroyers."

Joe's lips drew into a thin line. "If they're giving away their position with such a sloppy maneuver, then those shuttles either contain important people, or important things."

"Segment secure, Admiral," Captain Tracey announced. "We've pushed those cruisers back, should we move in for the second segment?"

Joe bit back a curse as he turned toward the main holotank and surveyed the battlespace. Just over four hundred Transcend ships had jumped in from the Styx-9 base, but they were almost an AU away, engaging the fleets closing in from the outer Karaske System.

"RMs in the tubes?" he asked.

"A pair," Captain Tracey confirmed. "Kill shots on the cruisers, then?"

"Reading my mind, Captain," Joe replied. "Finish

those cruisers, and let's go see who's running away from their warm beds onstation."

"Aye, sir," the ship's captain replied and turned to give fire control their orders.

Once they were selecting an optimal firing solution, she directed helm to come about and make for the three shuttles boosting away from Durgen.

Joe watched silently as the crew executed their tasks, weapons launching the relativistic missiles as the ship turned, flying over Durgen's upper reaches in pursuit of the shuttles.

"I suppose I should tell them to halt or something," he muttered.

"Only if you want to," the captain said with a sour laugh. "I'm pretty sick of Oggies, we could just blow them away."

"No," Joe drew the word out. "Even though they're only half-assing being sneaky, I still believe there are VIPs aboard."

"Got it, Admiral," Tracey said.

Something in her tone caused Joe to glance at the captain, and he saw a look of compassion in her eyes.

<Don't worry, sir. We'll find out where your daughters went.>

<Damn right we will,> he replied, watching in satisfaction as the relativistic missiles launched from their tubes and streaked toward the two cruisers, beams lancing out from the *Falconer* and breaching the enemy ships' shields moments before the missiles hit.

Twin nuclear blooms spread out around the engines of each ship, and when the plasma cleared, what remained of the cruisers was drifting away from the final jump gate segment, leaving streams of atmosphere, fuel, and debris in their wake.

"The rest of the Orion ships are falling back," Scan called out.

"I'll send the tug after that segment," Captain Tracey said, but Joe held up a hand to stop her.

"No, they could be trying to pull our attention away from these three ships. Seed another two RMs. We'll be back for the segment once we see which rats are trying to flee the sinking ship."

"Works for me, sir," Tracey replied, turning her attention back to the targeting solutions the weapons team was drawing up.

Joe followed along over the Link, watching as they picked targets on the Orion ships as well as the shuttles, opting to hit all three simultaneously.

*They'd better do it fast,* he thought as Tracey provided suggestions. *Those destroyers aren't going to sit there forever.*

Even as he formed the thoughts, he knew it didn't matter. The *Falconer* had stasis shields. There was nothing that the enemy could do outside of shooting their own ships.

"Solutions ready," Tracey announced. "Firing in ten, nine—"

"Ma'am!" Comm called out. "The lead shuttle is hailing us. They're surrendering."

"Huh," Joe shook his head. "Smart Oggies. That's a first."

"Patch them through," Captain Tracey directed

Comm.

A moment later, a man wearing captain's bars appeared on the main holodisplay. He looked worn, tired eyes below a bloody smear across his forehead. Joe couldn't tell if it was the Orion captain's own blood or someone else's, but he didn't much care.

"We're sending you a docking vector," Joe said without preamble. "Tell your three destroyers to run back home or we'll tear them apart."

"I already have," the man said. "I'm Captain Jera, I assume you're Joseph Evans."

"Admiral Evans to the likes of you," Joe replied in a low growl, annoyed that the man wanted to play games even now.

"Of course," Jera replied, nodding quickly. "I'm surrendering to you because I've decided that my final orders were invalid. A clone of Garza told me to rescue an AI. No way in all of core-damned space I'm going to die for either of those two."

A coarse laugh broke free from Joe's lips. "Well, I can't say I agree with your logic, but I'm happy to take advantage of it. Tell me, did this Garza clone tell you where to go after you rescued the AI?"

"I wouldn't call it a rescue," Jera snorted with derision. "Animus put up quite the fight. More like an abduction."

"And your destination?" Joe pressed.

"Rega." Captain Jera's tone was defeated. "The clones and the Widows are headed to Rega."

\* \* \* \* \*

Joe ran a hand through his hair as he absorbed the news that Admiral Lukas of the Transcend's 551st fleet had just related.

"*All* the gates?"

"I'm afraid so. And with the QC hub at Khardine gone, we can't reach half the places that have gates to spare. At best, we're going to be able to bring in five for our jumps out."

"OK, that's not so bad," Joe said. "Though I get the feeling that you're not going to be jumping with us to Rega."

"I can peel off forty ships." Lukas's eyes were filled with compassion, though his voice carried only a modicum of the emotion. "Orion is pressing harder on the antispinward front. Svetlana and Mardus have distracted them to some degree, but not as much as we'd hoped."

"The intel my daughters have could turn the tide against Orion," Joe pressed. "Give me a hundred, and I can secure the *Dream*, end Garza's operations, and we'll have Praetor Kirkland on the run in weeks."

"Joe…" Lukas breathed the word gently. "My orders have come directly from the Field Marshal on the *I2*. I'll give you another wing. That'll be sixty ships total, but that's all I can do, I already have the strategy for the counterattack we're mounting in Cerden, and if I give you any more than that…."

"OK," Joe nodded. "I get it. I'll talk to Tangel and see what else she can send."

The other man gave him a knowing look. "Good

luck."

With the holo gone, Joe let out a shuddering sigh, pent-up emotion that he'd not acknowledged suddenly threatening to break him completely.

"What the hell is more important than finding Cary?" he asked the empty ready room in a hoarse whisper.

The easiest way to find out was to contact Tangel via the *Falconer*'s direct connection to the *I2*. But the last thing he wanted to do was burn up the blade having a prolonged conversation with his wife about their daughters.

The only thing worse would be a short conversation.

He'd already sent an update on the situation, tagged with 'I'm sorry', and that was all he was mentally capable of at the moment.

*She's not vindictive, she's not rash or illogical. Tangel will understand.*

Joe clung to that and the knowledge that the many decades he'd spent with his wife would bear them through this trial.

Squaring his shoulders, he turned and walked to the door and checked the bridge's OOD, finding that Captain Tracey was still conning the ship.

<*Captain, the battle is won, why don't you catch some shut-eye?*>

A rueful laugh came from the woman on the bridge. <*Sir, I appreciate the concern, but I've got the mods to pull sixty hours before I start to flag. Once we have confirmation from the techs that the gate was indeed jumping the* Perilous Dream *to Rega, I'll be able to relax.*>

Joe realized he was clenching his fists. <*Well, at least*

*that'll make one of us.>*

*<We've pulled data from Durgen Station on the Regulus System.>* Captain Tracey's voice had taken on a note of concern.

*<I've reviewed that as well,>* Joe replied. *<Admiral Lukas is peeling off sixty ships to come with us.>*

*<Sir…Regulus is one of Orion's largest shipbuilding and training systems. We could be facing tens of thousands of enemy ships.>*

*<Or hundreds of thousands.>* Joe tried to add a note of wry mirth to his voice and failed, sounding only tired instead.

*<Well, we have stasis shields, and unless they shoot us straight up the ass while we're thrusting, we can weather a heavy barrage.>*

Joe barked a laugh both aloud and over the link, *<Captain…that was quite the double entendre. Please tell me that was deliberate.>*

*<Shit,>* Tracey muttered. *<It wasn't, but I sure wish I were that clever on the fly.>*

*<Well, you're going to have to be, because when we jump into Rega, we're going to have to find the* Perilous Dream *in what might be the busiest system in Orion Space…and then survive long enough to reach them.>*

The *Falconer*'s captain didn't respond for several long seconds. Finally, she said, *<And then what, sir?>*

*<And then we board that ship and take my daughters back.>*

# REGA

**STELLAR DATE: 10.13.8949 (Adjusted Years)**
**LOCATION: ISS *Falconer***
**REGION: Rega System, Quaor's Void, Orion Freedom Alliance**

"Location confirmed," Scan called out a second after starlight reappeared around the ship. "This is Rega, and we're only a light second away from the *Perilous Dream*'s exit point."

Joe nodded in approval, knowing that the jump exit his daughters had programmed into the gate, and where they *actually* dropped into normal space could be two entirely different things.

Still, it was all they had to go on, and the search had to start somewhere.

An image of the Rega System was already on the main holotank, and a marker lit up at the *Falconer*'s position. All around them, icons began to appear, highlighting ships and stations, confirming the position of planets and moons, filling in what Joe had to admit was an even busier system than he'd expected.

<*Tallying ships…*> Ella announced. <*It's difficult to spot them all, there's so much engine wash and ionized plasma here.*>

"Rough guess?" Joe asked.

<*Seven million?*> the AI offered. <*Plus or minus a few hundred thousand. Once we've moved more and can triangulate, I can improve my estimate.*>

The members of the bridge crew glanced at one

another, and Joe knew all too well what they were thinking.

"OK, everyone, we dropped into stealth the moment we arrived, so the number of ships here helps us— spotting any emissions we give off will almost be impossible."

<Also, the majority of the ships in this system are civilian and construction. I count just under a million warships,> Ella added.

"Oh, only a million," the scan officer whispered, glancing at Helm.

"Scan, deploy drones. I want as much data as we can get as fast as we can get it. We need to find the Perilous Dream."

"Aye, sir." The scan officer had the good grace to look embarrassed. "We've not yet picked up any ships with her profile, but there are traces of ionized plasma that closely match her engine signature."

"Good," Joe nodded. "The moment you get a lead, let me know. We have sixty ships waiting back at Karaske that we can jump in to scout further."

Though he voiced the words with confidence, the more he watched the main holotank update, the less convinced Joe was that calling the Transcend ships in to help scout was a good plan.

The more ships they brought into Rega, the more likely they were to get spotted. He harbored no illusions that the Falconer could withstand a concentrated attack from even a fraction of the ships in the system.

Stasis shields or no.

"There are three options," Captain Tracey said as she

approached Joe's side. "Either she's here for something, or she's jumping out."

"That's only two."

"The third is that she never jumped here to begin with."

He nodded silently, considering what that would mean.

Tracey continued a moment later. "But we have to assume that's not the case, otherwise we have no leads. Rega's clearly important, but what could Cary be doing here?"

Joe had been trying to come up with an answer to that question as well. The problem was that there were dozens of likely scenarios.

The main consideration was whether or not Cary was acting in interests aligned with her people, with Orion, or was playing some game that benefited the Widows. He only wanted to consider the first, but knew he couldn't.

Even so, the wave she'd given as her shuttle took off told him that she had a plan, that whatever crazy mission she was undertaking, it was with the intention of damaging Orion.

*What could it be?*

"Ella, what would you flag as the most significant installation in this system?"

<It's a bit premature to be able to gauge 'significance', especially without any clear metrics. However, if I were to use 'biggest' and 'most ships', that would be Dock 1.>

The main holodisplay updated to show a massive structure consisting of hundreds of concentric rings. It was easily a thousand kilometers across, and the notation next to it showed over eight thousand ships docked with the structure.

"Seems pretty significant to me," Captain Tracey muttered. "For a bunch of luddites, these Oggies sure can build ships fast."

"They've got the population to do it the old-fashioned way and still churn them out," Joe replied. "I'd hoped we were wearing them down more than this, though."

<*Feels a lot like pissing into the wind...or I imagine it does,*> Ella said.

"Yeah, that metaphor's not quite right, though I guess both are things you don't want. So, given our target of Dock 1—such an inspired name—what can we see on scan?"

<*Well, the station is six light minutes from here, and based on what we know of the* Perilous Dream, *they could have reached it in the time it took us to follow after.*>

As the AI spoke, a three-AU-wide sphere appeared on the holotank, showing the maximum distance the Widows' ship could have traveled. Given that the *Falconer* had jumped to a position only one AU from Rega's star, that encompassed the most populous swathe of the system.

"Dock 1 is well within that range," Joe said, hand rising to his chin. "The question is why they'd have gone there to begin with."

"You know your daughters best of all, sir." Captain Tracey's voice contained a clear note of hesitation. "Do you think they are acting in the Alliance's best interests?"

He nodded in response. "That's the assumption I want to operate under until evidence comes up to the contrary."

"Understood. We should look at this from the perspective of them making a strike against the enemy."

Joe glanced at Captain Tracey and saw an expression of sincerity on her face. She wanted to believe that his girls and Priscilla were acting for the Alliance and of their own agency as much as he did.

"Right." He nodded. "So are they trying to blow Dock 1? Or would they have some other plan."

<From what I can pick up on local chatter, a lot of those ships are in for refit. They came in after one of the skirmishes on the front, and many are nearly ready to go back out.>

"Skeleton crews, then," Joe said.

Tracey cocked an eyebrow. "You think they're going to try to take them?"

"There are over a thousand Widows on the *Perilous Dream*. If Cary can control the clones as well as I think, then she could seize a fleet in short order."

"We have more ships than crews," Tracey countered. "She could have brought her Widows back to Pyra. There are still hundreds of Nietzschean vessels in orbit."

Joe nodded slowly, considering what he would do with a few hundred freshly refitted Orion vessels. "You can't sail through Orion space in a Nietzschean hull, though—not unless you want to stare down every gun-barrel in the star system."

"And if you're going to make off with a few hundred ships, people might keep an eye out for them, as well." A look of understanding came over Captain Tracey's face.

"Just like word's going to spread that the *Perilous Dream*'s gone rogue."

<*I have it,*> Ella said a second later. <*The* Dream *is on Dock 1. Far side of an inner ring. Took me a bit to confirm it.*>

"Well then," Joe turned to the ship's captain. "We have our destination. Let's go take a look-see at what they're up to."

"We're not storming the *Dream*?" she asked.

"Maybe…I'm curious what Cary has in mind."

# WHEELS WITHIN WHEELS

**STELLAR DATE: 10.12.8949 (Adjusted Years)**
**LOCATION:** *Perilous Dream*
**REGION: Karaske System, Orion Freedom Alliance**

*One day ago...*

A1 resisted the urge to hit Garza. The man couldn't seem to grasp the fact that the AI he'd trusted with his life had betrayed him, and his inability to cope with reality had set him to repeating the same few ideas with different wording in a futile attempt to get a more satisfactory answer.

"You can't be serious," he insisted as the pair walked through the *Perilous Dream,* E12 following behind.

"Do you know me to be fond of practical jokes?" A1 asked. "Honestly, what Animus was doing was logical—for its purposes at least. Alas, those purposes ran contrary to our own."

Garza shook his head. "Well, he wouldn't have done it to me. He would have realized that I'm the original."

A1 sighed, the sibilant hiss echoing eerily in the spare corridor. "You should have trusted me. I would have provided you with properly subservient clones. Not a host of doppelgangers who believe they're the real thing."

The general snorted. "Yeah, I don't think conditioned beings like your Widows would have passed muster on the missions I sent my clones on."

"You'd be surprised," A1 said with a slow shrug. "My Widows have done chameleon infiltrations. More empires than you know have been toppled by my careful hand."

The grizzled man turned his head to regard her with both of his grey eyes. "More than I know? What have you been up to, Lisa?"

Cary only knew of one empire that Lisa Wrentham had toppled without Garza's knowledge, but it was enjoyable to toy with the man. Eventually she'd convince him that he was a clone—something that he seemed to have already forgotten from their conversation on the docks—but before that, he'd provide a brief bit of amusement.

"I keep my own counsel," she replied enigmatically. "It was long ago. What I want to focus on now, is how we take out the praetor. It's time you tell me your plan, beyond the obvious, of course."

A1 kept her eyes forward for a moment, not deigning to glance at the man next to her. A part of her mind reeled in shock at the audacity of what she was doing, while another part held a cold satisfaction that she was finally rising above the level Garza had held her at for so long.

*If I hadn't rejected Finaeus, I wouldn't have had to hide here in Orion for centuries, toiling under this repressive regime's edicts.*

The reflection gave A1 pause, and she resisted the urge to shake her head.

"It's as I've told you before," Garza interrupted her thoughts. "I control nearly all of the Guard's admiralty. Once I have secured Farmin and Selah, we'll be ready to move on New Sol and take the system."

"And then you become praetor."

Garza nodded. "Exactly. Then we finally do what has to be done to end this feud between Kirkland and the Tomlinsons."

"Which would be?" A1 prompted.

"You'll know when the time comes."

A1 shook her head. "Well, if you're not going to tell me, then you're not much more use than the other one. I'm starting to think that none of you know Garza's real endgame, not that it matters. I'm not going to do this his way, I was merely curious."

"What are—" Garza froze mid-word and mid-stride. He would have toppled over if E12 hadn't rushed forward to grab him.

"Stick him with the other one," she directed the Widow. "I want to be on the bridge when we jump."

"Of course, A1."

As E12 directed the Garza clone away, A1 felt a modicum of guilt for the compulsion she'd put on her sister. The woman inside the ebony armor was not a Widow, she was a young woman named Saanvi, but she should have trusted A1 to do the right thing, not work against her.

*She'll understand when it's done, when no more of our people have to die in this stupid war.*

Her conscience mollified, A1 continued on her way toward the bridge while ensuring the gate was ready to deploy and take them from the Karaske System.

\* \* \* \* \*

Priscilla's eyes snapped open, and she felt a surge of elation.

*It worked.*

She checked her Link connection, ensuring that it had been keeping up appearances that she was functioning properly for the last five minutes. It wouldn't do for the others to realize she'd been temporarily offline.

When she'd crafted the updates that allowed Cary to assume complete control of the Widows, she had done so with the knowledge that she was handing a very powerful weapon to a rather unstable person.

*Stars, Tangel and Joe are going to tear a strip off me for letting things get this far.*

Because Cary's conditioning had affected her too deeply, and her dive into Lisa Wrentham's memories had affected her further, Priscilla had built a failsafe into her own mind, a way to reset and remove the Widow programming and conditioning, should certain alterations be attempted.

<*Took you long enough.*>

The message came from Faleena, and Priscilla glanced across the small datanode that the pair had set themselves up in once they'd captured the real Lisa Wrentham—who was still standing in a corner nearby.

<*You too?*> Priscilla asked.

<*I'm not stupid,*> the AI scoffed. <*It didn't really work properly on me, anyway. Well, it did, but I'd sandboxed the entire Widow programming setup. When A1 sent her little update, all it did was corrupt throwaway data.*>

<**Cary**, *Faleena. She's not A1, she's Cary.*>

The ebony figure standing a few paces away shook

her head. <*No, Priscilla. She is not. Cary is now A1, just as Lisa Wrentham became A1. Through whatever error was made in her conditioning and her own actions, she's come to think of herself as a Widow.*>

Priscilla nodded slowly. <*I get that, but I don't want **us** to forget who she is.*>

Faleena walked toward Priscilla and placed a hand on her shoulder. <*She's my sister. I could never forget who she is. But right now, I'm worried about my other sister. We need to find out if she put the whammy on Saanvi as well.*>

<*The whammy, is it?*>

<*Seems apt.*> Faleena shrugged. <*A1 sent the two of us orders to remain in place for the time being, which means that if we start mucking around in the ship's networks, she's going to know about it.*>

<*What **is** her plan?*> Priscilla resisted the urge to tear her helmet off and throw it across the room. What she really needed was to let out a good scream and vent some frustrations.

<*Well, it involves going to Rega,*> Faleena said as she turned to the console and pulled up the astrogation displays. <*That seems like an odd choice. From what we pulled out of the databases, Rega is jammed full with Orion ships. Depending on current projects, there could be millions of vessels insystem.*>

<*Maybe there's something she wants,*> Priscilla suggested. <*Though I can't imagine what it would be. From what I can see, the* Perilous Dream *is a lot more advanced than most Orion ships.*>

Faleena was silent for a moment, and then she turned to Priscilla. <*We have to assume that she's still trying to do the right thing, it's just her methods that have become…shady. If becoming A1 had caused her to side with the enemy, she wouldn't be holding two Garzas captive and running from Karaske when it came under attack.>*

*<Or keeping us alive,>* Priscilla added. *<But that's all a bit weak, she could still be working against us. The next few hours will tell the tale.>*

*<Well, she hasn't stealthed the ship,>* Faleena said. *<That's something.>*

*<Something good or bad?>* Priscilla mused as she looked down at the astrogation display. *<Wow…that's a big dock.>*

*<And we're moving toward it.>*

*<Faleena.>* Priscilla turned to face the AI. *<At some point, we're going to have to take Cary in hand and stop her from doing something truly insane. But she's ascended now…or very close to it. How are we going to stop her?>*

*<I might have an idea…like…the seed of an idea, a germ, a microbe.>* The AI sent along a nervous laugh.

*<OK, I get the picture. What is it?>*

\* \* \* \* \*

"E12, I want you to personally oversee the service teams. Ensure that none of them leave the bays, and that Widows handle all materiel transport from the hand-off points."

"Yes, A1."

E12 turned on her heel and strode off the bridge toward the port-side bays where the ship would soon mate with Dock 1. She'd marveled at the size of the aptly named station, and wondered why A1 was going there. The ability to question her leader evaded E12 every time she tried, but that limitation didn't quell her curiosity.

The *Perilous Dream* wasn't so low on supplies that they *had* to restock. Much of what the ship required to function, it could produce on its own. With access to raw materials and a few exotics, it could ply the darkness for decades without need of resupply.

That led E12 to assume that the reason they were stopping at Dock 1 was something other than the stated purpose, though she knew not what that could be.

The knowledge that her sister was keeping the truth from her hurt more than the fact that she'd forced compliance—something that E12 knew she *should* be upset about, but couldn't bring herself to get worked up over.

An alert appeared on her HUD that she needed to replenish sustenance, and E12 diverted to visit an F&W facility. She hated the process for food and waste, and had been avoiding it, hoping that her time as a Widow would be done before she had to endure the ordeal again.

However, A1 appeared to be in it for the long haul, so E12 decided that she may as well get the event over with.

She entered the facility, which was a narrow space lined with narrow saddles down one side, a trio of tanks behind each. Two other Widows were present, sitting still on their perches. E12 walked past them, sitting down near the end of the room where she could keep an eye on the others.

A service door was on her left, and she checked that it

was unlocked — should she need to beat a hasty retreat.

*Why would I need to do that?* she wondered. *I'm not in any danger here.*

She mulled the concern over, and decided that it must be because, as a Widow, she was often sent on dangerous missions, and always needed to be alert.

Her musings were interrupted by the F&W system making its connections between her legs. The experience brought back the memory of Cary trying to get out of using the automated waste systems aboard the cruiser they had piloted during the Defense of Carthage.

In that instance, it had been she who had insisted that her sister remain in place and use the hookups.

*Wait…Cary? Yes, my sister. A1, my leader.*

The thoughts banged against one another in her mind, an irreconcilable quandary that she couldn't put together. She pushed them away, instead watching the readouts on her HUD shift to show the removal of waste, both biological and artificial, as well as the refilling of her food reservoirs and the recharging of her SC batteries.

Five minutes later, the process was done, and the hookups retracted, releasing E12 to carry on her way. She somehow felt cleaner, lighter, and more limber. Her mass was almost identical, though, and she wondered if the spry feeling was psychosomatic, or something programmed into the Widows to make the event more desirable.

The thoughts about the F&W system filtered out of her mind as she walked back into the passageway that led to the lift bank. She sifted through the available

Widows, putting together a security team that would ensure the *Perilous Dream* remained secure.

It was surprising to her that there was no dedicated security team, but she supposed that since the vessel hadn't left the A1 system in over a century, there was little need for one. The ship was designed to be run by one person if needed be, and A1 often did just that.

In some respects, it was surprising that she'd detailed E12 to manage security, but it was also unusual to be docked at what amounted to be a non-secure facility—and one with a large civilian presence.

*Why did she choose to dock?*

The question flitted through E12's mind as she stepped onto the lift, but it was gone again before she could fully grasp it. In all honesty, it didn't matter. A1 had never led the Widows astray, and she wouldn't now.

R49 was waiting with a team of Widows in Bay 14 when E12 arrived. The outer doors weren't open yet, but one of the hatches had connected to Dock 1, and a group of uncertain-looking naval personnel was standing just inside.

*<Do they check out?>* E12 asked R49.

*<Everything is in order, I was just waiting for you before we opened the main doors—though I'm not sure if they'll have the courage to bring the cargo in.>* R49 added an audible laugh to her statement that carried across the deck, causing the service crew to glance their way.

E12 let out a sigh and shook her head at the men and women waiting near the hatch. *<I'll have a quick talk with them, then we'll get this process underway.>*

*<Good. Do you know why we're doing resupply here, E12?*

*A1 has not shared any details with us.>*

A laugh lisped its way out of E12, and she shook her head. *<When has A1 ever given us the full picture? I trust her, though.>*

*<As do I.>*

She separated from R49's group and strode toward what she found herself thinking of as the 'regulars'. There was something so boring about their unevolved humanity. Barring a few small mods—such as the Link— they were largely unchanged from birth, their entire beings determined only by the randomness of their genetics, and interactions with their environments.

Such un-deterministic evolution was almost abhorrent to E12.

A small part of her cried out that Saanvi was the product of the same evolution, that before her alterations to pass as a Widow, she was very nearly a standard human as well.

She shook her head, silencing that part of her as she approached the CPO standing at the front of the group.

"You've cleared our security checks," she said without preamble. "I'm authorizing you to begin your resupply. However, no member of your team is to go further into the ship than this bay. If there is any need to do so, you must come see me, and we'll determine the best course of action."

"Err…of course," the man responded, looking E12 up and down, clearly searching for some sort of identifying marker.

"You may address me as E12," she said. "Do you possess a HUD that can flag me as such?"

The petty officer nodded. "Uh, yes…yeah, it's placed an ident tag on you."

"Good, we'll open the main doors. I'll be watching the proceedings, as will the members of my team."

The other naval personnel behind the CPO shared a few glances and shrugs.

"That'll be fine," their leader said. "We have the first batch of supplies waiting on the dock, so it will just be a matter of bringing it in on the hover pallets. However, there will be a bunch of upgraded SC batts arriving tomorrow. We'll need access for our R&R teams to install them."

"That won't be necessary." E12 held up a hand to forestall further discussion of the matter. "Our technicians are more than capable of handling an installation such as that."

"You have technicians?" one of the naval ratings asked, glancing around the bay.

E12 nodded, not wanting to bother explaining that any one of the Widows was more competent than the R&R teams on Dock 1. They did, after all, possess the skills and memories of Lisa Wrentham.

*Well, I do not,* Saanvi considered. *Though I can certainly still install a new SC battery.*

What she was curious about was *why* A1 needed new batteries. E12 wasn't privy to the detailed maintenance logs, but would have been surprised if the ship's batts were performing below expected levels.

E12 activated the bay doors and nodded to the team. "You may begin bringing in our supplies."

Without another word, she turned and walked away,

though she continued watching the station personnel via her helmet's rear optics. After a few seconds of glancing at one another, she saw the CPO shrug and direct his people to begin their work. He then stood to the side, alternately watching the bay doors and the Widows.

The ship was berthed on Ring 7 of Dock 1, and once the doors were open wide enough to glimpse the decks beyond, E12 felt a sensation of comfort to see the bustling activity of the Orion Guard crews.

Not that seeing a hundred Oggies strolling by gave her any comfort; rather, it was the knowledge that a vibrant world beyond the *Perilous Dream*'s sterile confines still existed.

<E12,> A1's voice entered into her mind a moment later. <*I'm sending up several containers with some of our more recent nanotech research for Rega's R&D stations. Ensure that they are transferred to the correct couriers when they arrive.*>

<*Of course, A1,*> E12 replied. *Curiouser and curiouser.*

# WAITING GAME

**STELLAR DATE: 10.15.8949 (Adjusted Years)**
**LOCATION:** *Perilous Dream*
**REGION: Rega System, Quaor's Void, Orion Freedom Alliance**

A1 watched the activity in the loading bay, noting that E12 was behaving exactly as she should. Yet another pang of guilt slipped into her thoughts as she considered the ramifications of what she'd done to her sister.

She'd done her best to convince E12 that her plan was the best way forward, but her sister hadn't given her a chance to prove its efficacy—which was entirely illogical.

In just a few short days, A1 had taken Lisa Wrentham out of play, seized her ship, captured two of the Garzas, and destroyed their base of operations. She'd also taken possession of the metamind that Animus had been constructing, and was certain that her father would have finished the job on Durgen Station and captured that foul AI.

And now she was at the heart of Orion's military power, the Rega System, about to sow destruction through the enemy fleets before taking the fight to New Sol and ending the Orion War with a single, decisive blow.

Then her own people could stop dying to bring about a peace that they shouldn't have had to fight for in the first place.

"A1, I have a message from Admiral Vega," the Widow at the comm station said. "He wants to know why you're shipping fabrication machines to the cruisers on Dock 1."

A frown creased A1's brow, and she shook her head. "These Orion admirals always look a gift horse in the mouth. I'll respond directly."

"Yes, A1."

<*Admiral Vega,*> A1 reached out to the man in charge of the ships she was seeding her packages on. <*I understand you are not interested in the fruits of my labors.*>

<*It's a pleasure to speak with you, A1.*> The admiral seemed nonplussed by A1's brusque manner, his own mental voice smooth and calm. <*Many of us in the Guard had begun to wonder if you were still alive, or little more than a myth that Garza maintained to keep the expansion districts in line.*>

<*I have been busy on a variety of fronts,*> A1 said without a hint of rancor at the man's insinuations. <*One of which has been researching improved stealth technology. As you know from the data we managed to gather from the failed attack on New Canaan, our enemies possess impressive personal stealth systems. I have been working at replicating those abilities, and the fabrication systems I'm sending can produce new armor that possesses comparable concealment systems.*>

<*Are you serious?*> Vega blurted. <*Are you saying that we'll have the ability to infiltrate positions completely undetected?*>

<*That is exactly what I'm saying.*>

<*And this level of technology…it is sanctioned?*>

A1 had expected Vega to balk at the idea of using technology that utilized restricted advancements, as determined by the Orion Freedom Alliance's charter—

but she knew he had a weakness.

<General Garza has authorized my research in this area. He wants to be certain that we do not have another incident such as the one at Lassik.>

A year ago, Vega had sent a team into a Transcend R&D facility a dozen light years behind the front in an attempt to disrupt enemy research on new nano-weapons. Unfortunately for his teams—and the support ships he'd sent along—the Transcend's detection systems were better than expected, and they'd spotted and eliminated his entire strike force.

Not only that, but they'd completed their development of new nanobombs that were highly effective against unshielded Orion ships.

All of which reflected poorly on Admiral Vega.

<I see,> came the admiral's response. <So this is his gift to me?>

<You're not the only one getting them, but we're here, you're here, it seemed logical to make a direct delivery.>

<Very well, but transfer them quickly—my fleet is preparing to ship out,> the admiral said, his tone sounding more like he was doing A1 a favor than the other way around. <Tell Garza I appreciate his gift.>

<You'll tell me,> A1 snapped. <Garza had nothing to do with the creation of these stealth abilities. You'd do well to remember that the Widows are behind the majority of the general's successes—including this one.>

A feeling of surprise at A1's vehemence filtered across the Link, but it was gone as quickly as it had come. <Of course. Many thanks, A1.>

The connection cut out, and the commander of the

Widows leant back in her seat, surveying the members of her bridge crew. Each one was diligently attending to their tasks, each doing their part to keep the *Perilous Dream* operating at peak efficiency.

None suspecting that the Widow they believed to be their long-time leader was betraying them.

*****

Priscilla scowled at the readout in front of her. "OK...that's odd."

"What is?"

The two women had breached the node's monitoring systems several hours earlier, allowing them to move freely about the node and speak aloud if they desired. Neither knew if A1 had checked in on them at all, but with each passing hour, Priscilla became more certain that Cary was going to leave them be until she'd completed whatever plan she had in mind.

A plan that was finally becoming clear.

"The stasis chambers. They're almost empty."

"Core...they are."

The two women looked at one another with wide eyes, Priscilla speaking first.

"She's sending them all out, but where?"

Faleena flicked a finger, updating one of the holodisplays. "She's shipping something out to ships in the 8912th Guard fleet.... Armor fabricators?"

"Shit," Priscilla muttered. "Widow stealth armor is as good as the ISF's now. If she gives that tech to the Guard, we're going to be up shit creek."

"So how do we stop her?" Faleena asked. "Cary could shred us molecule by molecule if she so chooses. But I still think we should give her the benefit of the doubt— that she *thinks* she's doing the right thing, at least."

"OK, then," Priscilla reached up and tapped a finger against her cheek. "We need to inspect one of these armor fabricators to see if she's doling out tech that absolutely cannot make it into general use in the Guard. If she is, we'll have to work out a way to sabotage it."

The AI snorted and shook her head. "Oh, so nothing too difficult, then."

"Hard, but not impossible." Priscilla nodded. "There are still ten of them slated to be shipped out. We just have to examine one before it leaves the *Dream*."

\* \* \* \* \*

Lisa Wrentham watched the two imposters move about the small node chamber with a growing sense of urgency mixing with the rage she already felt.

She didn't remember exactly what had happened toward the end of her meeting with the four Widows who had returned from the attempted assassination of Tanis Richards, but she had a strong sensation that something had been stripped from her.

It wasn't clear if she'd lost something permanently, or if she'd only revealed secrets that never should have been shared. Either way, it was clear that she needed to break free of the bonds that had rendered her body immobile, and get to Garza.

The general had to be warned that the ISF was

launching an incursion against Orion.

It had taken her some time to re-route her optical access, especially while ensuring she didn't alert the two women that she'd managed to retain a modicum of control. Though she was stymied as to how she would regain further input from her senses. Whatever means her captors had used to seize control of her had all but severed her cognitive functions from her body.

Movement in the chamber caught her attention, and she watched in surprise as the two women played rock, paper, scissors, going for best of five. She groaned at the thought of being bested by enemies who made decisions based on such random criteria. A few seconds later, a winner was chosen, and one of the two false Widows moved toward the chamber's exit, placing her helmet back on before moving into the passage beyond.

*Well now, just one? Those odds are much more favorable....*

# A SWITCH

**STELLAR DATE: 10.15.8949 (Adjusted Years)**
**LOCATION:** *Perilous Dream*
**REGION: Rega System, Quaor's Void, Orion Freedom Alliance**

Priscilla strode down the passageway as though she had every reason to be there. Technically she didn't—A1's orders were still for her to remain in the node chamber—but she'd received several notices to go to an F&W facility, which she logged as her reason for leaving the node chamber.

Her HUD's overlay directed her to the nearest chamber, which she entered, glad to see it was empty. Settling down on one of the saddles, Priscilla resisted the urge to chuckle at how similar the scenario was to when she functioned as Bob's avatar.

Though when ensconced in the *I2*'s bridge foyer, her physical body barely rated notice.

As the F&W system did its work, Priscilla fed a stream of nano into the saddle's control systems and initiated a breach. The facility wasn't subject to high levels of security, so it was the work of only moments to log a system failure and take the chamber off the active list.

Priscilla then altered the repair priority, setting it to the lowest possible value. Once that was done, she rose from the saddle and activated her stealth systems.

<*I'm moving out incognito,*> she sent to Faleena through the compromised systems. <*I'll keep you updated where I can.*>

*<Good luck.>*

She was surprised to hear the AI invoke luck, and wondered if Faleena had adopted the colloquialism from her sisters, or if she actually believed it.

*I suppose, given the fact that she's Tangel's daughter, she might actually have demonstrable luck.*

Priscilla shook her head, wondering if perhaps she should have insisted the AI leave the node instead.

*No, if I get captured, I want the lucky one to rescue me.*

With that thought in mind, she worked her way through the *Perilous Dream* to one of the mission prep rooms, where two of the armor fabricators slated to be delivered to one of Admiral Vega's ships were still present.

A pair of Widows was working to disconnect one of the fabricators, while the other was being loaded by a Widow operating a pair of cargo lifters into a crate with one side removed. None of the ebony figures were speaking aloud, and Priscilla doubted they were doing so over the Link, either.

She crept toward the fabricator being loaded into the crate and flicked a passel of nano at its control panel. Just as she flung the infiltration bots, the lifters slipped, and the fabricator shifted to the left, causing her nano to miss. She prepared another passel, but the fabricator repositioned and blocked the access panel.

*Damn, nothing for it, then.*

She'd noticed that the crate was much larger than the fabricator it contained. Not excessively so, but enough for her to fit alongside the device.

Carefully easing around the lifter, she stepped into

the crate. When the armor fabricator settled next to her, she reached out and dropped her breach nano directly on the control panel.

The tiny bots very quickly determined that the device was entirely offline, and Priscilla realized that it would take more than just a few minutes to access its systems and determine if Cary was indeed handing over the tech wholesale, or if she'd done something to diminish its effectiveness.

*I suppose I'll just have to go for a little ride.*

She leant back against the crate's side as the lifters latched down the fabricator, taking care to avoid their actions. Once they were done securing the cargo, the Widows stepped back, but didn't seal up the container. Priscilla was glad for the time, and waited patiently until a minute later, when two Widows strode into the prep room and stepped into the container.

She had to quickly move out of the way as the other Widows took up positions behind the device.

*A trojan horse, then, is it?*

It explained why the stasis chambers were being emptied out, and gave Priscilla hope for Cary's rationale behind disseminating the tech. She was infiltrating the Orion Guard ships.

The knowledge made her all but certain that the fabricators would be rendered ineffective somehow. Not that she planned to return to Faleena with nothing more than hope.

Once the pair of Widows had taken up their places behind the fabricator, the lifters sealed up the crate, and Priscilla felt it rise on the hoverpallet. She considered sending a message to Faleena, but with the other Widows nearby, she didn't want to jeopardize her stealth.

There was no other option, she'd have to ride it out and get back to the *Dream* once she'd finished her assessment.

\* \* \* \* \*

E12 watched the latest batch of fabricator-containing crates drift into the bay under the watchful eyes of their Widow escorts. She approached each one in turn, examining them carefully and scanning the contents to ensure that the Widows within were undetectable— something A1 had tasked her with after she'd noticed that the weight of the first crate to come through was off.

Now she checked each one, the weight of the Widows logged as part of the crate's mass.

The first three checked out, and she sent them on their way, but the fourth weighed too much. Exactly one Widow's worth too much.

She queried the data A1 had provided on the containers and their destinations, confirming that all were to have just two Widows within.

"Take it into the next bay," she directed the Widow who had escorted it.

The black figure gave a brief nod, and the container moved out, leaving a perplexed station courier team behind.

"I just need to verify the contents, and I don't want it to obstruct the loading process if something is amiss," she said, gesturing at the resupply cargo being moved into the bay.

"Of course," the courier said, and stepped back to the bay's entrance, seemingly glad to have the excuse to put as much room between himself and the *Perilous Dream*'s crew as possible.

E12 followed the suspect crate into the adjacent bay and prepared a nanocloud. The moment the side folded down, she flung out the cloud, noting that it settled on three distinct figures behind the fabricator. Two were supposed to be there; she addressed the one who was not.

"R329," E12 cocked her head. "Why are you not at your designated location with F11? You realize I'll have to contact A1 about this."

The stowaway Widow attempted to move, but E12 held up a hand, and the nanocloud sparked around her. "We can see you, R329. Any further attempts to escape, and we *will* take you offline."

"Shit," the other Widow muttered as she materialized. *<They found me!>* Priscilla sent to Faleena. *<Hide!>* Aloud, she said, "Saanvi, don't do this, we have to figure out what Cary is doing and stop her."

"Why?" E12 asked, shrugging. "I've already figured out what A1 plans to do."

"Which is?" R329 took a step forward, halting as the other Widows raised their weapons.

"Simple," E12 said. "She's going to end this war."

* * * * *

A1 watched with a growing sense of internal conflict as Faleena worked to evade the teams of Widows who were scouring the ship in search of her after the discovery of R329.

Faleena had escaped the node, leaving behind Lisa Wrentham—who A1 had quickly retagged as U71 and sent to a stasis chamber pending mental evaluation. Twice Faleena had been spotted, but both times, she'd evaded capture, seriously injuring several Widows in the process.

A1's clones were not without feeling, and the teams in pursuit were showing signs of anger and a desire for retribution against their aggressor.

*<Remain calm,>* A1 advised O21, who led the pursuit. *<I need F11 alive. I need to understand why she and R329 are working against us.>*

*<Of course, A1. We will see the task done with efficacy.>*

A feeling of dubious reassurance settled over A1. She knew that her control of the Widows was absolute, and even though she appeared to be operating in opposition to Orion, they would still follow her orders.

It was easy for them to do so when those orders treated outsiders as enemies, but hunting a fellow Widow was causing some cognitive dissonance for her simulacra. She considered telling them that F11 was a spy, but then worried that their measure of care in taking her safely would diminish.

That wasn't helped by the fact that F11 wasn't taking any care herself.

A brief flurry of shots lit up the ship's internal sensors, and A1 saw two more of her Widows go down.

She was considering changing her orders—allowing the pursuers to use lethal force—when O21 got off a lucky shot and tore a chunk out of F11's leg, dropping the fugitive to the deck near one of the port-side bays.

<Put her in stasis, immediately,> A1 ordered, knowing that if her Widows performed any medical intervention, they'd quickly discover that F11 was an AI housed in a biological body.

<As you wish, A1,> O21 replied.

Watching to ensure that her Widows did as they were told, A1 turned her attention to the team that was taking U71, the real Lisa Wrentham, to a stasis chamber. Her mind was torn as to whether or not she should let the Widows' progenitor live.

It was very likely that she'd not plumbed the depths of Lisa's mind, but at the same time, leaving her alive on the ship presented a serious risk.

*I'll have another session with her once we depart Dock 1, and then remove the variable.*

Her query as to the status of the ship's former commander was met with no response, and A1 pulled up visual feeds from the stasis chamber. Within, she saw that the two Widows who had been escorting 'U71' were laying prone on the deck. There was no sign of their quarry.

*Shit!*

A1 knew that if Lisa was loose on the *Perilous Dream*, the woman would be impossibly hard to catch. She knew more about the vessel than anyone, and it would only be a matter of time before she confronted the new leader of the Widows, outing her to the others.

*Stars, I need my sisters and R329 to be on my side. I can't do this alone, not with all these enemies surrounding me.*

She reached out to F11, who was laying prone and under guard as a stasis pod was brought to her.

*<Please stop fighting me. I need your help. Lisa Wrentham has escaped.>*

No response came from the woman, and A1 pushed harder, reaching past the standard Link interface into her sister's mind.

What she found was something familiar, but not at all expected.

*<Lisa?>*

*<I'll break free, it's only a matter of time,>* the former A1 hissed.

A1 shut down the Link and ordered O21 to hurry and get the wounded woman into stasis, carefully watching to make sure that Lisa wasn't able to give any sign that she was the Widow's progenitor.

*<E12, I need you to personally inspect the Widow with F11's ident.>*

*<With her ident?>* E12 queried. *<What does that mean?>*

*<F11 switched idents with U71—which means that the Widow O21's team just shot is Lisa Wrentham. Make sure no one finds out who she really is. And if they do…>*

*<I understand,>* came E12's reply.

*<I'm going to go speak with R329 personally. I need to know if she has any idea where F11 went.>*

*<Do you think she'll tell you?>* E12 asked. *<She's a very stubborn person.>*

A tendril of light slipped out of A1's hand for a moment as she considered her options. *<I think I might be*

*able to learn what I need to know.>*

# NON-ISSUE

**STELLAR DATE: 10.16.8949 (Adjusted Years)**
**LOCATION: ISS *Falconer***
**REGION: Rega System, Quaor's Void, Orion Freedom Alliance**

Joe hunched forward in the captain's chair as he watched the traffic coming to and from Dock 1.

The *Falconer* sat in a pocket a thousand kilometers above the station's central axis with little traffic. They'd lain in wait there for the past day, watching the goings on below, planning—and discarding—a variety of infiltration operations.

Despite how badly he wanted to go in and get his daughters, there was no plan that didn't result in a significant number of dead Marines, and he wasn't going to trade another parent's children for his own, no matter how badly he wanted them safe.

*Safe…now* ***that's*** *a fallacy if ever there was one.*

The thought settled him deeper into a foul mood, and he shook his head and sat up straight. The bridge crew aboard the *Falconer* was smart and would pick up on his angst. He needed them to be at their best, which meant not souring them with his mental state.

"Sir." The woman on comms glanced over her shoulder. "I've got increased traffic on the channels the tugs are using. I think they're getting ready to move a lot of ships off Dock 1."

"Does it look like a particular fleet group?" Joe asked, tapping into the signals and tasking an NSAI with searching for patterns.

"Ships in the Oggies' 8912th have been battening down the hatches for the past day," Scan chimed in. "They'd be my pick."

Joe nodded as he looked over the data the NSAI had brought up. "I agree with that assessment. How many ships have we tagged in that fleet?"

"Seven hundred we're certain of, another two hundred possible. Hard to tell from the chatter we can intercept," Comm reported.

"That's a healthy percentage of the ships at dock," he replied. "Given how many are deep in refit, it brings them down to just a few thousand ships here."

A snort came from behind Joe, and he glanced over his shoulder to see Captain Tracey approaching.

"I can remember when we used to worry about a few dozen Sirian cruisers coming at us back at The Kap."

Joe nodded emphatically as he rose. "I wouldn't trade stasis shields for anything, but sometimes I really miss those days."

"I think we all do," Tracey replied. "I sometimes wish we'd never left Kapteyn's Star."

"But then who'd save the galaxy?" Joe asked, laughing as he walked to the main holotank.

"Tangel, of course," the captain replied as she followed along. "She just would have done it at the outset of the FTL wars."

<Don't lose yourself in what-ifs,> Ella interjected.

"I won't," Joe replied. "The only 'what if' I care about right now is what we do if the *Perilous Dream* leaves with that fleet."

<I vote that we follow it,> the AI said. <I still say that this

*system is far too hot to engage under any conditions.>*

"There are a few conditions," Joe corrected. "If the *Perilous Dream* comes under fire, we defend that ship."

*<Of course, we—wait, that's odd.>* Ella paused, and Joe resisted the urge to press her for details.

Captain Tracey wasn't so patient.

"What is it, Ella?"

*<Sorry, I was verifying. I picked up a message on one of the tug comm channels. It was broken up, but I've stitched together a coded message for a connection point on Dock 1's general network.>*

"Coded how?" Joe asked.

*<Using the latest TSF verbal message cues,>* Ella said. *<I don't know if it's for us or not, though. It's entirely possible that there are TSF ops running here at Rega.>*

"Can't hurt to tap in," Tracey said. "We dropped the relays, we're buffered from backtrace."

Joe nodded. "Let's see who's out there. At the least, it could give us options."

*<Tapping in and sending the coded response. If it's authenticated, we can open an audible channel.>*

Joe drew in a slow breath, glancing at Captain Tracey, who was doing the same. She met his gaze and gave a half smile.

*<Authenticated. It's Faleena, sir!>*

"Shit!" he blurted out before accessing the datastream. *<Faleena! Are you OK, where are you?>*

*<Dad, stars it's good to hear your mind. I'm alright, and I'm on Dock 1, though I'm trying to get back aboard the Dream.>*

*<Back aboard? Are your sisters and Priscilla trapped*

there?>

<I had to get clear of the ship, they were running a very thorough sweep. Priscilla is in stasis, but Saanvi is under A1's thrall.>

<A1?> Joe choked out the word. <Do you mean Cary?>

<I do. It's gotten worse…. She used an update we'd made to ensure compliance with the Widows against us. She's really far gone, I'm not sure what to do…>

It was surprising to hear the fear and worry in Faleena's voice. Like his other two daughters, she always tackled problems head-on, ready with a host of plans to get the job done.

<Do you think you can do more good on the ship than off?> Joe asked.

<That was my thought, but I wanted to check in with you first. Priscilla and I both believe that Cary is not acting against the ISF's interests, but I don't know what her exact goal is, or what she's willing to sacrifice to achieve it. One thing I do know, however, is that she has sent most of the Widows off the ship, along with fabricators to make stealth armor.>

<How many are we talking about?> Joe asked.

<Over a thousand. A lot of them snuck into containers to ship along with the fabricators. I followed another team that got onto a shuttle heading to a cruiser. From what I can tell, they all went onto ships in the 8912th.>

All eyes on the bridge shifted to Joe, and he considered the possible implications of Cary's actions.

<She's going to try to take those ships,> he surmised. <Build her own fleet controlled by the Widows.>

<That was something I was considering,> Faleena said.

72

<Cary must have given them something that will allow them to take control of the ships.>

<Where do you think she'll go once she has them?> Joe already knew the answer, but was afraid to voice it himself.

<I can't think of anywhere other than New Sol.> His daughter said the words he didn't want to think. <She's already taken out Lisa Wrentham, and severely disrupted Garza's operations—>

<We finished that job,> he interjected. <We got Animus, and a TSF fleet crushed Orion at Karaske. If any clones are left, I doubt they'll set up shop there again.>

<There should be six more,> Faleena said. <But we got the impression some had already gone rogue.>

<Not important anymore,> Joe said. <What **is** important is that the next target up the chain is Kirkland. She's clearly going to make a play for the praetor.>

<There are dozens of other military targets she could hit first, but I'm inclined to agree that he's her ultimate goal. So what do I do?>

The next words turned out to be some of the hardest Joe had ever said.

<I need you to get back on that ship and be ready to help your sister when the time comes.>

<I was afraid you'd say that.>

There was a tremor in Faleena's mental tone, and for a moment, Joe's resolve wavered. He was about to change his order, when she replied.

<I got it, Dad. Don't worry, I'll keep her safe.>

<From herself.>

<Especially that.>

\* \* \* \* \*

<We've scoured the ship, A1. Either her stealth tech is better than what you shared, or she's no longer aboard.>

A1's lips pulled into a thin line as she considered O21's words. She didn't know what F11 planned, but if she was off the ship, at least her sister wouldn't be an immediate threat.

At worst, she'd get caught somewhere on Dock 1, then hopefully she'd get away and return to their father.

*I'm not evil,* she consoled herself. *I just have to do this, and I can't have people working against me. Not even my sisters or Priscilla.*

She sent an acknowledgment to O21, and ordered the Widows to finish the resupply and prepare to leave Dock 1. E12 was back in the loading bay, watching over the proceedings, and responded that they'd have the cargo secure in twenty minutes.

<Good. We'll be undocking in thirty,> A1 informed her.

<We'll be ready.>

The final tasks involved in departing consumed more of her time than she would have preferred; one of those was a prolonged discussion with Admiral Vega about how best to use the stealth capabilities she'd granted him. Not that she expected it to do the Orion Guard much good. The armor would all broadcast an IFF signal that would betray them to Allied forces, and not only that, but the fabricators would explode in a week—a failsafe to ensure that any ships her Widows did not take would be destroyed.

From this point on, every action was all or nothing.

Scan continued to update, showing the ships in the 8912th as they departed Dock 1 and began to form up in wings before moving toward the array of jump gates on the far side of the planet the station orbited.

The gaseous cloudtops a hundred thousand kilometers below moved through the steps of their intricate dance, unconcerned with the machinations of the humans above. A1 considered that the planets and the stars would see both the coming and the passage of humanity, that they would spin around one another and around the galaxy long after the last vestige of sentient life passed away.

*Or perhaps not. Maybe we're building something that will last forever.*

A1 wasn't sure why the melancholy thoughts had taken hold in her mind, but she pushed them aside as the *Perilous Dream* was cleared to disembark from Dock 1.

The bridge crew announced their board statuses in turn, and when all declared their systems in readiness, A1 triggered the release of the docking clamps, and received confirmation from the station that they had done the same.

"Tugs have grapple," Comm announced.

"Moving us out in the pocket," Helm added.

A1 nodded her acknowledgement, glad that the bridge crew didn't have to turn to see her—a benefit of the surround vision their helmets gave them.

She wondered why ships positioned key personnel in such a fashion that they had to turn to see the captain. A circular bridge where the crew all faced one another struck her as a better design.

*Something to test when this is over.*

The *Dream* continued to ease away from the station, and when they were two thousand kilometers away, the tugs released grapple and wished the ship a safe journey.

A1 sent a query back to Dock 1 as to a few administrative issues, a mask for the message she had for the team of Widows still on the station.

*<Engage.>*

*<Acknowledged.>*

There were still almost nine thousand ships on Dock 1. It was A1's intention that none of them rejoin the fight.

Helm brought the ship into a parabolic orbit that would see them pass around the planet once before approaching the gate array on the correct trajectory for their jump.

*<You following me, A1?>* Admiral Vega sent the message without greeting. *<I'm jumping out to the front, if you want to come and get your hands dirty.>*

*<I know where you're going,>* A1 replied. *<And I've no plans to follow you once we get to the gates. I have my own orders and destination.>*

*<Pulling strings behind the scenes, I imagine.>*

A1 let out a low groan before responding. *<I can take back the armor fabricators, you know.>*

*<Relax, Mother Widow, I was just teasing you.>*

She didn't dignify the statement with a response, and instead closed the channel. Orion seemed to have an overabundance of people who willfully used their position or station to belittle others.

*You'll get your comeuppance.*

She clenched her jaw, eager with anticipation for what her teams had planned.

# FLED

**STELLAR DATE: 10.16.8949 (Adjusted Years)**
**LOCATION: ISS** *Falconer*
**REGION: Rega System, Quaor's Void, Orion Freedom Alliance**

"Keep us within ten thousand klicks," Joe instructed. "I want to be in range to fire on the *Dream*, or any aggressors."

"Aye, sir," Helm responded, and the admiral looked to the scan officer.

"Anything untoward?" he asked.

The woman leading the scan team shook her head. "None of the ships have shields raised any higher than is normal for insystem travel. Just blocking stray rads and dust—same as usual around here, from the looks of it."

Joe had noticed that as well. The gas giant Dock 1 orbited functioned like a massive garbage scow in the Rega System, sucking up whatever flotsam and jetsam it encountered and pulling it into loose, slowly decaying orbits.

Normally, a massive station like Dock 1 wouldn't be found so deep in a gas giant's gravity well, but Rega was a tempestuous star, and the planet's van allen belts protected the stations and gates from the worst of its flares and CMEs.

The stellar soup they were flying through tested the limits of the *Falconer*'s stealth systems, but what they lost in effective stealth was compensated by the sheer volume of space traffic, which made tracking even visual objects problematic.

Silence fell over the bridge crew as they matched the *Dream*'s boost out toward the gate. The maneuver required little thrust from both ships, and Joe wondered if Cary had somehow picked it to allow for him to follow if he were present.

That didn't match what Faleena had suggested about her state of mind, but he was always prepared to give his daughter the benefit of the doubt.

*Even though that's led me here.*

He'd provided Tangel an update upon entering the system, and again when they began to move. She had told him she loved him, was glad that he'd made contact with Faleena, and suggested that he let Cary press forward.

That had surprised Joe tremendously. He'd expected her to either tell him to bring their daughters home, or come to Rega to do it herself.

The last thing he'd expected was for her to jump out to Star City with Jessica and Trevor, but that's what his wife had decided to do.

*'I'm hopeful we can find a solution there,'* she'd said.

Star City was the product of one of the most advanced human civilizations yet to ply the black. At its peak, their technology had rivaled the ISF's.

But now it was a near-vacant shell protecting the remaining few million Dreamers, the last of that culture to ascend into whatever realms pure-humans attained when they passed beyond their corporeal dimensions.

He supposed that was what would ultimately happen to Cary. She would ascend, and possibly before long. There was less holding her to the world than Tangel; his wife didn't have a complex three-being brain to recreate in higher dimensions.

He worried that Cary might leave once she was done with whatever she had in mind. A small part of him wondered if that would be better. He was certain that the daughter he had raised wouldn't return to him. Cary would never be the same.

"Sir!" Scan called out. "Four ships just jumped in, three light seconds from Dock 1. Their idents match vessels that fled Durgen Station in the Karaske System."

"Aw shit," Joe muttered. "This is going to turn sideways fast. Get us in close to the *Dream*. We're going to need to be her shield."

"Yes, Admiral," Helm said, and Joe glanced at Captain Tracey.

"Sorry about that, Captain. Heat of the moment, and all that."

The woman gave a rueful laugh. "I'll cut you some slack, sir. Not as though you've ordered anything I wouldn't have."

The *Falconer* closed with the *Perilous Dream* as the Widows' ship completed its transfer orbit and closed with the gate array.

Ahead, the ships of the 8912th were beginning to jump out, heading to the antispinward front, where they'd do battle with the same ships that Admiral Lukas had brought to the Karaske system.

There were still two hundred of them waiting to jump, easily enough to destroy the *Dream* before it made the gates.

"Helm, get us in front of the *Perilous Dream*," Captain

THE ORION WAR – STARFIRE

Tracey ordered. "If Cary's ship is going to take fire, it's going to be from that departing fleet."

"Their flag is still here," Joe noted. "Weapons, get targeting solutions on that ship. If we damage it, the enemy fleet will reorganize to protect it, and that should give the *Dream* a straight shot for one of the trailing gates."

The bridge crew set to their tasks, and Joe reconfigured the holotank to a battlespace view, tracking potential lines of fire and running damage estimates for the ship his daughters and Priscilla were aboard.

"The Karaske ships are broadcasting," Comm announced. "They're saying that the *Perilous Dream* aided a TSF strike force."

"Not too far from the truth," Tracey said, giving Joe a sidelong glance. "Their ship is still ten minutes from their gate. Even if Cary has a way to force it to activate, I don't see how she'll make it in time."

He nodded, hand on his chin while he considered the options. "We need a preemptive strike. Take the attention away from them."

"And then what about us?" the captain asked. "We're going to have to run one hell of a gauntlet to get out of this system if we give ourselves away."

"We still have twenty-four pico missiles." Joe fixed the captain with a level stare. "Fire six of them in stealth at the furthest gates."

The captain's face paled. "The gates are active, that could cause antimatter containment failure."

"Right." Joe nodded. "And that'll distract our Orion friends a little bit. Seed two more near their flagship."

His tone brooked no argument, and the *Falconer*'s captain gave a curt nod and turned to her bridge crew, issuing orders to the weapons team.

"Incoming!" Scan called out before the pico-bearing missiles had been fired.

Joe sucked in a breath as beams streaked out from a dozen ships in the 8912th, playing across the *Perilous Dream*'s shields. Given the firepower the enemy could hit the Widows' ship with, it was clearly a warning shot across the bow.

The response from the *Dream* was unexpected, however. The ship simply disappeared.

"It's got good stealth," the scan officer muttered. "Oh, got a ping! Hooray for Faleena."

The holotank updated, showing the *Dream* moving onto a new vector, angling for the jump gate the Orion fleet's flagship was lined up with. The gate was active, and if Cary's ship made it first, it could jump out.

"Missiles away," Captain Tracey called out. "Five minutes out."

Joe wished that they could speed things up, but if the pico missiles boosted too hard, they'd be clearly visible.

The ships in the 8912th were all braking, slowing and turning away from the gates, moving into a half-sphere that began to creep toward where the *Perilous Dream* had been a minute earlier.

Probing shots lanced out from the Orion craft, and one hit the *Falconer*, splashing against the conventional shields. Luckily, the ISF ship was much smaller than the Widows' vessel, and the next two shots missed.

A number of breaths released across the bridge when

the ship moved far enough away from the original impact that the seeking beams missed them entirely.

"That was too close," Tracey muttered.

"When the *Dream* jumps, we go through right on their tail," Joe instructed. "We'll have their vector, we'll know where they intend to come out."

More shots lanced out from the Orion ships, and Joe pursed his lips as one struck the *Dream,* highlighting the ship for the enemy to target. More beams streaked out, the relativistic particles joined by missiles that corkscrewed their way to the black ship.

Tracey directed her crew to intercept, and three of the missiles slammed into the *Falconer's* stasis shields— which had activated for a second before the ship returned to stealth.

<*They still think it's just one ship here,*> Ella said. <*They're trying to coordinate scan with the gates and monitoring satellites, but their data is conflicting.*>

"That us?" Joe asked.

<*No, Cary must be doing it.*>

"Impact in thirty!" Weapons announced, a countdown appearing on the main holo.

Then, just as the counter reached fifteen seconds, a wave of EM radiation washed over the ship.

"What the hell?" Joe swore, looking for the source of the pulse.

"It's Dock 1," the woman on comm said in a breathless voice. "It just went up."

"Went up?" Tracey asked, her voice cracking.

In response, Scan changed the forward holo to show a view broadcasting from a nearby surveillance satellite.

Dock 1's central spire was gone, and its inner rings were broken to pieces, careening through the remainder of the docking structures, tearing them to pieces. The bridge crew was still watching in awe, mouths agape, when the six picobombs hit, and six gates began to disintegrate.

The furthest one went first, breaking into five pieces. Somehow, the exotic energy in the center held in place for a few seconds before it suddenly exploded, a ball of plasma and high-energy photons sweeping out and engulfing two Orion cruisers.

"She had to have done that." Joe shook his head, unable to reconcile his little girl, the one he'd taken for walks and taught how to cinch a saddle, destroying a station with millions of civilians aboard.

"Maybe it was an accident," Tracey said. "Maybe the Widows did something they weren't supposed to."

A second gate exploded, and the Orion fleet began to scatter. The *Falconer* stayed close to the *Dream*, slipping behind to remain between the enemy flagship and their charge.

After almost a minute of inaction, Admiral Vega's ship turned to align its main railguns with the Widows' ship.

"Ready on the stasis shields," Tracey advised. "When that thing fires, we'll have only a second."

<*We've got this,*> Ella said.

The dreadnaught that was the 8912th's flag fired a trio of one-ton slugs. The *Dream*'s shields could have taken the barrage, but the kinetic energy would have knocked the ship off course and delayed its entry into the jump gate.

Instead, the blasts hit the *Falconer*'s stasis shield, brilliant flares of light heralding the destruction of matter. Scan blanked out for several seconds, and when it came back up, the *Dream* was gone.

"They jumped!" Comm announced. "Caught mention on the Oggies' network."

"Get after them," Tracey ordered. "We need to follow on the same vector."

"Aye, ma'am," Helm responded, and the *Falconer* surged forward, closing the final five thousand kilometers to the gate in a matter of seconds.

Beams from the enemy ships played across the *Falconer*'s shields, but the stasis field blocked them with ease. Joe focused on the gate and hoped the destination wasn't even more dangerous than where they were fleeing.

As that thought formed, the stars winked out, but only for a second. When they came back, he glanced at scan, waiting for an update.

"We're...nowhere," the woman said. "We've dumped out into interstellar space a dozen light years from Rega."

"And the *Perilous Dream*?" Captain Tracey pressed.

"Nowhere that I can see, ma'am. I don't think she's here."

\* \* \* \* \*

"Anything?" A1 asked as she surveyed the system the *Perilous Dream* had jumped into.

"No, A1. There is no evidence that the ISF ship in

pursuit was able to follow," the Widow operating scan reported. "So far as I can tell, your plan worked. The gate will have terminated the field almost immediately, meaning they only made it a few light years."

"Excellent," the Widows' leader replied. "Then we can proceed with the plan unimpeded."

She provided a destination and preferred vector to helm, then leant back in her seat, reveling in the deep connection to the ship almost as much as the plan she had set in motion.

# PART 3 – STAR CITY

## STAR CITY EXPRESS REDUX
**STELLAR DATE: 10.15.8949 (Adjusted Years)**
**LOCATION: ISS *I2***
**REGION: Interstellar Space, Inner Praesepe Empire**

"Everyone good to go?" Tangel asked as the final members of the command team approached the bridge's central holotank.

Jessica swept her gaze across the group. "I'm just putting it out there, but it's alright if you're nervous."

<*Who's nervous?*> Bob asked. <*I'm looking forward to running into some core AIs. It'll be like old times.*>

"Is there a reason why all AIs seem to be sarcastic?" Trevor asked from where he stood next to Jessica.

<*It's a coping mechanism,*> the ship's AI replied. <*Plus, I keep being told I need to practice, so I'm practicing.*>

"It's almost like you have Angela in your parentage," Tangel retorted, casting a quelling look at the nearest optical pickup before turning to Rachel. "Ship's status?"

"Green across the board, ma'am," the ship's captain replied. "First fleet is aboard and buttoned up."

"I bet Terrance and Earnest are not happy to be left behind," Sera commented. "Finally getting to see Star City is, like, the ultimate dream for those two."

Trevor shook his head and gave a wistful sigh. "You

can say that again. It's beyond astounding."

"Rub it in," Rachel muttered.

<I have several full-sensory recordings of it,> Bob said. <I can supply—>

"Not the same," Trevor held up a hand to forestall the AI. "Few will ever be able to say that they were there for the 'Defense of Star City'."

"Oh stars," Jessica groaned. "We fought off a few ships' worth of Oggies while our kids fired neutronium at the enemy fleet. We barely got to see the good stuff."

"I think we'll have plenty of chances to 'see the good stuff'," Tangel said.

"Promises, promises."

"I have word from Gate Control," Rachel spoke up a second later. "We're cleared for approach."

"Once more into the breach," Jessica whispered.

<You're so melodramatic,> Iris said, the AI's bubbling laugh echoing in her mind.

Jessica glanced back to see her silver-skinned doppelganger saunter onto the bridge.

"Nice of you to join us, Iris."

Iris shrugged as she reached Jessica's side. "What's the rush? This is just our first jump on the road to Star City."

"Not a rush, per se." Jessica shrugged. "Just figured you'd want to be here in case something went wrong."

"Wrong?" Iris glanced at Trevor. "She nervous or something?"

"Well, last time we tried to get to Star City, she had to duel an ascended AI, and then use weaponized Exdali that we couldn't put back. Oh, and we almost destroyed

Pyra. That was a bit nerve-wracking for all of us."

"You can say that again," Jessica muttered.

*<Well, unless the core AIs have managed to blockade the entire galaxy, the they won't be able to stop us this time,>* Bob interjected.

"There'll be no one to stop us this time!" Trevor intoned.

*<Pardon?>*

Iris barked a laugh. "It's from an old movie we watched back on *Sabrina*." She glanced at Trevor. "Easy now, Darth."

The hulking man held up two fingers and brandished them at Iris. "I find your lack of faith disturbing."

The AI squared her shoulders. "Your sorcerer's ways don't frighten me."

"OK, kids," Jessica muttered, shaking her head. "Let's focus here. This is a serious jump."

"T-minus thirty seconds," Helm interjected, nodding at the countdown on the forward display.

Tangel smiled at the group, glad to have them with her as they sailed into whatever it was they were going to face. At the very least, she'd get to see Jessica's eyes bug out of her head after they made the first jump.

"Thank you, Ensign," Rachel replied, and the group turned their attention to the gate that was growing ever-larger in the forward display.

No one spoke over the next half minute, other than Helm announcing "Jumping" a second before the *I2*'s mirror touched the roiling ball of not-space in the center of the mirror.

The silence stretched on as space disappeared and the

display showed only darkness, save for a countdown that stretched on for almost twenty seconds before stars suddenly snapped back into place.

<Welcome to the Large Magellanic Cloud,> Bob announced.

Tangel released the breath she'd been holding in, glad she could dismiss the worry that the core AIs would have blocked this route as well.

"Stars…" Jessica whispered. "Nice to jump and end up where we're supposed to."

"Technically, we did that when we jumped back to Pyra," Trevor said, and Jessica rolled her eyes.

"We're right in the pocket," Rachel announced. "Looking at a two-hour flight to the gate array."

"Very good," Tangel said as she swiped her hand through the air to shift the main holodisplay to show the Milky Way. "There you have it, folks."

Jessica cocked her head to the side. "Huh…does kinda look like a spaghetti bowl at this angle."

"Would Earnest have led us astray?" Trevor asked with a laugh.

Iris groaned and rolled her eyes. "That's so rhetorical, but in the opposite way you meant it."

"I think you have Earnest and Finaeus mixed up," Trevor replied, narrowing his eyes as he regarded the AI.

"No." Jessica's gaze remained fixed on the view of humanity's home galaxy. "Earnest has a tricky streak, too. He just hides it better than Finaeus. Trust me. He's the one that made me purple in the first place."

"Really?" Iris strode to Jessica's side, looking her up and down. "I thought that was your choice, when you got your artificial skin back in The Kap."

"Well, it was my choice to keep it, but Earnest did it as a joke when I was getting rebuilt after all the radiation."

"It's true," Tangel confirmed, enjoying the banter.

"I bet there's a good story there," Trevor said as he rose from his station. "How come you never told it?"

Jessica shrugged. "So that I'd have something new to surprise you with at times like this. Honestly, though, I spent seventy years there, I could tell you Kap stories for decades. Most of them involve something Trist got up to. That woman was a force to be reckoned with."

Tangel let out a low groan. "Also true."

"Can't ever forget that she was a thief before she was a governor," Jessica replied with a wink.

"Really?" Sera asked, fixing Tangel with a curious look. "You made a thief a governor?"

Tangel met Sera's gaze and shrugged. "I made a kinky pirate into a president."

Sera grimaced. "Touché."

"So, if I recall, Trist tried to steal some cargo that was bound for the *Intrepid*, right?" Iris asked.

"Yup," Tangel nodded, smiling at the memory. "She was duped into it and nearly died as a result."

"Yeah," Jessica nodded. "And then in true form, Tangel used her as bait to lure out one of the parties responsible for trying to destroy the ship."

"Still crazy to think that when all this started, we were just a sublight colony ship," Rachel said, her eyes glued to the view of the galaxy on the forward display. "Now look at us. We're colonizing another galaxy and waging a galactic war."

"Given that we've fought battles in the LMC, it's an *inter*galactic war." Trevor winked at the ship's captain. "Not many people know we're out here."

"Not like they could get here if they did," Jessica added. "Takes an ungodly amount of energy for the jump."

"Speaking of energy, I need a refill." Trevor patted his stomach. "Anyone else want anything?"

A flood of food requests came from the command team, and the big man laughed as he turned and walked away.

"So, what I heard was BLTs for everyone?"

"Seriously?" Jessica called after him. "I've shared the last three meals with Tangel. Anything *but* a BLT!"

"Hey!" Tangel exclaimed. "I'm standing right here."

* * * * *

"You ready?" Tangel asked as the *I2* closed on the gate that would jump them back toward the Milky Way, bypassing the core AIs' blockade and dropping the ship into the Perseus Arm.

If all went well, they would end up on the rimward side of the Stillwater Nebula. More specifically, half an AU from Star City, where Jessica, Trevor, and Iris's sixteen children—each one a powerful AI—guarded the massive dyson sphere and the final Dreamers.

Tangel wondered what the humans within Star City found when they Dreamt their way to ascension. Was it similar to what she and Bob were experiencing? Or was it something different? The fact that the billions of ascended humans from Star City had utterly vanished suggested that they had gone through a different sort of process.

"I'm ready."

Trevor's voice broke into Tangel's thoughts, and she looked to see his smile while Iris nodded silently.

"Good, because we're going either way." Rachel's lips twisted into a wry smile, and she glanced at her crew. "Helm, let's do this thing."

"Aye, ma'am. Going in."

The return trip to the Milky Way Galaxy seemed much longer, though it was almost two seconds shorter, by the counter on the display. Then the stars snapped back into place around them.

Rachel turned to the scan team. "Well?"

"Yes, ma'am, we appear to be where we intended to—oh! There it is!"

The forward display shifted to show a massive sphere, its shell illuminated by the dim glow of the system's second neutron star and the nearby Stillwater Nebula. Notation appeared next to it on the display, indicating the sphere's size. Most noteworthy was that it contained over seventeen trillion square kilometers of internal surface area, which was home to the Dreamers and Jessica's children.

"Thank stars," Jessica whispered. "I was starting to feel like we'd never see them again."

"I've got some...strange readings," Scan announced. "It's like—Shit! Exdali!"

The forward display shifted to show a wave of

darkness coursing toward Star City.

Tangel pulled up a three-dimensional view of the dyson sphere and surrounding space on the main holotank, drawing in a sharp breath as she saw that the encroaching mass of dark layer creatures spread across a million kilometers—and the I2 was directly in their path.

"Repulsor signal!" she called out, gritting her teeth as she considered options.

<Up and running,> Bob responded, a note of uncertainty in the AI's voice. <I don't believe that we can repel that many, not unless we deploy the fleet.>

"No time!" Tangel shook her head. "Helm. Max burn, keep us ahead of that wave!"

The I2 had jumped in three light minutes from Star City, yet they were only six light seconds from the encroaching wave of Exdali. At the rate the dark layer creatures were traveling, they'd meet the wave of darkness before getting a response from Star City.

Tangel sent a message anyway.

"Mayday, mayday, mayday. This is Field Marshal Tangel Richards—"

"Plus your parents," Jessica added, her lips twisted in worry.

"Yeah, them too," Tangel said, while shooting Jessica a quelling look. "You might not have seen them yet, but we have a shit-ton of Exdali about to swallow us whole. We're sending you information on how to generate a repulsor wave. If you can emit it from a dozen points, it will be enough to push them back."

"Mayday seems a bit strong, doesn't it?" Trevor asked. "We have stasis shields, and those can repel

Exdali, right?"

*<We have only run controlled tests against small creatures. The energy required to power the shields even then was immense.>*

"How much is immense?" Trevor asked, an eyebrow quirked.

*<To use Tangel's term, a shit-ton.>*

"That doesn't really help much."

Sera fixed Trevor with a measuring stare. "When an AI drops phrases like 'shit-ton', you should worry. It means 'you don't want to know'."

"Maybe we should just drop to the dark layer," the scan officer suggested. "It could be clear."

Jessica shook her head. "It won't be. The DL is swarming here. Even a few dozen AU out, it's still thick as you can imagine. We're going to have to rely on our repulsors and stasis shields."

"And pray your kids are listening," Tangel added.

"Our kids will figure out a solution." Iris's tone contained no trace of uncertainty. "They are sixteen of some of the brightest minds in the galaxy."

A deep rumble came from Bob. *<Spoken like a true mom.>*

The *I2* had completed its turn, and was boosting toward the city, the wave of Exdali falling a little further behind her with each minute.

At precisely six minutes, a response came from Star City.

*<This is Tanis Keller, Bastion of Star City—if we're being all formal. We're setting up that repulsor thing you sent, but first we'll use the tried and true method.>*

"Tried and true?" Rachel asked.

*<They're going to shoot the Exdali,>* Bob said.

Sera shook her head vehemently. "That's matter. Firing matter at something that eats matter isn't a good idea."

"You sure?" Tangel asked. "You're made of matter, and whenever you get shot at, it's matter too."

"And that matters, how?" Sera chuckled. "Still, it seems risky with these things. I've never seen something they don't want to eat."

*<Degenerate matter is different. Relativistic degenerate matter even more so. I'm interested in what will happen, though I'm more interested in how the Bastions keep it cohesive after extracting it from the neutron stars.>*

"You and me both," Iris muttered. "They wouldn't share that with us before we left. Children can be so ungrateful."

"Gave us a reason to come back and ask," Trevor replied with a grin. "You know…so long as we survive."

"There!" Tangel pointed at the holotank, where a grouping of objects appeared only a light second from the *I2*. Then they were past the colony ship, slamming into the wall of inky darkness.

The neutronium bullets were only a few hundred kilograms each, but at a high fraction of *c*, they impacted the Exdali with a tremendous amount of energy.

For a second, it appeared as though the things were unscathed by the barrage, but then the darkness began to break up and disperse. A moment later, the encroaching wave began to slow where the shots had hit.

*<They're breaking up,>* Bob observed. *<The Exdali's*

*bodies are falling apart.*>

"See?" Tangel nudged Sera with her elbow. "There's matter, and then there's *matter*."

"Who knew," the Hand's director said with a laugh. "Totally worth coming out here for this."

<*If we could send these bullets through a jump gate...*> Bob mused.

"That's barbaric," Trevor said, shaking his head, but not pulling his eyes from the display. "We can't just destroy the enemy willy-nilly without any sort of warning."

<*We can give warning.*>

"One thing at a time, people," Tangel admonished. "Let's just see if we and Star City can survive the day."

Neutronium bullets continued to fire from the dyson sphere, and more fire began to come from a structure encircling the second neutron star in the system.

It was significantly more massive than the one that lay at the core of Star City, the result of mass being funneled from one star to another.

Even for the people of New Canaan—who were actively working on moving their star—the work involved in transferring mass from one star to another was mind-boggling.

The rounds of degenerate matter continued to tear into the encroaching Exdali, shredding the forward lines, but not slowing the mass of things at a rate that would see them stopped before they reached Star City.

<*It's not going to be enough,*> Bob said.

"I was thinking the same thing." Tangel glanced at Jessica. "They have graviton emitters, right? They should be able to create a repulsor field."

The purple-hued woman nodded. "Yeah, I don't think it will be difficult, they should be able to force the things back."

Despite Jessica's certainty, nothing to that effect was happening.

Tangel pursed her lips. "Captain Rachel, deploy the first fleet. We'll corral the Exdali as best we can. If the bastions can get a broad enough graviton field up, we can open a rift and drive them back in.

"On it," the captain replied, her eyes narrowing as she began issuing orders via the Link.

Less than thirty seconds later, the first two cruisers were already exiting the *I2*'s main bay, and Tangel smiled, realizing that Rachel had already been preparing the fleet.

Tangel's mind wandered to the origins of the Exdali surging toward Star City. While their presence could be the work of core AIs, it also might be Orion. Both enemies knew that the ISF had used the dark layer creatures in the defense of Carthage. Figuring out how to get them out of the dark layer wasn't hard, either.

It was getting them back *in* that was problematic.

<*Thanks for the information,*> the response arrived from Star City a moment later. <*We're working on reconfiguring our station-keeping grav emitters to create the effect. It may not be soon enough, though. Anything you can do to help would be appreciated.*>

"We sure turned that around fast," Iris said with a soft laugh. "Good thing we're so resourceful."

<*It's not turned around yet.*> Bob's tone was ominous.

*<I've calculated the mass of the Exdali…. It's greater than that of Luna.>*

"Shit," Tangel muttered aloud. "Then we *really* have to get them into the dark layer. Even if the Bastions can kill them all, that mass hitting Star City will do a number on it."

"Sure wish the *Lantzer* was repaired," Jessica said, her gaze darting between Trevor and Iris. "I feel so impotent sitting around here."

"You're standing," Iris countered. "But I take your meaning. Next time, try not to get your shiny new ship torn to bits."

"Easy now," Trevor held up his hands, turning to Tangel. "We can fly tugs…. Would they help, and do you have spares?"

"Yes and yes," Rachel answered before Tangel could. "We have tugs coming out our ears, and never enough pilots."

Jessica was already on her way to the bridge's exit before Rachel was done speaking.

"Which dock?" she called out.

"Go to 17C," the captain directed.

"I'll join in," Sera said as she followed the other three off the bridge. "I can handle one of your scows."

*<Red…>* Bob cautioned.

"Kidding, kidding."

Tangel wished that Jason was aboard; his steady hand at the helm of a ship—any ship—was always welcome. Unfortunately, his duties back at New Canaan had called him home once more.

*Erin's ready to take over, though. Once we find Cary and*

*deal with Orion, we should hold elections. I'll get her primed to run.*

In all honesty, she'd expected to have Erin in place as governor years ago, but New Canaan's build-up, the Aleutian site in the LMC, and then the war had forestalled that. It felt unfair to still have Jason filling the role, but he was so stoic, she often forgot that he really didn't want the position anymore.

*Let's face it,* she laughed to herself. *He never did.*

"I love them all," Rachel said when the others had cleared the bridge, "but it's nice having all the extra cooks out of the kitchen."

Tangel snorted a laugh. "Where do I fall in that equation?"

"Stars." Rachel shook her head. "Admiral, this is *your* kitchen. I just follow your recipes."

"Oh I don't know about that," she replied. "I feel like you've got a pretty big stake in this enterprise."

A cough came from Bob, the rumble pealing in their minds like lightning and thunder on a clear afternoon. *<When you're done discussing who owns my body, can we focus on the task at hand?>*

"Are you telling me that you actually need us?" Tangel smirked.

*<You still serve a purpose.>*

"Ouch!" Rachel exclaimed. "You know I can walk and chew gum at the same time, Bob. The fleet is nearly deployed, and Helm has worked up the vectors. So long as the Bastions get the field going, we'll be able to herd the things."

*<Good.>*

Tangel shared a long look with Rachel, and then the two set to work providing final review of Helm's vectors and finessing the grid that the twenty ships of the first fleet were forming.

She felt a pang of guilt at how few people were on each of those ships—one of the destroyers had a crew of only two. The war had whittled down the sentient resources of her people to the point where the largest groups of New Canaanites were single platoons of Marines, and even a full 'toon was getting rare.

It took constant reminding that the reason for it was how thin her people were spread, not that they were losing that many.

But with a population of under five million, everyone from New Canaan had lost friends and loved ones.

*Jessica's kids better have a way to help. Another few years of this, and it won't matter that we saved New Canaan from Orion—we'll all be gone anyway.*

Outside the ship, the first fleet continued to move into position, arraying themselves in a long oval across the central light second of the Exdali's wave.

Tanis—it was strange for Tangel to think of another person bearing the name that had once been hers—was providing the firing patterns that her Bastions were using, and the ISF ships were staying clear of the neutronium bullets, adjusting their positions as needed.

"It's going to be close," Rachel said, glancing over her shoulder as she walked to the scan team's section of the bridge to review their probing of the Exdali mass.

<We're ready.> The message came from Tanis, now only delayed by seven seconds' travel time between Star

City and the *I2*.

Moments after the words came in, a wave of positive gravitons, attuned to the frequency that was anathema to the Exdali, washed over the first fleet.

The effect slowed the things' advance as the dark layer creatures bunched up in the center of their formation, pushed into place by the stronger field on the sides.

"They're not slowing as much as they should!" one of the scan officers called out. "I'm picking up refracted gravitons bleeding around the edges."

<Something's driving them,> Bob said.

<Jessica, you four strapped in already, or what?> Tangel called down to the bay where the tugs were stored.

<We're on the rails, ready to join in.>

<You have a new mission. Someone is pushing the Exdali in the ass. Get out there and take them out.>

<In **tugs**?> Trevor exclaimed.

<We've got stasis shields,> Jessica replied, a hungry edge in her voice. <It'll be like shooting fish in a barrel.>

A groan came from Iris. <You know that doesn't work, right? The water destroys the projectile before it reaches the fish.>

<Stop ruining things, Iris,> Jessica shot back.

Tangel couldn't help but laugh. No matter what they faced, it seemed like Jessica's little family always had time to crack a joke.

<Good luck,> she told them. <And kick ass.>

# DANCE WITH THE DEVIL

**STELLAR DATE: 10.15.8949 (Adjusted Years)**
**LOCATION: ISS *I2***
**REGION: Star City, Orion Freedom Alliance, Perseus Arm**

<Kick ass? Like we can do anything else,> Jessica added a laugh as she spoke on the team's private channel.

<Stars,> Sera muttered. <You three practically ooze Sabrina. Do I ever miss her.>

<You were aboard her just a week ago,> Iris said.

<That makes it worse.>

Jessica's tug shot out first, and the others followed a few seconds later. She switched her navigation system to run off her own scan, setting the feed from the *I2* as a secondary input.

<OK, people, let's fan out. Full boost, two above, two below,> she ordered.

<I'll go under with Iris,> Sera announced as she broke away.

<Good thing,> Trevor laughed. <I like being on top.>

Jessica snorted. <Since when?>

His only response was good-natured laughter, and Jessica smiled as her tug boosted at over one hundred *g*s, the dampeners only blocking two thirds of the force, the rest pushing her into the acceleration couch like a giant's foot, threatening to crush her.

She fixed her gaze on the holodisplay, her mind trying to deal with the view before her.

Seeing a representation of the Exdali wave on the bridge of the *I2* was one thing, but staring at the writhing mass while accelerating toward it was another experience entirely. Memories of the fear she'd felt aboard the *Lantzer* as they raced to the gate came back over her, and it took a moment for her to force herself to set it aside.

*Stop it, Jessica. That fight is over. We beat the Exdali there, we'll beat them again here.*

She wondered if she was the only one freaking out, and reached out to her husband on a private channel.

<*You good?*> she asked Trevor as the two tugs spread out, arcing over the dark layer creatures, scan sweeping the space beyond for evidence of any ships pushing the things.

She wasn't certain which would be worse: to find that the Orion Guard could weaponize Exdali like this, or to see a fishbone behind the wave.

<*You bet. Think I'm scared by some Exdali trying to devour our children? Nah, this is just another day at the office for us.*>

<*Nice try,*> Jessica replied. <*Damn, we've lost visual on Sera and Iris.*>

<*I2 still has them on scan. They're OK.*>

<*I know that.*> She didn't mean to come across testily, but something about the Exdali made her stomach churn. <*Do you think they found them or made them?*>

<*Do you mean the core AIs and the Exdali?*>

<*Uh huh.*>

Her husband laughed, his voice sounding calm and certain. <*No, I don't think the Exdali made the core AIs.*>

<*Funny man. Be serious.*>

<*OK, sorry.*> Trevor sent a reassuring feeling across

the Link. <*I think they found them and then altered them, or at least spread them around.*

<*Bastards.*>

<*That's the general sentiment, yeah. Wait, I've got something!*>

The two tugs had passed over the bulk of the Exdali mass and were arcing back down, searching the billions of square kilometers for any graviton emissions that would point to someone herding the things.

Trevor passed his scan data, and Jessica looked it over. There was no ship visible, but negative gravitons were bleeding out from a point near the center of the mass of creatures.

<*Iris, Sera, do you read this?*> she asked as the other two came back on the team's Link.

<*I do,*> Sera said. <*And I have another one a quarter light second further along the line.*>

<*I dropped relays,*> Iris added. <*Passing the feed to the I2.*>

Trevor snorted a laugh. <*Oh look at you, Missus Fancy Pants, dropping probes!*>

Jessica wondered if his injection of levity was for her sake. If it was, she appreciated it.

<*It's not hard, you should try it,*> the AI retorted.

<*We didn't have any,*> Jen said, her voice almost making Jessica jump.

<*Stars, Jen, I forget you're tucked away in Sera's head half the time. You never talk.*>

<*Not everyone is all about the talky-talky like you.*>

<*You clearly need to spend more time aboard* Sabrina,> Trevor commented. <*I used to be quiet and reserved, too.*

*Now look at me.>*

<Sooo, I've analyzed the pattern,> Sera said. <You know, doing what we're here for. It suggested ten ships, and I've found three more.>

<I was doing it too,> Iris protested.

<Look at that, my organic thinker is faster than yours,> Sera said with a laugh.

<She cheated,> Jen laughed. <Our tug has a big spatial vector analysis NSAI aboard. It crunched all four tugs' scan data in seconds.>

<Jen!> Sera admonished.

<You're not president anymore, you don't get special consideration.>

<Ohhh!> Trevor laughed. <Burn!>

<I've assigned targets,> Jessica said, laughing as she fed the updates to the team. <If those are ships, we'll just ram and slam them.>

<If they're **anything**, we'll just do that,> Iris said.

<What else could they be?> Trevor asked.

<Ascended AIs operating from extradimensional space,> Jessica suggested.

<Oh...shit.>

Jessica was halfway to her first target, her scan still unable to see anything other than the graviton bleed that was driving the Exdali.

While the tug had engines capable of moving a billion tons of asteroid without any strain, it possessed no offensive weapons, other than small beams for breaking up flotsam and jetsam. Those wouldn't do anything to a warship, but the tug's engines certainly would.

After a hard boost, Jessica spun the tug and pointed

her engines at the source of the graviton emissions, then fired a fifty-*g* burn for ten seconds.

Her ship's sensors couldn't penetrate the soup of gammas and plasma until fifteen seconds later. When she could finally see her target, she muttered a curse.

<*Fucking Orion! They're using those new four-hulled cruisers of theirs.*>

<*Spotted that as well,*> Sera replied. <*Those things have a ton of kinetics. If they clip you properly with a slug, they could push you into the Exdali.*>

Jessica nodded to herself, noting that the wall of dark layer creatures was only a thousand klicks from the Orion ships.

<*I have two grappling webs. I'm gonna fire one of those and bind up the rotating hulls,*> Iris announced.

One of the webs was present on Jessica's ship as well, and she decided to use it on her first target. She spun her tug again, boosting toward the enemy cruiser, stasis shields easily shedding the beamfire coming her way.

"That's right, you pieces of shit," she muttered. "Wanna take out *my* kids? Gonna have to deal with their mother, first."

She saw the cruiser turn its heavy kinetics, tracking her ship. Jessica initialized a jinking pattern to avoid the slugs that began firing at her. The rounds would foul the net before it reached the cruiser, so she had to get close before deploying it.

The onboard nav system calculated the enemy's firing rate, speed of projectiles, and the tug's maneuverability, presenting an optimal range for her to fire the net at.

"Seventy kilometers?" Jessica shook her head and

then quickly programmed an automated firing sequence, then gripped the edges of the acceleration couch as her tug boosted toward the enemy ship.

Fifteen seconds later, she'd passed the Orion cruiser, and her board showed that the net had fired.

<Hooked mine,> she announced to the group. <Tether's holding.>

The line connecting her tug to the cruiser strained as she fired her engines at max burn, slewing her captured prey to the side and sending it off course. At the same time, a graviton wave flowed through the Exdali from the far side, and the things slowed drastically.

One second, there was a ship caught in the net, the next, it was lost in the churning black of the creatures' bodies. An alert blared in the cockpit, and her tug jerked toward the creatures, their dark bodies surging up the cable.

"Shitting stars!" Jessica exclaimed, cutting the tether free and boosting away from the Exdali. <Watch out, those things are hungry! Ate my prey, then tried to eat me.>

<You're not supposed to be using your net to fish,> Sera said with a laugh. <Granted, the same thing just happened to me.>

Jessica didn't have time to reply, as her ship shuddered under a barrage of kinetics. Two of the cruisers had moved away from their herding positions and were slamming rounds into her tug, trying to force it into the Exdali.

She poured on the thrust, attempting to boost above the wall of creatures, but a massive round struck her ship and pushed it to starboard—right into the searching tentacles of a massive thing.

*<They got me!>* she shouted over the Link, getting no response as her stasis shields flared brightly around the ship, annihilating whatever part of the Exdali touched her.

She lost all bearings and didn't know if she was still moving into the things, or away. After a few seconds more, her CriEn module threw an alert that it could only operate at the heightened draw for one minute.

"Just great," Jessica muttered.

She had the ship's nav systems calculate the angle that her tug had entered the Exdalis, and worked out her current orientation. The ship's computer ran the numbers and triple-checked then, coming up with the determination that the tug was spinning like a top, but the gravitational mass of the dark layer creatures was great enough that it was blocking the ship's ability to use the dampener's strength to calculate vector.

"Well," Jessica muttered. "Might as well just pick a direction."

She programmed the tug's engines to fire for one second with every spin of the ship, and then held her breath as the small vessel followed her directions, every burn slamming her into the acceleration couch like a hammer blow.

Watching the timer on her HUD, Jessica noted that she'd been in the Exdali mass for twenty seconds. It counted up to thirty, and then forty.

*This can't be right,* she thought as it passed fifty.

At the speed she'd entered the wall of dark layer creatures, and with her consistent burns, she should have broken free—unless she was firing in exact opposition to her existing momentum.

Another thirty seconds passed, and she was still surrounded by the flare of her stasis shields as the Exdali smashed themselves against her ship.

"Oh wait…" Jessica whispered, suddenly realizing why she wasn't free of the dark layer creatures. "I'm *in* the dark layer."

Her ship's scan was useless, unable to see past the stasis shield and the wall of obliteration beyond. Her main panel was displaying the alert that the CriEn was going to drop into diminished power mode in ten seconds, and she had no idea if it was even possible to transition *out* of the dark layer when she hadn't activated the graviton fields to transition into it in the first place.

The CriEn countdown passed seven seconds, and she didn't wait any further, initiating a dark layer transition field and dropping into normal space.

"Did I—?"

Her words were interrupted as something hammered into her stasis shield, and then the CriEn shut down.

Directly in front of Jessica's tug was the surface of the dyson sphere, its white expanse stretching in every direction. The scan readings on her tug showed that she was only fifty kilometers from it, and drifting away ever so slightly.

A rasping breath left her throat as she realized that the shuddering had been neutronium bullets fired to keep her from hitting Star City—and to kill the Exdali she'd drawn out of the dark layer.

<Stars, Mom.> Tanis's voice was filled with relief. <We

110

*know you miss us, but try not to smash your ship into the place. We just got it fixed back up.>*

# THE CITY AROUND A STAR
**STELLAR DATE: 10.16.8949 (Adjusted Years)**
**LOCATION: ISS *I2***
**REGION: Star City, Orion Freedom Alliance, Perseus Arm**

"Sweeps are complete, Admiral," Rachel said as she turned to face Tangel. "The Exdali are all back in the DL...or dead and drifting."

"Good." Tangel let out a long breath, shaking her head that Orion was willing to utterly destroy Star City just because its denizens wouldn't join the OFA. *Hopefully that's why, and not that they're sitting out of the war.*

Chances were that the Bastions and Dreamers of Star City had no idea that war had spread across the inhabited section of the Orion Arm of the galaxy—and now into the Perseus Arm as well. It was Tangel's fervent hope that she could convince the Bastions to aid in the fight, primarily by explaining how they could keep degenerate matter from flying apart once extracted from their pair of neutron stars.

"We need to clean up the bodies," she concluded after drawing her attention back to the task at hand. "We know the detritus's trajectory now, but Exdali are almost as black as Elastene. They'll become a navigation hazard before long."

"I'll have crews get on it," Rachel replied. "Just...where do we put them?"

"Get them in a net," Tangel replied. "We'll kick it into the other star once they're all gathered up."

<I'd advise against that,> Bob broke into their conversation. <We don't know enough about the things. They might have the ability to reanimate, or maybe spawn new young from their bodies. I'd hate for the mass to come alive and then devour this system's other star.>

"OK, back into the dark layer, then."

<After I examine them,> the AI said. <This is a rare opportunity.>

"Umm…OK," Tangel reached up and grasped the end of her ponytail. "Just be careful."

<Of course.>

"I'll take a shuttle to the city," Tangel said. "I don't think we can fly in."

<We can fly in,> Bob said. <I've been talking with Tanis and her siblings. They've sent the coordinates for an entrance large enough for the I2.>

"Alright," Rachel said, her eyes turning to meet Tangel's. "Should we do that? I hate the idea of being trapped in there."

<I want to see it for myself,> Bob said.

~Why is that?~ Tangel asked privately, mind to mind.

~Professional curiosity,~ the AI replied. ~Humor me. I do it with you often enough.~

~Ouch!~ Her lips twisted for a moment, and then Tangel nodded. "We're going in, Rachel. Set a course."

"Aye, ma'am. Just gonna fly the ship into a dyson sphere…because our day hasn't been crazy enough yet."

<Now you're getting it,> Bob said.

The forward display shifted to Star City's shell, the white expanse filling more and more of the view as the I2 approached.

"Here's something crazy," Rachel said as the ship drew closer. "Even though it's a sphere, its surface is the flattest thing we've ever laid eyes on."

"Huh." Tangel nodded slowly. "You're right. Its circumference is greater than the Airthan ring's."

"It's not a competition," Sera said as she walked onto the bridge.

"No?" Rachel asked. "I mean…they built this thing millennia before Finaeus made the ring."

A laugh slipped from Sera's lips as she reached the holotank. "Oh I know, he was complaining about it on the flight to Airtha. He thought he was first to create a semi-rigid structure that large…and then they came here."

"The others not with you?" Tangel asked.

"No, they didn't want to wait. They followed Jessica with their tugs."

"Can't wait to see their ki—" Rachel choked off the last word. "Sorry, Tangel."

She gave a rueful laugh in response. "Trust me, I didn't *just* start drawing the comparison. It's been front and center in my mind all day. But what I've been remembering is that Jessica, Trevor, and Iris went ten years not knowing if their kids were OK. I've gone a few days. Their example is giving me strength."

Sera wrapped an arm around her shoulder. "We're here for you. We'll get them back, get it done."

Tangel nodded. "We know where they're going to end up. It's just a matter of when."

"Is Joe going to keep chasing after them?" Rachel asked. "Well…searching, I guess."

"No," Tangel shook her head. "He's released the ships that Admiral Lukas had set aside, barring a few that are setting up listening posts in New Sol."

"It's risky business." Sera paused and twisted her lips. "Every time we try to get a relay station into the New Sol System, they find it. But we don't need these to last forever. Just a few months, maybe a year, tops."

"Stars," Tangel muttered. "A year. If Cary takes that long to make her move on Kirkland, I'll eat my ponytail. She'll go in a lot sooner than that."

"She has to secure her fleet first," Sera said. "It'll take her a bit to gather those ships."

"OK, what did I miss?" Rachel asked. "I haven't read the whole briefing yet, just that she blew up some dock."

"Yeah." Tangel sucked in a slow breath. "A station called 'Dock 1'. At least a hundred million people aboard."

"Oh shit." Rachel breathed the words. "And the fleet?"

"From what Joe learned—mostly from Faleena—Cary sent Widows onto all the ships of a departing fleet. They think she did it to somehow seize the ships and use them for something."

"How many?" Rachel asked.

"Just shy of a thousand," Tangel replied.

"Really?" The ship's captain cocked her head. "A thousand run-of-the-mill Orion ships against New Sol's defenses?"

Sera pursed her lips, nodding in agreement. "Yeah, it's not even a pittance. We've no idea what she has planned."

"With any luck, we can get something from the Bastions that will help us against New Sol," Tangel said.

"I don't know if neutronium bullets are the sort of thing we want." Sera met Tangel's gaze. "Do we really need to go for an all or nothing option?"

"No, we don't. But I'm not above a really solid bluff."

"A bluff like this only works if you're really willing to carry it out." Rachel's voice was low, her eyes serious.

Sera laughed and winked at the captain. "That's a threat."

"Exactly."

"They might have something else," Tangel said. "Maybe we can work out how to make ships with neutronium hulls. They might be able to stand up to DMG weapons."

"I'll pass on captaining a death trap like that." Sera shook her head. "The instant the containment field fails, you're doing an impression of a pancake."

"Not to mention the mass," Rachel added. "Teaspoon of that stuff weighs as much as a small planet. How do you coat a ship in it?"

Tangel laughed. "I'm just spitballing, here. I mean, they starlift the stuff and then fire it. The energies required for that are staggering, but Jessica said they don't have CriEns."

<They don't need them,> Bob said. <They have something better.>

"What?" Tangel blurted out the word. "What's better?"

<Transdimensional energy.> Bob said the words as though it should have been painfully obvious that such

was the source of the Bastions' power.

"Maybe," Tangel allowed. "But they made Star City before they'd ascended. So how'd they syphon one star's mass to another before that?"

<We'll have to find out.>

"Sure took your extra-strength cryptic pills this morning, Bob," Sera said, her gaze fixed on Tangel. "I told you that you were nuts to keep god-like AIs around."

<I'm not god—>

"Sure, sure," Sera waved a hand, laughing softly. "I know that's how your type rolls. 'Deny, deny, deny'."

"There it is," Rachel said, pointing at the forward display. "Steady as she goes, Helm."

The lieutenant at the ship's helm nodded, her expression rapt as the *I2* eased toward a hundred-kilometer-wide portal set into the skin of Star City.

"It's like we're flying into our own main dock." Rachel's voice was filled with awe. "Intrepidception."

"You dipping into that old vid archive, too?" Sera asked.

The ship's captain nodded. "Something about the flat vids is soothing. Like you can enjoy the story as a story and not have to be a part of it—but even so, you feel sucked in. I don't know how to describe it."

"Sucked in seems apt," Tangel said as the *I2* began to pass through the dyson sphere's shell. "I thought I had gotten used to supermassive superstructures, but this…this is mind-blowing."

"And they built it without pico," Sera winked.

The blue haze at the end of the long shaft began to

gain resolution, green and white becoming visible in the far distance. Tangel held off on zooming the optics in; she wanted to experience the passage without cheating and jumping ahead, even though Jessica had sent her vids of the interior.

A minute later, the ship reached the end of the tunnel and passed out into open air. Below them lay the second sphere, covered in thousands of worlds' worth of space, broken into hexagons covered with oceans and dotted with continents.

The inner sphere was at a distance from the neutron star in the center of the structure that caused the outside of the sphere to experience one $g$ of gravitational acceleration. In a way, this made it an inverted dyson sphere, and a more practical one at that.

She briefly wondered how much air lay between the world sphere and the shell they'd passed through. A rough calculation told her that it massed more than Earth, and she wondered how the makers had ensured that storms didn't constantly rage across the interior.

*We have so much to learn…*

It was a comforting feeling, that for once the people of the *Intrepid*, those who had come forward in time five thousand years, finally didn't have to be the ones to come up with all the answers. Someone else could lend a hand on that front.

"There's Earth!" Rachel pointed to one of the tiny hexagons. "I can make out North America."

"All of Sol is there." Sera pointed to the surrounding hexagons. "Look, there's High Terra—they sort of wrapped it around. And there's Luna, Mars, and

Venus."

"And Eurpoa, Tyche, Ganymede…they recreated them all," Tangel added. "There, those are the planets of Tau Ceti. Amazing…"

Rachel scowled as she looked over the worlds represented below. "This doesn't really look like a city. In fact, I can't see any cities."

"From what Jessica said, they never fully occupied it before all the people here moved into the Dream and began ascending," Tangel replied.

"It's like a ghost town."

<We're going to Manhattan,> Bob said. <There's a city there.>

"Oh hell yeah," Tangel grinned. "I've always wanted to bring the ship down over New York. We'll stretch from Staten Island, past the Bronx and past Yonkers."

"Those can't be real names," Sera laughed.

"Totally. I wonder if they made all the cities and towns. On Earth, there was a town called New Canaan near there."

<The others are already in the Dream,> Bob said, a low rumble of laughter accompanying his words.

"Couldn't wait to see their kids, eh?" Tangel asked. "Not that I'm assigning blame here."

<I suspect as much, though their kids also have bodies.>

"So do you actually want to settle over Manhattan Island, Bob?" Rachel asked. "Or should we park a bit higher?"

"Going to take a lot of power just to float in one $g$ without orbiting," Tangel said. "Too bad we never put landing gear on the ship."

<Don't even joke about that,> Bob scoffed. <We have coordinates over the Atlantic, and there's an a-grav pad that will float us.>

"Ooooh...fancy," Rachel laughed while passing the order to Helm.

"I'm going to a shuttle," Tangel said. "No need for you to settle in before I go."

"Have fun," the captain saluted. "Make sure to get us all some shore leave down there. I imagine everyone is going to want to walk around this place."

Tangel nodded and waved absently as she walked off the bridge to the maglev station.

~So why did you want to come inside?~ she asked Bob.

~I wanted to see if the humans who ascended via the Dream are still here.~

The thought had occurred to Tangel as well. There was no reason to believe that the people who had ascended had left at all. If they had fully transitioned into higher dimensions, it was possible that they'd stayed within Star City afterward.

~Well, if they are here, they're not showing their faces,~ she replied. ~I didn't see any signs of them when we came in.~

~Nor did I, but that is far from conclusive.~

Tangel didn't speak further as she walked through the ship. Instead, she peered through the hull, looking down at the continent they were passing over. She easily recognized it as Europe, noting the familiar geology of the Italian peninsula, France, and then the islands of Britain and Ireland. She recalled many fond memories on Earth, and a few harrowing ones, such as the one against

Disker separatists in Dublin.

Moments later, the ship passed over the Atlantic Ocean, and Tangel took in the sweeping view, at one point able to see North America, Greenland, Europe, and Africa—courtesy of the flat representation of Earth.

She tried to peer through the ocean and beyond to the star within the inner sphere, but she was unable to see more than a dozen kilometers into the ground below before her sight was stopped by a luminous wall.

~*Can you see through to the star?*~

~*No,*~ Bob replied. ~*I think it's some sort of neutronium. It is a solid object in higher dimensions, as well.*~

~*That's annoying.*~

~*And useful. Want a bullet that can kill ascended beings?*~

Tangel snorted. ~*No way it's that easy.*~

~*To my knowledge, this is the only place in the universe where you can get neutronium bullets. So it's not **that** easy.*~

~*Good point. And we just so happen to have that ascended AI Jessica captured.*~

Bob's mind rumbled in slow consideration. ~*That seems inhumane.*~

~*It's not human.*~

~*For you.*~

~*I'm not human.*~

The AI laughed. ~*You're not so ascended that I can't bend you over my knee, Tangel.*~

She joined in the laughter, walking through the still-bustling administrative wing. Despite the fact that they were running on a skeleton crew, the entire war effort was coordinated from the hall she was walking through—even more so now that the primary

QuanComm hub in Khardine had been destroyed.

*<Do you miss her?>* Tangel asked, switching to the Link, though she didn't know why.

*<Priscilla?>*

*<Yes.>*

*<Do you miss Cary?>*

Tangel snorted. *<You know the answer to that.>*

*<Then you too know the answer to your question.>*

*<Well...>* She considered her next words. *<I wasn't sure if you missed people exactly, I was curious.>*

*<I think I do, in my own way—I don't feel complete without her aboard. I was wondering if this is what it might feel like if she were to die—as though a part of me is gone, never to come back.>*

Tangel nodded a she reached the maglev station. *<That's the general sensation.>*

*<How do you come to accept it?>*

*<You just have to figure out how to make peace with it. Accept the fact that you won't see them again, and figure out how to move on.>*

*<That's very vague,>* Bob pointed out.

*<Well, it's different for everyone. Are you worried about her? Can you not see Priscilla's future?>*

*<Cary's ascension and mental merge with Lisa Wrentham introduces many variables I cannot properly account for. My prior matrices required a certain number of knowns to operate with a desirable degree of accuracy. We have...we have moved beyond the point where we have sufficient knowns.>*

*<Everywhere?>*

*<Oh, no, of course not. Three nights from now, Karmen is going to have an argument with Lucida over repair priorities*

back at Pyra, and they're going to end up in a sexual relationship as a result of their tensions. Jessica will ignore it, and that will create the same atmosphere on the Lantzer— when she returns to it—as she had on Sabrina.>

<OK, so you haven't lost your mojo, it's just that the scope has changed.>

<Exactly. Which is why we're here. To improve our ability to perceive the true scope.>

# MEETING TANIS

**STELLAR DATE: 10.16.8949 (Adjusted Years)**
**LOCATION: Manhattan Island, North America**
**REGION: Star City, Orion Freedom Alliance, Perseus Arm**

Tangel stepped out of the shuttle and came face to face with herself.

"Stars." She smiled, shaking her head in disbelief. "When Jessica told me that you'd modeled yourself after me, I didn't realize she was being so literal."

"Hello to you too," Tanis said. "I studied you…a lot. From what I could tell, you are one of the best military commanders in human history. It seemed prudent to model myself after someone so accomplished."

"I'm not that good," Tangel replied. "I just read a lot."

"Well, she also gave me your name."

"That makes a lot more sense." She observed the being in front of her, noting that it was flesh and blood, a biological copy of what she herself had looked like years ago. But there was no intelligence inside of the form, it was just a vessel.

"You're wondering if I inhabit this form," Tanis said.

"No," Tangel shook her head. "I can see that you are not in there. Are you too big, or too uncomfortable with the mobility?"

Tangel's doppelganger laughed. "Perhaps a bit of both. I could squeeze my core in there, but it would not be well protected. We all have forms like this, but we don't use them too much. Most of our work does not require physical forms."

"Defending the Dreamers against Orion?" Tangel asked. "I took it from your comments that this is not the first time Orion has sent Exdali after you."

"It is not. However, this is the first time they launched an assault that large. If you hadn't shown up when you did…Well, let's just say that things wouldn't have gone well."

Tangel nodded slowly, glancing over her right shoulder to where the *I2* could be seen hovering over the ocean. "I find myself wondering if Bob had something to do with that."

*~I did not. In this case, I am innocent of manipulation.~*

"Oh! Now *that* was unusual," Tanis said. "Then it's true, Bob, you are ascended."

*~I am. Who has been outing me?~*

"You forget…." Tanis turned and gestured to the towers that rose up on the far side of Battery Park. "Our parents are already in the Dream. Five months have passed for them since they entered. We've had much time to talk."

"I'm eager to experience that. I would imagine it would aid in strategizing a lot."

"You cannot enter the Dream, not if what Jessica says is true."

"Which is?" Tangel cocked her head.

"That you too are ascended."

She wondered what that had to do with anything. "Not entirely."

*~It's a continuum.~*

*~Stop it.~*

"I'm sorry about your daughters and Priscilla," Tanis

said, her face growing serious. "I know you're here to seek help in finding them. My parents explained that as well."

"She's just stealing all my thunder," Tangel muttered. "Honestly, we would have come anyway. We need your help in the war."

"And it seems as though we need your help defending Star City."

"I thought you had a fleet," Tangel said. "Or Jessica said she told you to build one."

"We did. Orion has attacked us seven times in the decade since our parents left. We've fended them off, but the last three incidents, they have used those creatures. We're lucky they die to neutronium bullets, but we lost our last ships in the prior attacks. We are building more, but not fast enough, it seems."

"I think we'll be able to help you there, as well," Tangel replied. "And I do hope you'll be able to help us—even though I can't enter the Dream."

"It wouldn't make sense for you to do so. We cannot bring your ascended mind into the Dream, so you'd feel strangely detached."

*~Or you might permanently leave your corporeal body behind.~*

"Yeah, let's not risk that," Tangel gave a nervous laugh. "I told Cary I'd have this body for a long time. She'd be pissed if I lost it on a lark."

"Yes, it would be rather frivolous," Tanis confirmed.

Tangel looked around at the towers rising behind the AI who bore her name and face.

"Is the city entirely vacant?"

Tanis turned and surveyed the recreation of thirty-sixth century New York. "Other than my core, yes. Well, and our parents, of course. All of the Dreamers here have moved on."

A sensation of utter emptiness came over Tangel as she thought of the sixteen AIs who watched over the empty world that was Star City. She couldn't imagine what Jessica, Iris, and Trevor must have felt when they had to leave their progeny behind.

"Is it lonely?" she asked.

Tanis shrugged. "We have each other, and we have the Dream when we want to be with other people—though it's not the same as it was when we were growing up."

"Because your parents aren't there anymore?"

The AI nodded. "That, and the number of Dreamers is so low now that we have to simulate many of the people the actual Dreamers interact with."

"Oh? How low is it?"

Tangel wondered if there would be a point where the accelerated human evolution system would not have enough people for the final Dreamers to ascend.

"Hovering over a million," Tanis said. "We're going to have to change the setting in some fashion to remove urban scenarios very soon. We're thinking of trying something set in the ancient Roman era."

~I wonder if that is necessary,~ Bob interjected.

"Oh?" Tanis cocked an eyebrow and glanced toward the starship hovering over the ocean. "What are you thinking, great and powerful Bob?"

Tangel snorted. "I like that one."

*~Just that if the final Dreamers are close enough, there may be a way to catalyze a final mass transition.~*

"We've considered that," Tanis said. "It may be possible, but even though we are caretakers of these humans who seek ascension, we don't know enough about ascension itself to understand what their final triggers are. It seems that in some ways, it's a final critical mass of enlightenment across multiple lifetimes. Obviously, this is not a natural method for an organic being."

Tangel glanced up at the artificial sun as it slid across the sky, a strange melancholy settling over her.

"If there is one," she murmured.

"I understand that you did not undergo what I would call a natural process, but your daughter is ascending, is she not?" Tanis asked.

"Yes, but her path is a byproduct of the tweaking that was done to me."

"And are you fully ascended?" Tanis peered at Tangel as though she could see through her—which she probably could, to an extent.

"I don't know if ascension is a thing with a metric we could define as 'full'. Were I to try, I could leave this corporeal body behind, but I don't want to. I made a promise to my daughters that I intend to keep. And to Joe, too, though my promise to him is a bit different."

*~Tanis, could you grant me access to the Dreamer network? I would like to observe.~*

A look of concern crossed Tanis's features, but then she nodded. "OK, we agree that it would be safe enough if we slow the Dream down for a little bit." A smile settled onto her lips. "Actually, if we slow the Dream down, we could let you project into it, too, Tangel. Would you like that?"

"Yes, I think I very much would."

* * * * *

Tangel appeared next to a grill that was loaded with sizzling bacon and burgers. To her left was a two-story house, and to her right was a secluded yard lined with trees and filled with people talking with one another, Trevor and Iris in their midst.

"Took you long enough," Jessica's voice came to Tangel, and she saw the purple-skinned woman walk out of the house with a platter of buns and condiments.

"Look at you!" Tangel laughed. "When I throw parties at my lakehouse, you never carry anything out."

"That's because I'm not your mother, and you like preparing a party spread," Jessica countered as she set her tray on the table. "Plus, you have a zillion servitors."

"Fair point."

"And you always tell me I lay things out wrong."

"*OK!* I get it," Tangel said in mock annoyance, a half smile on her lips.

Jessica's gaze slid to her children who were now wrestling with Trevor and Iris, engaged in some sort of bizarre game whose rules were not documented, but built up over time from a thousand prior matches.

The smile fell from Tangel's lips as she pursed them tightly.

"I'm so sorry, Jessica."

"Sorry?" Her friend turned to look back at her, an eyebrow cocked. "What for?"

"For sending you away. Again and again. For never getting to share this with you. We always talked about raising children together, but instead, I sent you across the galaxy and you had to do it alone."

Jessica took a step closer, her eyes glistening. "Stupid holoprojection. I wish you were really here so I could hug you, Tangel. You did what you had to do, which is what you always do. You make the hard call, and quite honestly, you make the biggest sacrifices. I feel bad for *you*, not the other way around."

"Me?" Tangel asked, surprise lacing her tone. "Because of my girls?"

"Well, yeah, that too. But also because of how things went raising Cary and Saanvi, not to mention Faleena. I know how you are. I bet that while Cary was growing up, you spent half your nights away from her, trying to put together a colony and deal with all the other shit going on. And you hardly got to spend any time at all with Faleena before you had to go off and do this whole war."

"Do the war." Tangel snorted. "That's my thing, isn't it?"

"You know what they say, play to your strengths."

A laugh burst from Tangel's throat, and she wished more than anything to be able to embrace Jessica. "I guess I do at that. And it's not quite as bad as you're worrying it was. Cary and Saanvi had two mothers, Tanis and Angela. And I have both their memories. Yes, I do wish that I was there with them more in the flesh, and do I ever wonder if I made a terrible mistake sending them out—and making Joe deal with how much slack to give them…."

Her voice trailed off, and she turned to look at the ongoing match in the backyard.

"Stars, Trevor is big," she laughed as the man picked up one of his sons and tossed the full-grown man at his siblings.

"How modded is he, anyway?"

"Not much at all, just a lot of heavy worlder biology in his background," Jessica replied.

"I guess we're all just products of our environment," Tangel replied.

"Oh, I don't know that I'd say that," a voice said from the doorway into the house. "I think you alter your environment more than it alters you—the both of you do."

Her eyes darted to the left and fell on a tall man with olive skin and a long moustache. He wore a wide-brimmed hat and a brown coat and pants.

"Bob?" she asked, mouth agape.

The man shrugged. "The burgers smelled good, I wanted to try one. I figured this might be my best opportunity to really feel what it's like."

"I didn't expect *this*," Tanis said as she walked up the steps onto the deck, looking Bob up and down. "Is it safe for you to be in here in this way?"

"This is a shard," Bob replied. "I don't do this often, but it can be useful from time to time." The AI walked to the table and picked up a bun, then strode to the grill and selected a burger. "From what I hear, medium-rare is best."

Jessica nodded silently, her gaze meeting Tangel's, and she mouthed the words 'It's really Bob!', her eyes wide with amazement.

"I wonder if I could do that..." Tangel mused.

"Not unless you want to shard yourself," Bob replied as he turned and walked back to the table, selecting a bottle of ketchup from the condiments laid out there. "Which you can do, but I don't think it's a good idea just yet."

She was tempted to ask him why not, but decided that she'd had her fill of deep conversations for the time being.

Just then, a whoop of joy came from a dozen voices on the lawn, and Tangel turned to see a pile of bodies and no sign of Trevor or Iris. Then she saw a silver arm stretched out, slapping the ground in defeat.

The brood rolled off their parents to reveal Trevor and Iris sprawled across one another in a tangled mass of limbs.

"That looks uncomfortable," Bob mused as he applied mustard to his burger, then stared at it pensively. "I think I'll pass on that experience."

"Wise choice," Tanis said as she looked Bob up and down. "So, you going to eat that or just stare at it?"

The AI shrugged, opened his mouth wide, and took a bite. A smile formed on his lips as he chewed slowly, and then swallowed with his eyes closed.

"OK," he whispered. "Why did no one tell me that food was so good?"

Jessica snorted a laugh. "Pretty sure Tangel here gave

that away by orgasming every time she ate a BLT."

"Jessica!" she exclaimed. "I've *never* orgasmed from eating a BLT, or *any* food."

"There was that one time, I recall it vividly," the purple-skinned woman countered.

"That doesn't count, you drugged my food!"

* * * * *

They spent the rest of the evening in the Dream—which, even at its slowed rate, only amounted to ten minutes outside the immersive simulation.

Tangel got to meet each one of the sixteen bastions who were now the protectors of Star City and its denizens. Many bore the names of people from Jessica and Trevor's pasts, though none had adopted the features of their namesakes in the same way Tanis had.

Some were polar opposites, such as Troy, who was a garrulous young man, passionate about art and endlessly optimistic. He was all but attached at the hip to Kira, and Tanis had noted that the pair was planning to produce a brood of their own once the bastions' future was clear.

That conversation had led from one to another until eventually, all twenty-one humans and AIs were settled around a roaring fire in the backyard, idly discussing what they'd do when the war was over.

Tangel found it interesting that there were only two full humans present in the group, yet the AIs still chose to engage in activities that the humans found comforting. The bastions had confirmed that they did this sort of thing often, even though they could commune on far higher levels should they wish to.

"Sometimes, the level of communication you can have while being utterly silent and at peace with everything around you is far more profound than even a multilevel mind-to-mind merge," Amanda had explained at one point. "Maybe it's because we all grew up together and we just *know* what each other is thinking."

"No one knows what you're thinking," Peter countered. "It's like a nest of spiders in there."

"Plus snakes," Kira added.

"And rats," Tanis added. "Big ones."

"I don't know why I'm so nice to you all," Amanda mock-pouted.

"You've all talked about things you might want to do once the war is over and the Dreamers are gone, but what about Star City, itself?" Bob asked.

"What do you mean, exactly?" Tanis asked from across the fire.

"Oh dear." Tangel shook her head. "Never ask Bob what he means, 'exactly'."

"Really, Tangel," Bob cast her a look of mock indignance. "I've learned how to parse organic nuance better than that."

"But I'm not organic," Tanis countered, a smirk on her lips. "What if I actually mean *exactly*?"

"Staaaaahp!" Jessica laughed as she held up a hand.

Bob gave her a dark look and shrugged. "I mean that Star City could house a sizable fraction of all humans. Easily a quadrillion. It's also an ascension machine, so should we make the Dream available to all of humanity?"

"Maybe the people of Serenity, at least," Jessica suggested.

"Those are difficult questions," Tanis said as the side conversations faded away. "The problem with Star City is not the city, it's the star."

Bob nodded. "I suspected as much. The sphere protects the star, though at the same time, its very existence makes this system a target, and always will."

"What do you mean, the problem is with the star?" Jessica asked.

Tangel had begun to suspect, but held her tongue, wanting to hear it from her namesake.

"It's where they go," Bob said. "The ascended humans. They fully leave their corporeal bodies and move to higher dimensions, but they still exist in spacetime, and they've built their new home inside the neutron star at the center of the sphere."

"Yes," Tanis nodded. "Which is the real reason it is called 'Star City'. Everyone assumes that it's the dyson sphere, but that is just the city's shield. And that shield must always be preserved. That is our charge."

"So all this talk of what you'll do 'after'?" Trevor asked. "Was that just wishful thinking?"

Amanda shrugged. "Well, the universe is going to carry on for a long, long time. With luck, our ascended charges will move on before that, and we'll get to go out on our own."

"I might have a solution for you," Bob said in a quiet voice. "One that is good for both you and your charges."

"Oh?" Tanis asked. "What could that be?"

"We move Star City."

The words fell onto the group like a blanket of silence. The bastions looked at one another with varying levels of disbelief. Finally, Troy spoke up.

"Is that really possible? Far enough and fast enough that Orion would no longer pursue us?"

"Yes." Bob nodded slowly. "Though we will have Orion dealt with before long."

"There will always be another Orion," Tanis countered.

"Perhaps, but my plan would be to move Star City out of the galaxy by jump gate. We can send it anywhere you'd like—though I'd suggest the Small Magellanic Cloud."

The bastions exchanged looks with one another, their gazes carrying a wealth of thought and emotion. Tangel found herself wondering if they were speaking via the Link, or if they really did have such a strong bond that they could debate the issue entirely via human expression.

"We'll have to take you to the city," Tanis said at last. "It is up to the Woken."

"Woken from the Dream," Trevor nodded, a smile on his lips. "I like it."

"When do we go to see them?" Tangel asked.

"No time like the present," Tanis said as she rose. "But they want to see Bob in person, so you'll need to bring your ship through."

A grin formed on Tangel's lips. "Now *that* sounds like fun."

# THE REAL STAR CITY

**STELLAR DATE: 10.16.8949 (Adjusted Years)**
**LOCATION: Approaching ISS *I2***
**REGION: Star City, Orion Freedom Alliance, Perseus Arm**

Tangel rode the shuttle back to the *I2* with Tanis sitting in the copilot's seat, both women silent as they contemplated what Bob had proposed.

As the shuttle approached Dock A1, Tangel reached out to the ship's AI.

*~Are you thinking that if we help them move Star City, we'll get to keep the second neutron star and the neutronium-firing ring around it?~*

*~Yes.~*

*~Do you think they'll let us have it?~*

*~Maybe. At some point, they need to either hand over this technology to corporeals, or destroy it. But I think, given what they've done here, that they need to destroy these stars anyway, to fully remove the evidence of what they've done. And destroying a pair of neutron stars is no simple task—outside of slamming them together to create a supernova.~*

*~Which would not be a nice thing to do to the people at Serenity,~* Tangel added. *~Or pretty much anyone on this side of the Stillwater Nebula…or in the nebula.~*

*~Yes, it would be a very destructive act. An alternative would be to deplete the stars by firing their neutronium out of the galaxy. I think that would only take a thousand years or so.~*

*~Or we move the stars. Because that's a thing we do now.~*

Bob laughed, the sound less like pealing thunder and

more like a human's chuckle for the first time.

*~I have some ideas on how to do it, but it will take Finaeus and Earnest to pull it off. They are quite rare in their ability to make cognitive leaps regarding things of this nature.~*

*~You know…~* Tangel mused. *~If we can move stars, we can fix what the core AIs did a lot faster than doing things the old-fashioned way.~*

*~It is even amazing to me that we now consider inducing asymmetrical burning in a star to be 'old-fashioned'. However, I think that in a lot of cases, that still may be preferable. Neutron stars are much smaller and less…squishy…than stars still undergoing fusion.~*

*~Squishy.~* Tangel snorted. *~I've never thought of a star like that before.~*

*~You're welcome.~*

"You're talking to Bob without the Link," Tanis said from next to her. "I can see the energy coming off you when you do it."

"Really?" Tangel asked. "I didn't think that was visible."

"A sliver of it is," the AI responded. "If you know what to look for."

"Good to know."

"May I ask what you're talking about?" Tanis asked.

"That we'll need Finaeus and Earnest to move your star."

A grin split the AI's lips. "Now that's a development I can get behind. I miss Finaeus. He's like my crazy uncle."

Tangel snorted. "I think Finaeus is all of humanity's crazy uncle."

"That sounds about right," Tanis said as the shuttle drifted into the *I2*'s main dock. "You know, even though Star City dwarfs this ship, the *I2* is still really impressive. I think because of all the places it's been as much as anything else."

"Home sweet home," Tangel replied. "She's really been around. Touched another galaxy, even."

"Which we will too, if you can convince the Woken to leave."

"Do you think they'll go for it?"

Her namesake shrugged. "They're not really that concerned about us lower beings anymore. I don't know that we'll be able to convince them to care."

<*They'll care,*> Bob intoned. <*I'm certain they're worried about the core AIs. If we lose against them, Star City won't last long.*>

"Do you think that's why they tried to block Jessica from getting here?" Tangel asked.

<*Yes, and I'd be shocked if it wasn't the core AIs who gave Orion the ability to herd Exdali.*>

"It lines up," Tanis said. "Considering that Orion only attacked Star City twice before *Sabrina*'s arrival—and then they stepped up their aggression, even while fighting a war against you—an outside influence makes sense."

"It certainly does," Tangel replied, wondering what else the core AIs were going to attempt while she played firefighter for the rest of the galaxy.

\* \* \* \* \*

"OK, that's just weird," Rachel said, a nervous smile on her lips as Tangel approached with Tanis at her side. "I don't think the galaxy is big enough for the both of you."

Tangel chuckled. "Ironic that that is what we're trying to solve."

"Pardon?" Rachel frowned. "No, nevermind. I don't want to know what that means."

"Very nice to meet you in person, Captain Rachel." Tanis extended her hand. "I read about you in the archives *Sabrina* left behind."

The captain's brow lowered into a scowl. "Oh great, just what I need, my sordid tale spread across the galaxy."

"I didn't think it was sordid," Tanis said, glancing at Tangel. "Did I misinterpret something?"

"The only time Rachel did anything sordid—that I know of—was when she snuck out of the academy in a garbage bin, back in Victoria."

The captain's face reddened, and she glanced at her bridge crew. "Gee thanks, Tangel. Now everyone knows."

One of the nearby officers coughed and gave Rachel an apologetic smile. "Sorry, ma'am, we've all known about that for years."

"Well, shit."

"It wasn't me," Tangel held up her hands. "Probably Joe. You know how he is."

"Your Joe? Not likely," Rachel snorted. "I know who it was, I'll deal with them another time. So, where to?"

Tanis approached the main holotank. "With your

permission?"

"Of course," Rachel replied.

The tank shifted from its display of the ISF logo to a cross-section of the dyson sphere.

"We're going inside," Tanis said plainly. "The entrance to the interior is due north, where the Earth plate meets the Mars and Ceres plate. It's a hundred kilometers through the inner sphere, and then we'll be within the structure.

"There's an a-grav column that will take us down to the star. It lessens the full pull, but it's still going to be twenty $g$s at the surface."

"Uhhh…how far down are we going to go?" Rachel asked.

"Only halfway," Tanis said. "At the surface, acceleration is over one hundred billion $g$s. Even our most powerful a-grav systems cannot counter that. We'll stop at a thousand $g$s, and they will meet us there."

Whispers broke out amongst the bridge crew, wide eyes glancing about, some excited, some alarmed.

"Are you sure?" Tangel asked. "Is that necessary?"

*<It is necessary,>* Bob replied.

"And the heat?" Rachel asked. "I assume it's hundreds of thousands of kelvins inside the sphere."

"We use much of the thermal energy," Tanis explained. "Since the star has no wind, just gravity, it's a total vacuum in there."

"Plus a killer magnetic field," Tangel added. "I've been wondering if that is how you support the sphere."

"Well, *I* don't." Tanis winked. "But that's how the builders supported the structure, yes. We're going to go

141

right down toward the north pole, where the field has a gap." She turned to the helm officers. "Navigation is going to be difficult. You'll need to orient the ship by the three beacons behind us. The magnetic field inside the sphere is so intense that it polarizes the vacuum and creates a birefringence effect."

The pair of lieutenants looked at one another and then nodded.

"OK...really?" Rachel asked. "Is this worth the risk?"

"It'll be fine," Tangel replied. "We'll back down, OK? Then if things get hairy, we can boost out. The *I2* has enough thrust to blast out of the well at our stopping point."

The captain drew a deep breath and nodded. "No one ever said that life in the ISF is boring."

"That's for sure," one of the lieutenants at the helm commented. "Uh...ma'am."

"I've passed the coordinates," Tanis said. "Shall we get this show on the road? The sooner we can get the OK from our ascended friends, the sooner we can get to building the jump gate."

Rachel glanced at Tangel, and she preempted the question.

"The ascended humans all live within the neutron star in the center of the sphere. In higher dimensions, it's bigger and less dense...sort of."

"Further up and further in," Rachel said in a quiet voice. "Helm, let's get this done."

"Aye, ma'am. Going for our little jaunt."

The ship slowly lifted further into the air, drifting over the North Atlantic, passing between Greenland and

Iceland before crossing beyond the final stretch of ocean that separated the continents and islands of the Earth replica from the edge of the plate.

Ahead, the separator wall loomed, and Helm drew the ship up and over the hundred-kilometer-high slope, angling to starboard where the opening lay.

Unlike the passage through the outer layer of the city, this time, Helm turned the ship around and allowed the force of gravity to draw the *I2* through engines-first, the fusion burners emitting a soft glow as they fired, ensuring the descent continued at a measured pace.

Unlike the blue haze they'd seen last time, this long passageway ended in a reddish-grey glow. Tangel looked over the readings and saw that most of the star's emissions were in the X-ray band, though some visible light came from the tightly packed cluster of neutrons.

"That's a lot of redshift," she said. "I wouldn't have expected it, given the mass decrease the builders undertook."

"The star bled a lot of heat when they siphoned off its neutronium for the other star," Tanis explained. "It's cooler than a neutron star its age should be."

That reminded Tangel of the black dwarf Joe had reported in the A1 System. That star was also far cooler than it should be, and she wondered if it too had been cooled by artificial means. In all the furor that had followed, she'd not made a note to send a team to investigate that star.

*Still plenty to do after the war.*

The *I2* passed out of the shaft and into the huge space inside the sphere. The star lay over a million kilometers below the ship, its gravitational pull drawing the vessel down faster and faster, Helm letting the ship accelerate until it was traveling at five hundred kilometers per second.

~Do you see it?~ Bob asked Tangel. ~The city.~

Tangel had not looked down yet, not with her own eyes. She turned toward the back of the bridge and disregarded the input from her two-dimensional eyes, shifting to her fourth-dimensional perception.

~Shit! It's **huge**.~

Where the neutron star was a tiny point only twenty kilometers across in three-dimensional space, the luminous object that filled the fourth and fifth dimensions was much larger, stretching half a million kilometers from the center of the sphere.

She mapped the ship's destination against the city built of starstuff, and saw that the I2 would stop at the surface of the structure.

~It stands to reason,~ Bob said. ~Mass and density do not translate the same way. In the lower dimensions, neutron stars are the densest objects aside from black holes. But that doesn't directly align.~

~So it would seem,~ Tangel nodded.

"I can tell you see it," Tanis said from her side. "I've only glimpsed an impression."

"It's beautiful," Tangel whispered. "It's like a billion mobius strips made from hypercubes."

The AI snorted. "OK, even I can't follow what that could look like."

"Maybe someday you will."

Tangel didn't speak for the remainder of the twenty-minute journey. When the ship finally halted, docked with an invisible city in the center of a dyson sphere, she glanced at Tanis.

"Do we go out to meet them?"

~No,~ Bob replied. ~*They are already here. Come to my primary node.*~

Tangel strode from the bridge with Tanis on her heels, eager to meet her first ascended humans, curious what they would look like in the higher dimensions.

"Are you nervous?" the AI asked. "You look nervous."

"Anxious. Curious. Not nervous, no."

The pair reached the lift that would take them down to Bob's primary node, and Tanis smiled. "They're kind. You'll like them."

"I'm less worried about that and more concerned with whether or not they'll help us."

Tanis glanced at Tangel, a worried look on her face. "They might not. They're a bit sorry that they ever developed the ability to fire neutronium. It's not the sort of thing you can put back in the bottle."

"Oh trust me," Tangel nodded emphatically. "I know that all too well. I've got quite the collection of things that don't go back in the bottle. Hopefully, if we can move Star City, that will be a worthwhile trade."

The AI snorted. "It's certainly a better offer than Orion made."

A few minutes later, they reached Bob's node and walked inside. Tangel was ready to see just about anything, though what she saw was a luminous, multilimbed being that looked like every other ascended person she'd seen.

~Tangel, Tanis,~ it said, the tone sounding distinctly male. ~My name is Eric.~

~Eric is one of the leaders in Star City,~ Bob said, adding to the introduction. ~He's different than the others, though, in that he's an AI.~

"Very nice to meet you," Tangel said aloud, dismayed that she was seeing yet another ascended AI and not one of the Dreamers. "I didn't realize there were AIs amongst your people. The *Perseus* left not long after the solar wars, if I don't miss my guess."

~I joined up at Lucida,~ Eric answered her question equably. ~Before that, I was at Proxima. Things had become a little…tense there, and it was better for me to find my fortune elsewhere. The FGT put out a call for AIs, and the rest is history.~

Tangel's eyes grew round. "Wait. No…you're not *that* Eric, are you? Commodore in Alpha Centauri's space force before you joined up with Jason and Terrance's merry band of marauders?"

~You know your lore,~ the AI commented. ~Though we were hardly marauders.~

"Sorry, couldn't think of another 'merry band of' name, and I know some Marauders who are stand-up people."

~I'll forgive you, then.~ The AI sent across the impression of a wink.

There was a moment of silence, and then Bob spoke.

~Now that introductions are out of the way, I'd like to talk about what we can do for each other.~

"Actually," Tangel held up a hand. "Before we get

into that, I'd like to ask why you haven't been helping the Bastions deal with the attacks from Orion."

"Until today, the other bastions didn't know that the ascended beings were still here," Tanis explained. "They'd revealed themselves to me, letting me know to call on them as a last resort, but that they were trying to keep the core AIs from knowing they were still here."

~Or Orion,~ Eric added. ~Praetor Kirkland reviles ascended beings. If he knew there were millions of us here, he'd throw everything he has at us. Essentially, hiding is the safest thing for us, even if Star City already is a massive target.~

"You could join in the fight," Tangel countered. "Stop Orion, stop the core AIs. Live in peace."

~We came out here to leave humanity's endless wars and squabbling behind.~ Eric's tone was even and measured. ~If we reveal ourselves to aid in this war, another will come along. We'd end up becoming the galaxy's police, eventually reviled by all, hated more than what we rose up to stop.~

Tangel nodded in grim agreement. "I have the same worry, though I don't have the luxury of hiding—not anymore, at least. We tried it as best we could, and got two good decades before the war found us. I can't say I agree with your stance on this, but I *do* understand it. I'm not exactly eager for what the future holds for me after this war is over."

"You're not?" Tanis cocked her head to the side, regarding Tangel curiously. "What do you think will happen?"

"In a nutshell? For me, and probably Bob, the war will never end."

"That's depressing," Tanis replied.

147

Tangel gave a noncommittal shrug. "I'm resigned to the fact that I may get a decade or two here and there when things aren't on fire somewhere. Honestly, that's more than humans used to get. Maybe I'll be able to find some others willing to help, and we can rotate out."

~Or maybe humanity will learn how to not fight all the time,~ Eric added.

~We'll see how that goes without the core AIs' meddling,~ Bob said. ~But for now, we have more immediate issues to deal with. In a nutshell, Eric, you wish to remain removed from the current struggle, and future conflicts as well. In all honesty, that's going to be problematic, unless your bastions take up a more punitive response to incursions.~

~That has been on my mind as well,~ Star City's representative replied. ~In the short-term, that will just escalate things further.~

A feeling of agreement came from Bob. ~Which is why the best solution for you is to move Star City.~

~An exodus has been on our mind for some time. As you know, however, it is not as simple as just leaving. We would have to remove what we've built here.~

~I believe that is not necessary,~ Bob countered. ~I'm certain that we can move all of Star City. The sphere, the neutron star, everything.~

~Through your jump gates.~ Eric did not seem convinced.

~Yes, that is how we would move you. I think that somewhere extragalactic would serve you well.~

The visitor didn't respond immediately, and Tangel waited patiently, able to see by the strands of energy stretching out from Eric that he was communicating with other ascended beings. After several minutes, he finally spoke.

*~And in exchange, you want us to leave you our other neutron star and its neutronium manipulation systems.~*

"That is correct," Tangel said. "With that, we can achieve decisive victory and win the war."

*~Your picotech isn't enough?~* Eric prompted. *~With that, you can devour entire planets.~*

"On a planetary scale, picotech is very slow, and it would be possible to stop it with sufficiently high magnetic fields. There are also…sociological reasons to limit its use as a weapon. Neutronium is just a better bullet."

*~And it is matter transmutation. That would provide other benefits.~*

Tangel pursed her lips. She had suspected that the ability to manipulate degenerate matter in the way Star City had done was tantamount to the direct manipulation of atomic structures themselves. That meant the beings living within the dyson sphere possessed femtotech—something she knew Earnest had been working on cracking for some time, but had not yet unlocked.

"We've been good stewards of the technology we have," Tangel countered. "All I want to do is to stop this war and strengthen humans and AIs for what is to come."

*~The conflict with the core AIs,~* Eric said.

"You know that everything going on right now is due to their manipulation. There is no question that we *must* defeat them. I plan to succeed, one way or another, but access to your technology will make the war shorter and less destructive. Not only that, but it will ensure a longer peace after the conflict."

~An imperial peace,~ he countered. ~Is that what you want?~

"Stars, no," Tangel gave a vehement shake of her head. ~I can't think of anything I want less—except for an eternal war.~

~I can't argue with that. I will discuss this with our elders. If they agree, we will put it to our full population. It may take several days for us to come to a conclusion. Also, we will require you to demonstrate the ability to move a star through a jump gate before we accept this deal.~

Tangel gave a nervous laugh. "Trust me, I also want to see it safely done with something less precious than Star City the first time."

~We will reach out when we're ready to discuss further,~ Eric said, and then turned and walked away.

The world he walked through was not the same as the one surrounding Tangel, though she could see both. The other ascended being's stride took him down a long ramp that led to a tower rising above the gleaming structure that was Star City.

She'd done her best not to stare at it during the conversation, but Tangel paused now to take it in, to follow the twisting structures that seemed impossible even in her perception of higher dimensions. It was clear to her that the denizens of the city existed in higher planes than she could perceive. She was curious if Bob could see all of it, but decided not to ask just yet.

A slow breath slipped past her lips, and she met

Tanis's gaze.

"I wish I could see it," the AI said. "Perhaps someday."

"Someday," Tangel replied, and then reached out to the bridge. <*Captain Rachel, take us out.*>

# SUPPOSITION

**STELLAR DATE: 10.17.8949 (Adjusted Years)**
**LOCATION: Palatine, Euros**
**REGION: Earth, New Sol, Orion Freedom Alliance**

The Orion Guard's top admiralty met deep within the Guard Command complex in what they called the 'Star Chamber'. Praetor Kirkland rarely visited it, usually preferring to summon the Guard's commanders to his own offices.

Today, he didn't have the patience required to wait for them to arrive.

He stormed down the long corridor that led to the chamber, his gaze fixed on the doors, willing the men and women within to sense his approach and ready themselves for what was to come.

*Of course, they'll know I'm coming, and I imagine they know why.*

A minute later, he reached the end of the hall, and as he neared the two massive slabs of stone, they swung aside, admitting him into the inner sanctum of his people's military.

The sixteen commanding admirals of the Orion Guard sat around the circular table, all eyes on him as the officers rose and nodded in greeting.

"Praetor Kirkland," Admiral Myka spoke first. "We were just discussing the latest reports. I assume that is why you are here."

"It is. I look forward to how you'll explain the defeats we've suffered."

"Well, for starters, they've been minor," Myka replied as she waited for Kirkland to take his seat. "We've lost a few systems in the Expansion Districts and on the rimward edge. What happened at Karaske and Rega was something else entirely."

"Oh?" Kirkland pressed. "Those were Transcend and ISF ships at Karaske. Karaske! That's deep within our borders. How did the enemy know that system was significant? Garza is too careful to have led his enemies there. Stars, half of you didn't even know that's where he based his operation."

The admirals glanced at one another before Myka cleared her throat and responded. "That was a betrayal, sir. Lisa Wrentham directed our enemies to attack Karaske. We also believe it was her Widows that destroyed Dock 1 in Rega. It seems like she's switched sides."

"Nonsense," Kirkland shook his head. "I've known her for thousands of years. She wouldn't just turn on me."

"Her ship was—"

Kirkland's hand sliced through the air. "Lisa Wrentham is not her ship! Yes, it is possible that the *Perilous Dream* has been taken by our enemies and they're using it against us, but I will not hear of Lisa's betrayal. She's lost more than you could know to join the true cause."

"And the reports that her Widows were fighting against Orion Guard forces on Durgen?" Admiral Myka pressed. "Could our enemies have taken control of her Widows?"

"No." Kirkland shook his head. "That is not possible. Lisa assured me herself."

"Are—" Admiral Prel began, but the praetor cut him off.

"We have Transcend fleets operating inside our borders, they've taken the *Perilous Dream*, and the Transcend's civil war has come to an end. It feels like the tide is turning against us, people. I want to know what you intend to do to stop this."

"We've no word from General Garza," Myka's tone betrayed no emotion. "Are you suggesting that I take control of the war effort?"

Kirkland locked his gaze on Myka's. He knew that some of the admirals in the room with him were fully Garza's creatures, more loyal to the general than their own praetor. He'd never been able to discern where Myka's loyalties lay.

*Well, maybe if I elevate her above Garza, she'll become more loyal to me.*

He knew the logic was weak, but he needed a clear commander. Without it, the admirals would fight for days amongst themselves.

"I think that's possible," he replied. "First, tell me what you plan to do to gain the upper hand."

A smile cracked Myka's lips apart, and she summoned a holodisplay above the table. "For starters, we have to stop defending points we don't care about. We must put all our attention into two, singular strikes...."

Kirkland leant back in his chair and interlaced his fingers, nodding slowly as the admiral explained her plan.

*Yes, I think this just might work.*

# PART 4 – PIVOTAL

## CONSIDERATIONS

**STELLAR DATE: 10.16.8949 (Adjusted Years)**
**LOCATION: TSS *Cora's Triumph***
**REGION: Interstellar Space, Inner Praesepe Empire**

Terrance gave Earnest a mock scowl as they walked onto the *Cora's Triumph*'s bridge. "Just like Tangel to swoop in, get all the glory, and then fly off."

"Trust me," Earnest said with a heartfelt sigh. "This tears me up inside. I want to see Star City more than I can say, but getting to the bottom of what the core AIs are up to is even more important. Plus, we might be able to use their tech to aid in accelerating Project Starflight."

"I get that," Terrance glanced at Earnest, noting the glimmer in the man's eyes. "And stopping this entire star cluster from going boom is kinda important."

"Oh?" Captain Beatrice cocked an eyebrow from where she stood next to the holotank. "Just kinda? If I'd known that, I wouldn't have put up such a fight when those core ships attacked."

"Heard you gave 'em what for," Earnest said, his voice growing quiet.

"We did," she replied, her voice lowering. "As did you."

Terrance nodded solemnly. "It was hard-won, but worth it, Captain. We got what we came for, and we're one step closer to shutting down the core AIs."

"Well," Earnest held up a hand. "Shutting down might be a bit of an overstatement.

"Pardon my eternal optimism," Terrance said with a rueful laugh. "So, are we ready to move on to our friendly neighborhood drone sphere?"

"Sue's finishing the final integration of the data we got from the C&C," Earnest nodded toward a panel that was initializing on the forward holodisplay. "We're setting it up in an NSAI core and sandboxing the hell out of it. Not going to risk some trojan getting into the ship."

"I appreciate that," Beatrice drawled. "Should we set a course?"

Terrance glanced at Earnest, who nodded and said, "Bring us to fifty thousand klicks. That will be close enough for a lag-less interface and far enough that we can run away if necessary."

"Still some light-lag at fifty thousand," the captain said.

"Sorry, less laggy," Earnest said with a long-suffering glance at the captain. "You've been around these scientists too long. Their pedantry is wearing off on you."

Beatrice laughed. "I suppose it is. So how come you're immune? You're the ultimate scientist."

"Comes from being married to Abby. I've had to get regular inoculations to be around her."

Terrance snorted and covered his mouth. "Sorry, I just imagined the largest syringe ever with 'Withstand Abby' on the side."

"If you hadn't been the one who got us together, I'd

take offense to that," Earnest countered. "Ah, Sue's done, we're online. Going to send the initialization commands now."

"One hour till we reach a fifty-k orbit," Beatrice added. "Or do you need us to rush it more than that?"

"No," Earnest shook his head. "It'll take a bit to sort through the control interfaces, figure out what they do. This system was not made for humans to operate."

"Good thing we have you." Terrance met Beatrice's gaze, and a sly smile formed on his lips. "An hour or so should be enough, right?"

"Only if you shut up for a minute or two," Earnest muttered, the smile in his eyes contradicting the scorn in his voice.

Even so, Terrance took the hint and walked to the far side of the holotank, watching the drone swarm grow larger with each passing minute. As the engineers worked their way through the control systems, data began to appear alongside the object on the display, noting mass, number of drones, types of drones, and resource limits.

It turned out that there was a moonlet beneath the swarm, but it was over half gone, its mass converted into the single-use machines that fell into the star they were moving once their task was done.

The waste bothered Terrance until he considered that, with the time between optimal burns—and the fact that the core AIs planned to obliterate the entire cluster—it didn't really matter how efficient they were with the use of resources from one small rogue body.

In turn, it made him upset that they were going to

destroy an entire open cluster...for what remained reasons unknown.

"What do you think their goal is?" he asked Beatrice, who had been silently standing at his right shoulder.

"The core AIs?"

The question was rhetorical, but he nodded anyway, signaling her to continue.

"Well, I suppose it'll depend on whether or not they're doing this in other clusters surrounding Sol. The wave of supernovae this will cause won't reach the core worlds for centuries, easily enough time for people to move. But if they do this here, in Hyades, the Pleiades and others, the result will be the sterilization of the Inner Stars."

"But like you said, it'll be slow."

The ship's captain nodded. "Right, but where are all the people going to go? They're going to have to travel across a hundred empires to get to unclaimed space, and what if the core AIs have done the same thing in clusters further out? Humanity will fall into a final war where we battle it out over the tiny slivers of the galaxy that are still habitable."

"That seems a bit melodramatic," Terrance said. "Maybe if we hadn't discovered the core AIs' plan, and if we didn't have jump gates...."

"There are just too many people to relocate them all through jump gates...and some will remain, fighting over the scraps. You have to admit that, at the least, it will weaken us all beyond the worst of the FTL wars. You can hide from a war, but you can't hide from a dozen supernovae shockwaves."

He nodded, evaluating her words. "If you consider that they started this awhile back, and that everyone thought the *Intrepid* would appear five hundred years from now, I can see them playing a long game to have our disruption come into play right around the same time as the supernovae shockwave starts to hit populated areas."

"A lot of long games being played," Beatrice muttered. "I wonder how long it'll take to find out if they're doing this elsewhere."

"Well, there are over twelve hundred open clusters, and more than two hundred globular clusters in the galaxy. Plus a number of star-forming regions that they could mess up. So maybe two thousand locations we have to check out, and since all of them are likely slow zones, it's not going to be a fast process. Probably take decades...and that's if they're all clear."

"And if none of them are further along than Praesepe."

Beatrice's words caused a sliver of fear to take hold in Terrance's mind. If there was the possibility that a star cluster could fall into a cascade of supernovae, it would take some drastic measures to prevent the event—though he had no idea what measures those would be.

He chatted off and on with Beatrice for the next hour, the pair moving on from a discussion of what dangers the core AIs posed, to what Terrance had busied himself with during the two decades New Canaan had been at peace.

"I enjoyed losing myself in the establishment of our economy more than I thought I would have," he said. "I thought I was over that sort of thing, but it came back with a vengeance. We were trying to make something where everyone could have enough security to explore their personal interests, while still incentivizing everyone to work in the colony's best interests. I think we did rather well with it—until we had to toss all that aside and go to a war footing."

"I imagine that will take a bit to reorient," the captain said. "My home is a bit lucky—it's in the Vela Cluster, which sided with Khardine almost immediately. The civil war never made it to our astrosphere, so other than some general disruption in trade, things remained largely unchanged…. At least, that's what I've heard from my brother back home. I do wonder if he's just telling me what I want to hear so I won't worry."

"Airtha was such a fool," Terrance muttered. "She should have sided *with* New Canaan, not fought against us."

"Same thing is true for Orion," Beatrice added. "Ultimately, we all want to stop the core AIs from fucking around with us. From what I've heard, the schism between Tomlinson and Kirkland hit its breaking point when they learned about the core AIs. Rather than pissing off, the *praetor* should have worked with us to stop the core devils. Instead, he delayed the Inner Stars' uplift, and now he's stopping us from going after the real enemy."

"Yeah," Terrance nodded emphatically. "From what I can see, the core AIs played Kirkland like a fiddle…Jeffrey too."

"Well, they are a bunch of all-powerful AIs. Stands to

reason that they'd be able to mess with us."

"They're not all-powerful," he corrected. "From what Tangel distills it down to, they just have better eyesight."

The captain snorted. "That's an interesting way to put it. Though from what I've seen, they can also shred matter and blast you with photonic and electric energy. That seems like more than good eyesight."

Terrance barked a rueful laugh. "Yeah, it does, doesn't it? I never said I really agreed with her assessment, just relating her thoughts on the matter."

"Do you think we'll all ascend eventually?"

He turned and stared into the captain's eyes, trying to discern whether she was excited or scared by the prospect. Her eyes were unreadable, but her right hand was clenching and unclenching.

"Maybe," he allowed. "But I think you generally have to want it."

"Did Tangel want it?"

"Well, that's a different sort of scenario. I don't claim to understand all the ins and outs of what she went through, but if there is such a thing as fate, it had her squarely in its sights."

"Was it fate, or was she manipulated?"

Terrance shrugged. "If anything thought they could manipulate Tangel, they got a rude awakening."

"You put a lot of stock in her."

"Yeah, well, she always comes through."

"I think we've figured it out," Earnest said from behind the pair, and Terrance turned to see Sue standing next to the engineer.

"When did you get here?" he asked.

"Twenty minutes ago," the AI smirked. "I'm like a ninja."

Earnest rolled his eyes and gestured to the holotank, which showed the drone sphere shrouded in darkness.

"You're going to love this, Terrance," he said. "They're using a formulation of Elastene that still has the Enfield markers in it. I guess there's no reason to mess with a good thing."

"Damn," Terrance felt a twist in his gut. "How many times are my company's inventions going to be co-opted by fucking evil bastards?"

"Easy now," Earnest placed a hand on his shoulder. "Your family made a lot of good stuff…. It's no wonder that everyone uses it even six thousand years later."

"Hooray. So, what have you learned?"

"Well, all the stellar alterations they've made are logged in the data we pulled, and the drone moon is all but automated, though it possesses no C&C of its own, and we blew up the last one."

"Right," Sue joined in. "So for now, the *Cora's Triumph* is that C&C. We've already programmed our first major correction for two of the core's blue giants, and if they shift like the models predict, we should have the stars back to a stable pattern in fifty years."

"Really?" Terrance was surprised by the speed, given how long it had taken to shift the stars off course.

"We're not trying to hide what we're doing," Earnest explained. "We can go a lot faster than the core AIs did."

"Ma'am?" the comm officer spoke up. "A courier jumped in back at the gate array. A message from the field marshal just came on sublight."

"I guess we don't have a QC blade that links up with the right places," Beatrice muttered. "Put the message up."

The forward display shifted to show Tangel standing at the edge of a city, the faint sound of waves slapping against the shore in the background.

"Terrance and Earnest. I've worked out a deal with the people of Star City. They're going to give us their technology, and their second neutron star, on the condition that we move Star City."

"Good thing we have the ability to do that now," Beatrice said, gesturing to the display on the holotank.

"This is where you're going to say something really terrible," Tangel continued. "But this was Bob's idea, and he thinks it's possible, so you can get mad at *him*. We're going to move Star City out of the galaxy, with a jump gate."

"What the ever-loving fuck," Earnest muttered. "There's no way at all, under no circumstances...just, no!"

"I'm bringing Finaeus here, and Terrance...an old friend of yours is waiting to meet you. You're not going to believe who."

"That woman!" Earnest shook his head. "I swear, someday she's going to ask me to move the galaxy."

Terrance barely heard the engineer's outburst, wondering who it was that Tangel had met, a tiny hope welling up inside that it just might be Khela.

# RECALLED

**STELLAR DATE: 10.16.8949 (Adjusted Years)**
**LOCATION: *Sabrina*, Airthan trojan asteroids**
**REGION: Huygens System, Transcend Interstellar Alliance**

"We've got company!" Cheeky cried out, spinning the ship and punching the fusion burners up to their full thrust. A-grav system warnings lit up across her board as the strain on the ship's frame caused it to twist violently.

A depressurization warning flashed in the main hold, caused by the bay door unseating, and she pursed her lips, knowing that Nance was going to give her a tongue-lashing over the abuse she was putting *Sabrina* through.

<*I see them!*> the ship's AI called out. <*Just don't break me to bits, and I'll take them out.*>

Cheeky grunted her acknowledgment and held her course for ten seconds while Sabrina unleashed the unassuming freighter's beams on the two destroyers that had dropped stealth only ten thousand kilometers away.

<*Think they can sneak up on me?! Taste my hot breath, assholes!*>

"Oh gawd…gawd!" Cheeky grimaced. "That was terrible! Don't mix things like that…ewww."

<*What…ohhhh…wow. Yeah, not what I meant at all.*>

"I think I got all the sense when we sharded," Sabs said from where she sat at the scan console. "OK, you tore a hole clear through one of them, it's dead in the water, but the other is trying to limp away."

<*Not for long,*> Sabrina replied. <*Hold steady another*

*sec.>*

Cheeky complied, and a shudder rippled through the deck as both railguns fired in unison, a trio of slugs bursting from each weapon, streaking across the small gap between the ships and smashing the destroyer's starboard engine. The Airthan craft's other burner winked out a moment later, and it slewed to the side, spinning slowly as it drifted through the black.

"That the last of them?" Cheeky asked, wiping a hand across her brow. "Who would have thought that Airtha would have 'true believers' and that they'd be fucking nuts? Don't they know they lost and Airtha is dead?"

"You shall not defile her holy shrine…" Sabs intoned. "Only Airthans shall tread in that sacred place."

*<More like airheads,>* Sabrina scoffed. *<Sucks that we're stuck here on cleanup duty and not dealing with a real threat.>*

"Or hunting for Cary," Cheeky added. "But it has to be done, right? We didn't fight so hard to secure Airtha, only to have these dorks take it back."

*<You done turning my ship into a pretzel?>* Nance called up. *<Because we're leaking stuff down here that should never be leaked.>*

*<Yeah, all's clear. What did we crack open?>*

*<Oh, you know, the usual, just a tank full of stuff that we pretend we don't grow things in for food in a pinch.>*

*<Why can't you just say 'shit',>* Sabs asked.

Nance snorted. *<Because I have you to say it for me.>*

"Admiral Krissy on the horn for us," Sabs announced.

Cheeky sat up straight, somehow feeling like she was talking to her mom when Krissy called—which was more than a little strange, since it was she who was married to the admiral's father.

"We've cleaned things up around the trailing trojan asteroids," Cheeky reported. "Two more destroyers out here. They haven't dumped any pods yet."

"Stars, they're like freaking cockroaches," Krissy muttered. "I'll see that boarding and cleanup teams get sent out. I need you to get to High Airtha and pick my dad up before heading to the main gate array."

"Ummm sure…. Where we headed?"

"Tangel has requested you all get to Star City. Well, she kind of demanded Finaeus—you know how she is—but suggested that you be the ones to courier him over."

<Story of my life,> Sabrina chimed in. <Couriering Finaeus.>

"Either that, or searching for him," Sabs added.

"OK," Cheeky responded to Krissy while shooting Sabs a quelling look. "We'll drop a beacon and be on our way. Did Tangel say *why* she wants us at Star City? Not that I'm complaining, I can't wait to see the kids again."

"She only said that she needs Finaeus to build a…and I'm quoting here…star gate."

"A stargate?" Cheeky glanced at Sabs. "Didn't we watch an old 2D about that?"

"Sure did," the AI nodded. "Though the series was better than the movie."

"Uh, sure," Krissy said with a long-suffering look on her face. "Just get a move on, Tangel seemed like there was some level of urgency."

"You bet." Cheeky brought the ship onto a vector that would get them to High Airtha in a few hours. "One delivery of a grumpy old man, coming right up."

"Thanks, Cheeks," the admiral said. "Give him a kiss for me."

"Uhh…is that weird? He's your father, and I'm his wife. I kiss differently than you."

"Can't you just give him a peck on the cheek?"

Cheeky cocked her head. "I don't think I've ever given anyone a peck on the check. Usually it's between the che—"

"Gah! Cheeky. Enough." The admiral groaned and shook her head. "I'm sorry I asked."

# THE NEW BUILDERS
STELLAR DATE: 10.17.8949 (Adjusted Years)
LOCATION: Manhattan Island, North America
REGION: Star City, Orion Freedom Alliance, Perseus Arm

"Not a lot impresses me anymore," Terrance said as he approached Tangel, his eyes filled with wonder. "But this does."

She smiled and clasped his outstretched hand. "I thought you might like it. So far as I know, this place is unique—that alone is something uncommon in this universe."

"We flew over El Dorado." Moisture formed in the corners of his eyes. "The planet and the ring. Jason's going to have to come out here some time."

"You could always visit AC when the war is over," Tangel suggested. "No reason why not."

Terrance shook his head. "I can think of a few. It's not the same...filled with people, and ones I'm not too keen on, given their participation in the Hegemony. Here, it's pristine, looks like it did when I grew up."

"I feel the same way. I made a trip over to Mars, climbed Olympus Mons. Relived my childhood, all the good stuff."

The one-time executive nodded soberly. "That's something you can't do back in the Sol System. Not without clambering over the ruin of the ring, at least."

"Yeah, though I plan to do that someday, anyway. I feel like I owe it to my family to stand there and remember. Do you realize that only a few thousand living people have stood on terraformed Mars?"

"Proud to be one of them." Terrance smiled and placed a hand on her shoulder. "Maybe we can remake it."

"Maybe." She placed her hand over his. "Sorry I was all cryptic when I said there was someone here and didn't say who it was. I was feeling almost giddy then, but now that I'm a bit more melancholy, it seems foolish of me to have toyed with you like that. Especially because you probably thought it was Khela—which it's not."

"I didn't know you knew about her."

Tangel twisted her lips. "Well, I didn't until Bob told me about her. Anyway, the person is Eric."

Terrance's eyes widened, and his mouth fell open. "Eric...*my* Eric?"

"Yeah, I guess he was with the *Perseus* worldship, came out to Serenity with them, and then left with the builders to come and make Star City."

"So he ascended." The words fell from Terrance's lips like lead weights. "I thought there were only ascended humans here."

"A few AIs, as well, as it turns out," Tangel said. "Him, and a few of the Bastions. When they ascended, they just flitted down to the neutron star in the center of the sphere and built a city on it in the higher dimensions."

A snort burst from his lips. "Sure, of course. That's what *I'd* do, build a city on a neutron star. So is he here, or do I have to go down?"

"We convinced them to come up for the next chat. It's

a bit dangerous inside the sphere. The magnetic fields could rip the *I2* to shreds."

"I've read that about neutron stars."

"Oh? You're an astronomer now?"

"Tangel, you left me with the FGT's top stellar engineers for weeks. I have at least two or three degrees now, mostly earned while getting drunk and discussing what could happen if various stars in Praesepe crashed into one another."

"Which is?" Tangel pressed.

"Not good. So much not good."

She chortled. "I think the drunk version of your degrees are lacking some specifics—but I get the sentiment."

"Thanks for waiting," Earnest said as he stepped out of the shuttle and walked across the grass to where Tangel and Terrance waited. "Bob was bending my ear—well, my brain—about a thousand different topics. Guy can be exhausting."

*<I can hear you out there.>*

"I know, that's my passive-aggressive way of reminding you that I'm still organic. I can't think as fast as you can."

*<You're organic like I'm still an AI,>* Bob retorted.

"What does that mean?" Terrance glanced at Earnest, an eyebrow cocked in question.

"Mods," Tangel said in a singsong voice, gesturing at the scientist. "Honestly, he rivals me for lack of original parts at this point."

"Yeah, but where you're all muscles, I'm all brains," Earnest countered. "Actually…that's a lie. You have three brains, so you've got me beat there as well. Why do you need me here, again? I was all ready to play with my drone swarm."

Tangel looked over Earnest's shoulder to where the *I2* hovered above the Atlantic Ocean. "Oh, I don't know, probably because I'm commander of the largest war in humanity's history. That takes a lot of concentration. I'm reviewing four after-action reports from the fronts, seven intel feeds, and working with two planning teams on an attack in the Trisilieds and the Hyades."

Terrance looked at Earnest and mouthed 'showoff'.

"There they are." Tangel pointed toward the sky, and Terrance and Earnest turned to gaze up.

"Where?" Terrance asked.

<Sabrina *is over two thousand kilometers away still,*> Bob admonished. <*You know they can't see it yet.*>

"Well, they were accusing me of being a showoff, so I figured I'd best live up to it."

The trio chatted about the state of the war, the ISF fleet, and shared news from New Canaan while they waited. Tangel was glad to hear that Erin had finally returned to Carthage to discuss a run for office with Jason. Elections were coming in the following year—provided the war was over—and neither Tangel nor Jason wanted to be in power.

Ten minutes later, *Sabrina* was settling down on the cradle vacated by the shuttle that had brought Earnest and Terrance. The trio turned toward the ship, once again sporting the blue and silver colors that had been present when Tangel was first aboard.

The craft had barely settled into the cradle when the

airlock door opened and Finaeus leapt out onto the still-rising ramp.

"It can't be done!" he shouted. "I don't care what Bob says. It's madness!"

"Glad he's ready to consider options," Earnest said out of the side of his mouth.

"Why not?" Tangel asked as he drew near, waving at the rest of the ship's crew as they exited the ship.

"Gravity, my dear ascended fool. *Gravity.* The two stars in this system are in an intricate dance, living deep in their gravity wells, carving deep gouges through spacetime. Add to that the propensity that neutron stars have for starquakes—ones that smash out gravitons like they have nothing else to do—and you have a thing that *cannot be moved.*"

Earnest was nodding. "I've been thinking about that, too. If we remove this star and sphere, the other one is going to streak clear out of the system…at a healthy clip, too."

"Not to mention the angular momentum of Star City when it lands wherever we put it. It might just tear itself to shreds."

*<Not if we slow down these two stars, first. We move them further apart, and then swap them at just the right time.>*

"I'm sorry," Finaeus waved a hand toward the *I2.* "I forgot that we have two ascended fools giving out terrible advice. Swap *what*—"

The words died on Finaeus's lips, and his mouth formed a wide 'O'.

*<Gravity moves at the speed of light. We pull Star City out at the same time that we drop two other smaller mass stars*

*into its L3 and L4. Then we land Star City somewhere with a similarly massed star as its new counterpart. That star will flare like mad, but we can shield the city from it.>*

"Oversimplified, but it could work," Earnest said. "Maybe our ascended friends aren't such fools after all."

"Well, thank you," Tangel said.

"*Maybe,*" Finaeus wagged a finger at Tangel. "So do we get to work now, or do we have to have a meeting with more glowy balls of light?"

"Don't pay attention to him," Cheeky said as she reached the group and wrapped Tangel in an embrace. "He's just grumpy because the trip was so short that we didn't get to have any shenanigans."

"Plenty of time for that," he groused. "This is no overnight project. Going to take months, easy."

Tangel nodded to Nance, Sabs, Amavia, and Misha. "You three are welcome to join us for this conversation, it should be interesting."

"Fate-of-the-galaxy interesting, or *actually* interesting?" Misha asked. "Because, frankly, I'm getting a bit bored with constantly having to save all the shit that's burning down around us."

"Well," Tangel tapped a finger against her chin. "I suppose it's a bit of column A and a bit of column B. Moving stars is no mean feat."

"Yes," Finaeus nodded. "Stars. A lot of stars. There'll be a test star, maybe more than one if we fail, then braking stars, and maybe others for balancing mass and testing vector change. Fascinating stuff!"

"I thought you thought it was stupid," Tangel said.

"Oh it probably still is." A broad grin stretched the

engineer's lips wide. "But it's my kind of stupid. Besides, how will I ever build a ring around the galaxy if I don't first practice moving stars?"

"Good point," Earnest nodded. "Gotta skill up."

"Granted, it would be nice if our first major project wasn't moving a star that was also a city."

Tangel placed a hand on Finaeus's shoulder, a sly smile forming on her lips. "Well, if you hadn't run off and become an antiquities dealer in the Inner Stars for a few decades, you'd be further ahead."

"Not to mention sending us to Grey Wolf, where we jumped halfway across the galaxy," Cheeky added. "Chop-chop, mister, we have lost time to make up for."

"I think I'll go for a walk through the city," Misha said. "Just look around, soak it in. I'd love to go to the real Earth someday."

Tangel would have loved to go on that same stroll, but she didn't have an option to do so. Even if her input wasn't necessary, she still needed to manage the plan.

"I'd like to join you," Cheeky said, her lips twisting with indecision. "But chances are that they're going to need me to fly a ship that's going to move those stars...or move something that moves stars later."

"I don't know that we'll get that far today." Finaeus gave Cheeky a light peck. "If you want to wander around, feel free."

"That's my plan," Sabs chimed in. "Sabrina can listen in to all that nonsense, I'm going to soak up the sights."

<I see how it is.>

"OK, then. Everyone who wants to go to boring meetings about moving stars, with me," Tangel held up a hand. "Everyone else, group up around Cheeky."

With a dose of good-natured laughter, the crowd split up, and Tangel led Terrance, Finaeus, and Earnest toward one of the nearby towers. On the way there, she passed Jessica and Trevor.

"Bailing before we start?" Tangel asked.

"Cheeky told me there's going to be ice cream," Jessica shrugged. "I'm not one to say no to a walk on the shoreline followed by some frozen milk."

Terrance snorted. "Sound logic. Why am I going to the meeting, again?"

"Eric?" Tangel prompted as they continued on their way.

"Right! Eric. Plus, I'm also shockingly good at corralling engineers and keeping them on task."

"Seriously? Do you really think we need that?" Finaeus asked.

The former head of Enfield Technologies fixed the ancient engineer with a serious look. "Didn't we just talk about you running off and becoming an antiquities dealer?"

"I was retired…and running for my life. Retirunning. It's a valid excuse. Look, if you know someone else who can make a stargate, feel free to call them up."

Earnest winked. "I thought it couldn't be done."

"Oh for starssakes," Finaeus muttered. "You going to throw that in my face forever?"

Tangel smacked a palm against her forehead. "You said it five minutes ago!"

"In *this* spacetime. In another spacetime, it might be centuries ago."

"I'll send *you* to another spacetime," Tangel gave a soft laugh as well as a narrow-eyed glare to keep Finaeus on his toes.

Once inside the tower, the group walked through tall, empty halls until they came to a meeting room where Tanis, Kira, and Troy waited, along with Eric and two other ascended beings.

The two new denizens of Star City confirmed her suspicion that ascended humans would appear to be very different than ascended AIs. To her organic eyes, their forms were vaguely humanoid, but indistinct, as though all of their defining features had been smoothed over. They also appeared to have six arms, and were over three meters tall. The visual caused her to wonder if it was at all possible that humans had ascended in the past and whether some ancient mythology had been based on encounters with those ascended beings.

*Or it's just logical for people to envision deities that look like things they can relate to.*

<Which one is Eric?> Terrance asked her as they walked into the room.

<The tentacled one. I guess that's normal for AIs, since they don't have bipedal self-images like we do.>

<I suppose that makes sense.>

"Eric," Tangel said aloud. "Thank you for coming to us this time. The city is something to see, but the journey is not for the faint of heart."

~Understandable. And since we're not hiding ourselves anymore, there's no reason not to come up to the surface.~ He gestured to the other ascended beings. ~Corin and Bill were two of the chief engineers behind Star City.~

177

"Shit...Corin?" Finaeus shook his head, mouth agape. "I wondered where you wound up. You weren't on the roster for the *Perseus*."

*~A story for another time, Finaeus. I was glad to know you were well when you were here a decade ago, though I do wonder how you think you can move our city.~*

The ancient engineer snorted. "Well, it's Bob who thinks it can be done. He just wants Earnest and I to do the legwork."

*~Do you want to sit, before we get down to brass tacks?~* Eric asked.

"I'm OK standing," Earnest said. "So long as someone brings some drinks. Like brandy. This is definitely a brandy sort of conversation."

"I'll have some synthesized," Tanis said, only to have Finaeus hold up a hand in protest.

"Stars, no. If we're to have fortifying drinks, it has to be the real thing."

<*I have a servitor coming with a selection,*> Sabrina said, her voice lilting with laughter.

"Always knew you were the best sort of AI," Finaeus said.

<*Are you conversing with Eric?*> Tangel asked Terrance privately.

<*I am...it's amazing to think he's been alive—well alive-ish—all this time. He and I had a complicated relationship when we parted ways. It's good to be able to look back on it now with better perspective.*>

<*That's good. I'd be interested in knowing what happened, if you're willing to tell.*>

Finaeus, Earnest, and the two ascended engineers had

fallen deep into the details of how one could move a star and not have the changes in gravitational forces acting on it create irreparable damage.

Tangel continued to half listen to it as Terrance suggested that he tell the tale along with Eric. She initiated an expanse—a replica of her lakehouse on the *I2*—and Eric appeared as a grizzled old soldier.

The three took seats around the fireplace, and Terrance began to explain the events that had taken place at Proxima Centauri almost six thousand years before.

"Back then, even though the Phobos Accords had been signed in the Sol System, there was still a burgeoning trade amongst the near-Sol colonies for shackled AIs. A lot of AIs fled Sol during the outset of the Second Solar War, only to find themselves enslaved by cartels and unscrupulous corporations."

"I recall reading some of that," Tangel inclined her head. "Some vigilante groups went around freeing them, right?"

"Indeed," Eric replied. "I led one such group, though we were unofficially-officially sanctioned."

"Phantom Blade." A melancholy smile settled on Terrance's lips. "That's where Jason and I met, and where I met Eric, here. We stopped the illegal trade at El Dorado, and found that some of the AIs had been sent to Proxima, so we took a ship, the...."

"*Speedwell*," Eric supplied.

"Right!" Terrance snapped his fingers. "The *Speedwell*. Anyway, due to some rather bizarre circumstances, a truly insane AI who styled himself as 'Prime' snuck aboard the ship."

"Inside Jason's sister," Eric added.

"Yes...which made for more than a few complications." Terrance's gaze settled on Eric, and he drew in a deep breath. "We had come to realize that Prime was in control of her, and had hunted her across C-47, the primary hab in Proxima at the time. Prime was working on taking control of the whole place, and we were at a loss for how to stop him while saving Jason's sister, so..."

"So I assumed control of Terrance's body, and shot Prime out of her head."

Terrance snorted. "You still have such a way with words."

"I don't feel shame for that—the shooting. I *do* hate that it caused you anguish, and breached our trust. Even so, given the options at the time, I would do it again."

"Trust me," the former executive clasped his hands and stared at his lap for a moment. "I'm glad you did it. I couldn't bring myself to, but it had to be done. You saved Proxima with that one action."

He turned to Tangel before continuing.

"Prime was an AI unlike any we'd seen before, and few since. Others, like the Psion AIs, wrought atrocities on humanity to further their ends. Prime did it because he was, at his core, deeply broken. I'm certain he derived whatever his version of joy was from torturing humans."

Tangel's brow lowered. "I'm surprised I'd never heard of this before."

"It was kept quiet," Eric explained. "Some people knew about a rogue AI named Prime, but it sort of got mixed up in Phantom Blade's mission to rescue shackled AIs, so a lot of people assumed Prime was being used by people, and not the other way around."

"He could turn people into sock puppets faster than you could say...well, 'sock puppet'," Terrance added.

"On the plus side, the attack vectors he used greatly improved Link security. So much of the protections people have around their minds now come from how Prime was able to control people."

Tangel looked from one man to the other. "So that's when you decided to take your leave, Eric?"

"The AI council at Proxima was not pleased with what I'd done.... I'd violated the Phobos Accords and a host of ethical considerations. I was removed from Terrance, and ordered never to embed in a human again."

"Did you abide by that?" Terrance asked.

A grin formed on Eric's lips. "No."

"Not surprised. How a rule-breaker like you made it to the rank of commodore, I'll never know."

"Commodore," Tangel mused. "That's a title that's fallen out of use. I rather like it."

"God-empress not available?" Terrance laughed.

"Not funny," Tangel chastised. "Besides, as is clearly evident by the company we're sharing these days, I'm the new girl on the block. There are many who are far more ancient and evolved than I."

Eric fixed Tangel with a penetrating look, his head tilting to the side. "I'm not so certain that's true. Older, yes. Perhaps wiser, too. But you're on a different track than anyone else. Well, you *and* Bob. Neither of you are anything like the people of Star City, nor like the other ascended beings we've come into contact with."

"Other ascended beings?" Tangel asked.

"Not something I'm privy to discuss." Eric's tone brooked no dispute, and Tangel settled back in her seat, regarding the ascended being skeptically.

"So that's our story," Terrance changed the subject. "I'm glad that you made it safely to Lucida and the FGT, Eric."

"Stars, that was an interesting period. So much of the mess you're dealing with now comes from there. I thought we could escape the schism growing in the FGT, but we didn't go far enough."

"Or maybe you went just far enough," Terrance countered. "To be exactly where we needed you to be to help end this."

Eric shook his head. "As I told Tangel, there will always be another conflict, another great war. There is no end."

"Perhaps," she said, peering into the former AI's eyes. "But the core AIs clearly spread the Exdali around the galaxy as a way to slow human expansion. I wonder if some similar solution might be possible…without all the death and destruction."

"A solution for human expansion?" Terrance asked. "That sounds draconian."

"In our prior meeting, Eric mentioned that his people had no interest in becoming the galaxy's police. I don't much like the idea, either, but at present, we're in a situation where, if we don't keep things under control— after this war, that is—we'll end up doing it all over again."

"So what are you suggesting?" Terrance asked. "Surely not something like what Praetor Kirkland enforces in Orion, keeping the majority of his people living in technological poverty."

Tangel shrugged. "I don't have a solid answer yet, but the idea that I can't shake is what if FTL was no longer possible? Would that be enough to stop most major wars?"

Eric nodded slowly. "It might. It would at least constrain the scope of most conflicts. There still might be marauding fleets, but they would likely move slower than the speed of civilization—meaning people would expand and rebuild faster than marauders could attack."

"Not to mention, you'd see them coming," Tangel replied. "Like we did with the Sirians. Even with our fledgling civilization, we were able to hold them back."

"Until they got FTL," Terrance added.

Tangel nodded soberly. "Exactly."

"Well, this has been enlightening," Eric rose from the chair. "And it seems as though our engineers have worked out a trial subject."

"I've been following along," Tangel said as she rose as well. "An interesting bit of symmetry."

"What is?" Terrance asked. "I've not been able to follow both conversations."

A smile lit Tangel's face. "They're going to build the first test stargate at Grey Wolf. It's their plan to jump that star here."

"Well, that should be interesting."

* * * * *

"Grey Wolf?" Jessica asked, her eyes wide as she settled into a seat in *Sabrina*'s galley. "You're going to move a dwarf star surrounded by black holes out *here*?"

Tangel couldn't help but laugh at the incredulous look on Jessica's face.

"Well, I'm not," she teased. "I'm going to keep fighting a war. Earnest and Finaeus are going to move that white dwarf."

"And the black holes." Jessica's expression remained deadly serious. "It's surrounded by black holes. In a ring, spinning really fast."

"So I've heard," Tangel replied. "My understanding is that the complexity and density are both a key part of the test. Then the team will use Grey Wolf's matter to build the larger stargate here, as well as begin the starbraking."

"How long is all this going to take?" Jessica asked. "This seems like a *massive* project. Wasn't the hope to get the neutronium tech so that we could use it as a war-ending deterrent?"

"Yeah," Tangel sighed. "It was. However, they're also starting work on a gate capable of jumping neutronium rounds. I pushed for that as a requirement."

"I guess if you can move a star, then neutronium bullets shouldn't be too hard. Wait, I thought it was impossible to push a black hole through a jump gate, due to some sort of mass interaction between the pseudo black hole that is the gate, and then the real one?"

<*That was my understanding as well,*> Sabrina chimed

in.

"Well, Airtha disproved that," Tangel said. "Remember when we encountered the first DMG ship out in the Large Magellanic Cloud? That had a rather massive black hole inside—for something that can be contained in a starship, at least. Anyway, it came in via jump gate, so we know it can be done. Earnest and Terrance have been working on solving that one for weeks now, and they both think they've figured it out."

"Well, that sounds promising."

Sabrina laughed. <Their solutions are contradictory.>

"Oh," Jessica grunted. "Less promising, then."

"They're going to start testing it out soon with some low-mass black holes," Tangel said. "Apparently, it's pretty easy to smash neutronium together and get a wee black hole."

"I need a beer," Jessica rose and walked to the cooler. "I mean…what in the stars are we even talking about anymore? Smashing neutronium…."

"Grab me one, too," Tangel said. "Whatever's good."

Jessica peered into the cooler for a minute. "Stars, I'm gone for a week, and they don't properly restock."

<Things have been a little hectic,> Sabrina said. <Try the Huygen White. Everyone raves about it.>

Jessica pulled two beers from the cooler. "OK, I suppose I'll grant a reprieve, then. I heard about the 'true believers' in the Huygens System. What a mess."

She handed one to Tangel as she sat, and the two women pulled the tops off, tapping the bottoms of the bottles together once before taking a drink.

"I'll admit," Tangel said after taking a sip of the beer,

rather enjoying the flavor. "Things don't seem to be slowing down in the 'shit's getting weird' department."

"You can say that again," Jessica nodded, then took a long pull from her own drink.

The two women sat in silence for several minutes, soaking in the companionship along with the draft. Tangel's thoughts raced in a thousand directions, thinking of the latest reports, the various fronts the war was being fought on, the progress in the LMC and New Canaan, and a hundred other concerns.

But the one that lay in the back of her mind, a consistent hum of worry that she was unable to dismiss, was the worry over her missing daughters and Priscilla. Sera was on the *I2* organizing hundreds of Hand agents in Orion space to search for any news about the whereabouts of the *Perilous Dream*, or the ships from the 8912th fleet that had begun to go missing.

So far, there had been no reports of either, and Tangel took it to heart, knowing it meant that Cary hadn't yet made her move, and that maybe Faleena, Saanvi, and Priscilla would be able to stop her.

*Maybe.*

"You've got quite the far-off look," Jessica said, looking over her bottle's neck at Tangel. "The kids?"

Her lips pursed, and a wordless nod was all she could manage.

"I know that feeling—well, sort of. I knew where my kids were, I just didn't know if they were OK, or if I would ever get back to them."

"I'm sure you knew you'd be able to get back here eventually," Tangel said after she found her voice again.

"Once the war was over."

"Well, if I survived. I've come close to biting it a lot more often than I would have expected. Too close too often to assume I'd see this through. I imagine you don't feel that way now."

"Because of what I am?" Tangel asked.

"Or even before. You're the sort who has always laughed in the face of danger."

"Stars." Tangel shook her head after a moment of silence. "Every time I think that I'm secure—that our *future* is secure—I hit a wall. Even after the war started, when I ended up alone on Pyra, I really thought that was it."

"And then you merged and ascended."

"I still would have died without Rika showing up to save me."

Jessica cocked an eyebrow. "Doubtful."

"Well, then there was Xavia. She kicked my ass. Took Bob to save me, and again with Airtha."

"We expected to need his help with Airtha—sort of. That mission did not go to plan *at all*. Speaking of, what's the plan with Sera's sisters? I miss them."

"Sera wanted to wait till both Finaeus and Earnest could work on them. They're going to take Cheeky-level reconstruction to put back together again, and she wanted the best of the best."

<*They're planning on starting said reconstruction soon,*> Sabrina informed the pair. <*I've been reminding them hourly about it.*>

"Don't you think that's excessive?" Jessica asked.

<*With those two? No. If they don't do it soon, it won't get*

*done, since they're going to flit off to Grey Wolf before long—
well, they want us to take them. I'm not sure I'm ready to go
back to that place, though.>*

"Cheeky either, I imagine," Jessica added. "I can go
back with you. The *Lantzer* is still undergoing repairs."

"Despite the fact that you tore your ship in half, it will
be repaired in another week," Tangel said. "I had it
shipped back to New Canaan so they could use pico to
regrow the frame and hull."

"Seriously?" Jessica asked. "You shipped my ship and
didn't tell me?"

"Uhhh…" Tangel felt her cheeks flush. "Sometimes I
forget things, sorry."

*<She's not perfect!>* Sabrina laughed.

"Stars, am I ever not," Tangel replied. "When it's
repaired, your fleet will be ready as well. It's not huge—
five hundred ships, and I have a crew of a hundred for
all of them—but you're getting fifty AIs. My thought is
that you'd crew the cruisers, and remote the destroyers
and fighters."

"Has our mission changed?" Jessica asked. "Last plan
on the books was that we were to aid Corsia in her slug-
fest with the Trissies."

"I changed my mind," Tangel replied. "You're going
into the Hegemony. Now that the League of Sentients is
hitting them from the rimward side, and Scipio is on the
move again, antispinward, I want to tighten the noose
further."

"Spinward or coreward?" Jessica asked.

"Neither. I want you to jump to Kapteyn's Star."

The other woman's eyes grew wide, and then she

barked a laugh. "They say revenge is a dish best served cold, but this—"

"It's not revenge," Tangel countered. "It's going to be forward recon. I want to see how they respond to an incursion that deep in their space. You'll hit, but be judicious in your use of force. From there, you'll need to assess your next targets. Maybe Gilese or Epsilon Eridani."

"Or maybe Sirius," Jessica growled out the words. "If we want payback, that's the place to deliver it. Those assholes are at the root of so much shit that's gone wrong."

"I'm with you," Tangel nodded emphatically. "But the intel we've gathered through Petra's network suggests that they have a massive fleet—possibly one of the single largest reserve forces in the Inner Stars. I'd like them to keep it there until we can wrap things up with Orion. Then we can bring the weight of the Transcend's military to bear."

"That'll be a game-changer."

"I can't wait. Finally, we'll get to fight this war the way we should have been able to at the beginning."

Jessica nodded absently, and Tangel saw that the admiral was tapping into the intel on the Kapteyn's Star System.

"They kept the names," she said quietly. "I hadn't expected that."

"I know…somehow seems like a slap in the face, doesn't it?" Tangel asked. "We built all that, the first ones to terraform a tidally-locked superearth around a red dwarf, and the Sirians just do a smash-and-grab on it after we're gone."

Lavender eyes met Tangel's blue ones. "We're going to go to Sirius before this is done, right? I'm not one for 'sins of the fathers' and reparations, but I feel like they deserve some comeuppance."

"I can't make promises." Tangel heaved a sigh and took another sip of her beer. "But I'd love nothing more. Trust me. And the Jovians…. My goal has always been to eventually make peace with the Hegemony, which means I'll have to sit across the table from them and treat with the people who destroyed my homeworld."

"*Our* homeworlds," Jessica corrected. "Those fuckers turned Earth into a nuclear wasteland. My family had taken care of the unique ecology around Lake Athabasca for a thousand years, and then boom. Nuked from orbit."

"We can't let that get to us." Tangel reached out and took Jessica's hand. "You're right about the sins of the father. They don't pass to the children, that's not justice. For us, they destroyed our birthplaces. For them, it is so far back that it might as well have been pre-spaceflight."

Jessica nodded, remaining silent for almost a minute before saying, "Next time we fly to a new colony world, let's make sure we avoid the supermassive stream of dark matter."

Tangel gave a rueful laugh. "I'll make a note."

# NEXT MOVE
**STELLAR DATE: 11.02.8949 (Adjusted Years)**
**LOCATION:** *Fortune Favors*
**REGION: Kapteyn's Star System, Hegemony of Worlds**

The ship's name was *Fortune Favors*, which Prime hadn't even realized until a nav beacon at Kapteyn's Star's heliopause connected, requesting various bits of information having to do with permission to enter the system, and licenses to haul salvage.

He thought it strange that such things were necessary. The ship's logs showed that it had departed from Kapteyn's Star a scant two weeks ago, and that the vessel's licenses had in fact been issued by that same system.

A desire rose within Prime to somehow mess with the navigation beacon; feed it false information, or perhaps breach it entirely and use it as a means to learn more about ships entering and exiting the star system.

He was about to follow that line of thinking, when instead, he accessed its general datastore and found a public feed with all current ships, their vectors, and logged destinations.

*Well, that was unsatisfactorily easy.*

He already knew much about the system colloquially referred to as 'The Kap' by its inhabitants. There were two terraformed worlds, one named Tara, and one Victoria. They had originally been turned into life-supporting homes for organics by the *Intrepid* while under the command of Jason Andrews.

Prime would have razed those worlds, but from what the system's public records told him, that task had already been completed by the Sirians several thousand years before. They'd attacked the system and killed all its inhabitants. For some reason that wasn't noted anywhere in the histories, the aggressors had chosen to keep the names of all the worlds within the star system.

Over the millennia, it had gained its independence several times, fallen to other nations and empires before eventually being subsumed by the AST, which later became known as the Hegemony.

Though it technically fell within what was known as the 'core worlds', the inappropriately named star systems closest to Sol, Kapteyn's Star was poor. Though it sported several planets, the star had not been formed from the remnants of a supernova. As such, it was not rich in heavier metals, and contained no elements above iron at all.

It was a waste.

<We need a better ship,> Virgo said. <This one cannot maintain a transition to the dark layer for more than a few days. It cannot reach the star system where the colonists settled.>

<Do you really want to go there?> Prime asked. <It will take us at least ten years.>

<What are ten years? I've spent thousands drifting through deep space, watching bits of my memory and processing power be whittled away by neutrinos and cosmic rays.>

If Prime possessed eyes, he would have rolled them at Virgo's melodrama. <Even so, the reports I've picked up tell me that we do not need to go to New Canaan. The Intrepid

has been in many systems. Recently, it was at Aldebaran, which is far closer.>

<I saw that as well. If it has been in many systems, then it will be hard to track. But it will eventually return home, and we will be waiting for it.>

<And if it gets there first?> Prime asked, annoyed that Virgo was pressing this point once again. <They are strong at New Canaan. Far stronger than we are, even if we sneak in. No, what we need to do is find out where they're going to be, and lie in wait. Perhaps stir up local resentment while we're at it.>

<All well and fine, but how do you expect to do that?>

<Have you been following up on the war that is raging across the stars?> Prime asked, working to keep any ire from being discernable in his mental tone.

<There is little else of interest, of course I have.>

<Then you know that the Hegemony plays a major part in that conflict.>

Virgo sent an affirmative sensation. <Yes, as makes sense, they are one of the more advanced groups, but they are bordered on all sides by other peoples. Much of this war is their need to expand.>

<Yes, to control more space. They think that will give them strength. However, that is not the reason to pay them any heed. What matters is that, win or lose, their hegemon will end up in the presence of those we seek.>

<Not only that,> Virgo mused. <But if we can aid the Hegemony, we can bring about the downfall of our enemies that much sooner.>

<If they're capable of such a thing. I'm not convinced the Hegemony can win any way.>

<Then we'll enjoy watching the organics perish.>

<Virgo, you may be mad, but you're my favorite type of mad.>

The other AI laughed far longer than appropriate— which was bothersome, as it was clearly an affectation— then said, <Well, then, should we shop for a new ship?>

# JOE STRIKES BACK

**STELLAR DATE: 12.30.8949 (Adjusted Years)**
**LOCATION: ISS *Cora's Triumph***
**REGION: Outer New Sol System, Orion Freedom Alliance**

*Two months later...*

"Sir," Tracey said, her voice laced with concern. "We have a problem at post fourteen."

The tension Joe already felt in his shoulders increased, making his neck feel like it was in a vice. He triggered his biomods to release targeted relaxants into his muscles, and stretched his neck side to side before turning to the *Falconer*'s captain.

"Were they detected?"

"Worse," her brows knit together. "Captured."

"Shit," the curse slipped from his lips as he brought up the details on post fourteen, half an AU away from the ship's current position.

It remained Joe's fervent belief that Cary planned to strike at New Sol, where she'd take out the praetor and the Orion Guard's admiralty. He was certain it would be a lightning strike, enabled by her ship's stealth capabilities and the fleet she'd taken control of.

To that end, he'd infiltrated the outer fringes of the New Sol System, setting up twenty listening posts to keep an eye on system traffic, both physical and network.

Like other important capital systems, New Sol was protected by interdictor fields that would block ships from jumping deep into the gravity well, dumping them back into normal space before they reached their destinations.

Because of that, Cary would need to approach the system under stealth, at sublight speeds. Which was why Joe had spent the past two months setting up the twenty listening posts.

They were nearly complete; only number fourteen had needed its final component, the QC blade that would send updates to the hub on the *I2*, should it detect anything.

That was what made the capture of the team at post fourteen all the more concerning. They'd been transporting the QuanComm blade. That was something that could *not* fall into enemy hands. Even if it meant blowing the entire operation, Joe had to ensure that Orion didn't get QC technology.

"Where at?" he asked as the captain brought up the pertinent information on the holotank.

An oblong asteroid nearly shimmered into view. A label reading 'Polux' hung above it, as well as a notation that it was just over seven hundred kilometers in length and three hundred across. It was a former gold mine, the valuable ore extracted, leaving a honeycomb of tunnels stretching through the rock. Home to only a few million people, the vessel was mostly empty space and old equipment not worth salvaging.

"This is where we got the last message." She pointed at a location near the spaceport on the asteroid's southern pole. "They'd secured the package, and were en route to their internal transportation when it looks like a random patrol picked them up."

"Sergeant Bella," Joe shook his head. "Dammit. I'm going to go after them."

"Sir?" Captain Tracey blurted out the word. "Alone?"

"I'll take a team, but not many. Half our people are still headed back from their outposts.... Who do we have that's fresh?"

Tracey brought up a roster and flipped through it. "Sergeant Hector and his team got in yesterday from their listening post."

"Have him and two of his best meet me in the armory, and then bring the ship to within a hundred thousand klicks of that rock. When we pass into the sensor shadow created by the equatorial bulge, we'll deploy the pinnace and get down there."

"You sure, sir?" Tracey asked, the unspoken part of her question being 'that it has to be you?'.

"Yes. I'm sure. We'll wrap this up fast and get gone. By then, the FOB and the jump gates should be ready. We'll be back at the I2 in just a few days."

Tracey nodded, her expression stoic.

The crew of the *Falconer* was more than ready to get home—the I2 feeling more like a home to many of them than New Canaan after years away from the colony. Yet at the same time, it felt like running away—and none of them wanted to do that.

Least of all Joe.

Even so, he needed to be with Tangel, and she with him. There was a hole inside of him caused by fear and worry for his missing daughters. That hole could only be filled by finding them, but his wife had the same hole, and being together again might help.

*She doesn't blame you...she's said she doesn't blame you.*

Even if he did believe her, he still blamed himself.

"Good luck, sir," Captain Tracey finally said, those three words conveying that she understood where he was coming from, and wished him every success.

At least, that's how he decided to take it.

Once down in the armory, he greeted Sergeant Hector and corporals Tim and Ourey.

"This is a stealth mission. Our primary goal is to secure the QC blade. Ideally, we should make it appear like a robbery of some sort, though that'll depend on what sort of suspicions they're harboring regarding our team. At six AU from the next closest major outpost, we're looking at easily a day before any sort of reinforcements arrive, so that puts us on the clock."

"And if they figure out what they have their hands on?" Sergeant Hector asked.

"We've removed all identifying marks from the blades and described them as environmental NSAIs. At worst, the Oggies are going to realize that they have something more important than an NSAI, but chances are that they won't flag it as a QuanComm blade. We'll play things by ear, depending on what they think it is, but likely our best option will be pirates of some sort."

"And worst-case?" the sergeant asked.

"We get our people out and have Tracey blow the rock."

\* \* \* \* \*

*<Jenny's shuttle got a nice rent in it from a piece of space-*

*crap,>* the captain called down as Joe's team was doing their final armor checks. *<Which means we don't have a stealth-capable bird right now.>*

Joe nodded absently as he slapped Tim on the shoulder to signify that the Marine's seals were tight and his assorted gear checked out. *<OK, then, we're going to dive. How close do you think you can get us to Polux?>*

*<Figured you'd ask that. Ella and I are working it up, there are a few places where they have absolutely nothing on the surface, but those also put you too far from your target. OK…I think we have one. There's an old ore refinery just forty klicks from where we think our team is being held. We can get the* Falconer *within sixty klicks of the surface there. Good enough?>*

*<It'll have to be.>* Joe surveyed his team, knowing they would do it without question. *<Get us in, we'll be ready.>*

*<Use 'lock 13B, sir. And good luck.>*

*<We're ISF, Captain.>* Joe tried to add as much levity to his voice as he could. *<We don't need luck.>*

*<Hell yeah. T-minus fifteen.>*

*<Roger.>*

"Admiral?" Sergeant Hector asked. "You've got a look like you just ate something that didn't agree with you."

"There aren't any stealth birds that can take us in," Joe said. "So we're gonna jump."

"Fine by me." Tim shrugged. "I was orbital drop back in Sol. Piledrove into half the rocks in the system."

"I went boots-first down onto Venus," Ourey added. "Though that was non-combat, an asteroid should be no biggie."

"Landfall for me," Hector said. "Came down hard and blew away Trissies like there was no tomorrow. Oggies on a rock like this'll be no sweat. Sir."

"Glad to hear it, people, because Sergeant Bella is probably getting treated to the pointy sticks right about now, and we don't have a lot of time to spare."

He led the way out of the armory and to the airlock Captain Tracey had indicated, passing his team data on the drop point and what they knew of the route to the sector station where Bella and her team were being held.

"Seems like a pretty straight shot," Sergeant Hector said. "The first stretch, at least."

"Should be," Joe agreed. "But remember, once we get close, we have to swap gear to look like locals. This all goes to shit if the Oggies figure out that the ISF is hanging out in New Sol."

"Good times," Tim replied. "And we still have to get the QC to the listening post."

"That's correct."

The group stepped into a lift that would take them down to Deck 4, and Joe turned to face the other three.

"Hector and Tim, you'll be on QC duty. You find that thing and get gone. Ourey and I will get Bella, Lance, and Ferra out."

"We can boost out from the refinery to get back to the *Falconer*," Hector nodded uncertainly. "But how are you five going to get off Polux? Shooting your way out of a sector station is going to set off a bit of a hunt."

Joe patted the pouch on his thigh. "Got three skinsuits here. We'll all get stealthed and sneak off on some ship or another, then blow its pods and get nabbed by the

Falconer."

<Seems a bit iffy,> Ella chimed in. <Systems tend to track pods. You know, to make sure they find people, and that the pods don't slam into things.>

"I'm counting on you to fake them out somehow," Joe replied, with a wink at the optical pickup in the corner of the lift.

The doors opened and the team filed out, walking the last few meters to their designated airlock in silence. When they arrived, Joe cycled open the inner door and put on his helmet.

<Remember,> he advised his Marines. <I'm not risking lives on this. We run into trouble, you get out any way you can, I don't care how noisy it is. The Falconer is onstation to unleash hell if needs be.>

A trio of affirmative responses came back, and the team stepped into the airlock.

\* \* \* \* \*

Joe felt like it had been forever since he'd managed to still his mind. From the moment his daughters and Priscilla departed the Falconer, an undercurrent of worry had been running in the back of his mind.

More like a waterfall of worry.

He'd felt a few moments of peace, but the entire time, the one thought that continued to circle was that if his daughters didn't come back, he'd never be able to live with himself.

Exactly what that meant wasn't clear, but he knew it wouldn't be good.

But as he and the three Marines surrounding him drifted through the black to the old refinery hunkered down on Polux's surface, he felt a stillness settle over him.

They were entirely EM-silent. No Link, no comms. Nothing other than the sound of his own breath rattling down his throat.

His eyes soaked in the view around him, the asteroid dotted with old structures, its surface pitted deeply, scarred by humans scraping away its insides. They were coming in on the leeward side of the asteroid, and starlight streamed from New Sol, adding a bright glow around Polux's irregular edges. Beyond the grey stone, the glow lit up the hulls of ships passing by, their engines trailing streams of hot plasma in their wakes as they moved about their business. Further out, distant ship engines twinkled in the black, adding to the backdrop of stars that shone around New Sol.

For just a moment, he was able to push the worry from his mind, forget about the war, the years-long struggle of the colonists who just wanted to find peace. Even concern about his daughters diminished as he watched the stars and ships wheel about in silence, a celestial dance that shouldn't be buried in fear and worry, but rather celebrating a galaxy that was *alive*.

*Stars, I'm getting poetic in my old age.*

Though it wasn't just his age, or any general sense of melancholy. Joe had always loved staring out into the black, existing in calm silence, at peace with the universe. That had been why he'd first signed on to be a fighter pilot in the TSF, and gotten assigned to the

Scattered Disk. Out there, everything was shrouded in darkness; even Sol had been a pinpoint of light, lost in the starscape.

30 SECONDS TO BRAKING

The words appeared across his HUD, spiking his adrenals and shattering the calm that had suffused his being.

Below the words lay his velocity relative to Polux: 41.2m/s. It would require a hard burn to match $v$ with the asteroid, and the refinery only rose a hundred meters from the surface. That meant the burn would be constrained to two seconds.

*Just like the good ol' days*, he thought, remembering what it was like to do heavy burns with no a-grav dampening the bone-jarring thrust.

Single pings came from each of the team members, signaling their readiness, and he acknowledged them all. Then the refinery's towers and platforms were directly below him, and his armor fired its a-grav systems, followed by the single burn chem boosters attached to his calves.

Before he knew it, his boots had slammed into an old landing platform, and his maglocks had activated, keeping him from bouncing back into space.

The team's stealth systems were still active, but small clouds of dust spread around their impact points, and now that they were shrouded by the refinery's structure, they activated their IFF systems.

Outlines of the Marine's figures appeared on Joe's HUD, and Corporal Tim took the lead, moving in the bounding lope that was characteristic of moving through near micro-gravity.

Though there was no atmosphere on Polux that would dirty and corrode the structure around them, the asteroid frequently moved through several dustclouds that hung at lagrange points in the New Sol system. As such, the towers, gantries, and platforms around them were pitted from micro-impacts, with a few larger scrapes and rents sprinkled throughout.

The team steadily moved deeper into the facility, headed for an underground causeway that had long since fallen into disuse. It was very nearly a straight shot to Polux's south pole and the more populated regions.

After ten minutes, they reached the sealed portal that led from the refinery to the subterranean passage, and the team formed up as Tim initiated a breach.

<Airlock, sir,> he reported. <Looks like the causeway is still aired up.>

<We'll have to manage,> Joe replied.

He would have preferred vacuum. Though air made it easier to fool optical sensors, with light bending and shifting as it passed through the gases, there was the issue with disrupting currents in the air, and any dust they kicked up taking longer to settle back down.

The lock's outer door opened, and the team moved inside, trusting the total lack of EM around them and not taking the time to do the maneuver two-by-two.

Joe hated the thought of being sloppy, but knew that every second Bella's team spent in custody was a second closer the ISF's presence was to discovery.

Air hissed in around them, and a minute later, the inner door opened, and Tim moved out with Ourey following after. They gave the all-clear a few seconds later, and Hector followed with Joe bringing up the rear.

They walked down a short corridor that led to a bay filled with old loading equipment. On the side of the bay, open doors let out onto the underground causeway.

No traffic passed by, but there were lights interspersed through the tunnel, only half functional, leaving sections in deep gloom.

<Looks entirely unused,> Tim commented.

Joe shook his head. <Not entirely. Look at the dust patterns around the maglev track. Trains come through here from time to time.>

<Noted, sir.> Sergeant Hector's tone was all business. <Tim, you stay in the lead. Ourey, I want you to stay a hundred meters behind. Leave a few drones, I want to know if this egress stays clear.>

A pair of affirmations came from the corporals, and Tim took off, moving at the maximum threshold of his armor's stealth systems.

Hector followed after a few seconds later, and Joe moved forward, staying a few bounds behind the sergeant.

They had just under two hundred kilometers of tunnel to traverse before reaching the junction with another subterranean road that would be more heavily trafficked. The group reached a steady speed of one hundred and fifty kilometers per hour, only once having to slow and move to the edges of the tunnel when a maglev train went by.

When they reached the junction, the Marines found that there were very few station cars and only three active maglev lines. They carefully crossed the lanes to one of the two inactive lines, and continued on their way in silence. After another seven kilometers, the causeway branched off into a number of smaller underground concourses, with the maglev lines disappearing into discrete tunnels.

Tim moved to one of the side passages that was designated for foot traffic and compact station cars. A few vehicles moved in and out of the entrance, and further down the passage lay a commercial area with foot traffic and service businesses for the remaining mining activity on Polux lining the sides.

<Looks clear,> Joe said when he reached Tim's side. <We need to find a spot where we can swap to civilian gear.>

<Some of these places seem abandoned,> the corporal replied. <I'll scout ahead.>

The rest of the team waited at the junction while Tim worked his way down the passage. Five long minutes later, he signaled that he'd found a place they could change, and the rest of the team joined him in an abandoned office that had once handled the leasing of deep-tunnel atmosphere scrubbers—at least, that's what Joe gleaned from the sign 'Tommy's Atmo-Scrub' that was stretched above the entrance.

Inside, old desks and holotables were arranged in orderly rows, with a few wide-open spaces in the center that may once have been—by the presence of magnetic hold-downs—the location of floor models.

<OK, let's make this speedy,> Joe said.

He pulled off the case on his back and opened it up to reveal a loose coverall to wear over his armor, and a long cloak that pinned to his ankles in the style that was common for low-*g* workers in the region.

They used their cloak almost like a sail to steer themselves while bounding through the air. It was something Joe had seen used back in Sol, but not often in the ninetieth century, when most stations had at least half-gravity via a-grav systems.

The weapons they held were already Orion Guard issue, scavenged from recent battles and worn-down enough to look like they'd passed through a few owners before ending up in the hands of civilians.

Helmets would be a dead giveaway that they were up to no good, so each member of the team placed theirs into a pouch on their hip, something common enough on stations where you didn't quite trust the seals.

Even though he still wore a base layer of transparent flow armor, Joe felt naked as he led the team out of the office and down the passage.

They garnered a few looks from the locals; it was clear by their size that the four were not low-*g* dwellers, and though each one tried to move easily, they were Marines, and they were ready for action.

After another ten minutes, they came to a wider concourse, the Polux Sector Station a hundred meters to their right. Here, light a-grav was in play, 0.2*g*s of force tugging at their feet.

<Remember,> Joe said to his team as he set the maglocks on his boots to a lower level. <Our ROE is to remain as non-lethal as we can, but we're going in shooting. Pulse to start, but don't hesitate to switch over to projectiles the moment they start shooting back. We're pirates, and we

*have to act like we don't give a fuck.>*

The Marines sent non-verbal acknowledgments, and he wondered if it was because they were keeping EM to a minimum, or if it was a result of their distaste over shooting up a police station.

He didn't ask—not wanting to think about it too much himself—and took the lead, striding down the concourse as though he owned it. Two bots stood guard outside the station, and he didn't slow as he walked past them, watching twin beams streak out from Marine rifles and hole the machines.

Before the guard drones' bodies even hit the deck, Joe lobbed a pair of directional pulse grenades into the room and shouldered his rifle, adding a barrage of concussive blasts to the fray, bowling people over, civilian and sector police alike.

His HUD outlined the room, the three doors leading into corridors in the back, and the four still-conscious police who were crouched behind desks.

Stepping to the side, he made room for the Marines to enter, and they spread out, weapons trained on the doors and the desks, ready for anyone to make a move as they advanced.

A woman popped up from the left and fired a pulse pistol at Tim, who responded with a focused blast from his rifle, the force flipping her desk and slamming it into the cop. She went limp just as two men eased around their cover and opened fire on Tim.

Joe put a round in one man's shoulder—tearing his arm half off—before he got off a second shot, and Ourey hit the other with a pulse blast.

Hector rushed forward, covering the downed cops, while Joe circled around to the fourth officer. She moved suddenly, and he almost fired on her until he saw that she was only raising empty hands above the edge of the desk.

"Come out," he grunted. "Where are the prisoners?"

She scrambled to her feet, a look of obstinate resistance on her face despite the fact that she'd given herself up.

"Prisoners?"

"The three you captured earlier today. We know you're holding them here," Joe growled. "Do you really want to see people die, just to hold on to some suspects?"

"Suspects?" she asked, cocking her head to the side, and Joe held back a curse, knowing that was a word hard-bitten pirates wouldn't use.

"Yeah, we hacked your database, and that's what you're calling our friends, 'suspects'," Hector said as he approached. "We're getting a bit *suspect* of you, so talk, or we just make you a spec."

<Thanks,> Joe said. <Almost cocked that up. Kinda weak insult, though.>

<Don't worry, Admiral,> Tim chuckled. <What Hector lacks n finesse, he makes up for with grade-a asshole.>

"OK!" the woman squeaked as Hector sighted down his rifle, aiming at her head. "Door on the right, take the first right, it'll lead you to our holding cells."

"Better not be an ambush," the sergeant said. "If it is, I'll make it back here and put one in your head."

He fired a light pulse blast, but it was enough to

knock her out, given that he'd fired at her head.

<*Ourey,*> the sergeant directed. <*Keep an eye on this mess.*>

<*On it. I'll plant a few surprises at the door, as well.*>

The sergeant waved in acknowledgment, and then directed Tim to take the lead once more.

Once through the door, they could see the corporal pause at the first intersection and plant a mine on one wall before looking back and nodding. Joe and Hector moved in, while Tim disappeared down the right-side passage.

When the admiral and sergeant caught up, the corporal was standing in front of a large cell, staring in and shaking his head. Joe approached and sighed, unable to resist joining Tim in his expression of disapproval.

Within, Bella, Lance, and Ferra were reclined on their bunks, appearing entirely relaxed, as though they hadn't a care in the world.

Then the sergeant realized who was standing outside the cell and leapt to her feet.

"Easy there, sailor," Joe growled before she blurted out either 'sir' or 'admiral'. "Glad to see you swabs are enjoying the good life. There's work to be done, though, so get your asses in gear."

Tim moved to the cell's controls and placed an Orion-issue breach kit overtop, then set his hand on it to add some ISF nano and get the job done faster.

"Where's the cargo?" Joe grunted as the three Marines moved out of the cell.

"They said it was in holding," Bella replied. <*No clue*

*what it was, they just stuck it with the other junk they'd impounded.>*

*<I've breached their network,>* Hector said, providing the team with an overlay of the station. *<Not too complex. Holding is marked on the map.>*

The mine in the intersection went off, its pulse blast sending a shockwave through the corridor.

*<Lone guy,>* Tim said. *<I'll secure holding.>*

*<Check for our armor,>* Bella called after him.

Hector took aim and shot out the sensors in the cell and hall while Joe fished the three stealth skinsuits from his thigh pouch.

*<In case it's not there, get these on so you can go poof when the time comes.>*

*<'Poof', sir?>* Ferra asked. *<Is that the technical term?>*

*<It is now.>*

Bella finished stripping off the simple coveralls she wore and grabbed one of the suits. *<What's our exfil plan?>*

*<I vote we all just go poof now, and then find a transport to disappear on,>* Ourey suggested. *<Oh, and two cops came back in, but I popped them with pulses.>*

*<Pirates wouldn't just disappear inside the sector station,>* Joe said as the three Marines finished pulling their coveralls back on. *<We have to lay down a bit of a trail.>*

*<I have the QC,>* Tim reported. *<The armor's here, but it's all torn apart. Nothing's missing that I can see, though.>*

*<Leave it, then,>* Joe ordered. *<It's all Oggie tech anyway. Let them wonder where the leak is.>*

Three minutes later, the team was formed up at the entrance to the sector station—excepting Tim and

Hector, who had already left out the back, headed for the listening post where they'd install the QC blade.

The concourse was nearly empty, most smart people not wanting to be around for the aftermath of whatever happened when marauders hit a sector station. A few civilians were peering out of doorways, or crouched behind station cars, and Joe tagged them, not wanting to add further collateral damage.

"Drones." Ourey pointed down the nearly empty concourse at a trio of armored bots.

"Do what you do best," Joe said, assigning two targets to the corporal while he took the third.

Their weapons barked several times, and the machines ground to a halt. Not waiting to see if they had backup, the group of five moved back down the concourse, headed to the offices where they'd changed the first time.

Other than several more automated security systems, they didn't encounter any resistance, and five minutes later, the group was divesting themselves of anything that couldn't be concealed under stealth.

<*OK,*> Joe addressed the four Marines. <*We're going out the back and heading to the spaceport. Ourey, set up burn charges. I want to melt this place to slag, give them no clues about what happened to us.*>

<*You got it, Admiral,*> the corporal replied as he set to his task.

<*Do you think there will be ships leaving, sir?*> Bella asked. <*I'd expect them to put the port on lockdown, with the chaos we're causing.*>

<*There's always someone who's too important—or self-*>

important—to stick around,> Joe replied. <We'll figure something out. Also, do we need to scrub down your transport?>

<No, sir. We followed protocol. It was already clean as a whistle.>

<Good. Ourey?>

<All set, sir,> he replied. <Five-minute timer.>

The admiral nodded and let Sergeant Bella set the order, falling into the middle of the group.

Even though they hadn't made demonstrable progress in finding his daughters and Priscilla, he had to admit that it felt good to be doing *something* other than sitting on the *Falconer* and giving orders.

*Maybe I need to get back in the thick of things more often.*

It should have only taken thirty minutes to get to the spaceport, but with the attack on the sector station and the explosion at the abandoned office, Polux had dropped into lockdown, and all but a few concourses were closed off, forcing the group to sneak through crowded checkpoints before they finally reached their destination.

Polux's southern spaceport was set in a deep crater, with a grav shield arching overtop. Once, it had handled massive ore haulers, and three cradles were big enough for long-haul freighters and military cruisers, though they were all vacant.

A host of smaller freighters and a few passenger transports were dotted throughout the port, along with a pleasure yacht and a smaller passenger ship with the name 'Krilla Industries' on the side.

<There's our ride.> Joe highlighted the smaller

passenger vessel. *<Let's move, that ship will be taking off before long.>*

*<What makes you think that, sir?>* Bella asked.

*<See that guy standing out front, looking like someone's poured lava down his shipsuit?>* Joe asked. *<He'll be the captain, and inside is an irate executive who doesn't want to wait for the lockdown to be lifted.>*

Ferra chuckled. *<Poor guy. I flew commercial ships between Troy and Tyre for a few years in New Canaan. We didn't bring many of the 'my shit don't stink' types along to the colony, but I sure seemed to get my share on my run.>*

The group moved slowly past stacks of cargo, threading their way around the docking cradles until they reached the passenger ship. It wasn't large, only forty meters long, and likely not rated for interstellar travel at all. The captain was now pacing, continually glancing toward the port's control tower—more a control ledge, jutting out from one side of the crater wall—and then back at the open entrance to his ship.

*<Does that thing even **have** escape pods?>* Ourey asked as they approached. *<And if it does, can we all fit?>*

*<It'll have them,>* Joe said. *<Enough for forty people, if they're abiding by local regs.>*

He led the team past the pacing captain and up the ramp. Once aboard, they turned right, walking into the main cabin, where an irate man was speaking to a holoimage displaying a woman who Joe assumed to be in charge of the port.

"I wish I could help you, but our protocol must be followed. If I let you take off, we could be facing serious fines. You—"

"If I cared about your fines, I wouldn't have called you in the first place," the man growled. "I'm certain Polux would love to have my business, but they're not going to get it unless you can prove that you can pull strings for me. I have an important meeting on Jova, and if I'm late, I'll lose a lot more credit than I ever stand to make here."

*<Why do people never just try to appeal to others' better natures?>* Bella asked.

*<Really, Sarge?>* Ferra quipped as she moved past the man who had begun listing a litany of things that he'd do to ruin the woman's life if she didn't let him take off. *<This coming from someone who doesn't **have** a better nature is rich.>*

*<Stay sharp,>* Joe admonished. *<We need to hack the ship's piloting system and sensors to hide our mass, otherwise they'll know we're here the moment this bird lifts off.>*

*<On it,>* Ourey reported. *<This thing isn't too different from some models that we had back in Sol. Amazing how old shit still gets recycled.>*

Joe had noticed the same thing when they'd entered, but chalked it up to there only being so many designs for a small, short-range shuttle.

"No! I won't ho—*fuck*!" the man swore as the holo in front of him froze.

*<I'm going to see what I can do to help our friend out,>* Joe said.

He tapped into the spaceport's network, pulling up their regs for lockdown, and looking over the condition sets under which a civilian ship could still take off. Given the level of breach that the station administrators had assigned after the attack on the sector station, there weren't many exceptions that the executive could use.

Not giving up, Joe continued to flip through the list until he came across an item labeled 'Economic Hardship'. He accessed the criteria, and saw that if a civilian ship being denied takeoff would constitute gross negative hardship on the economy of Polux, it could be granted permission. He noted that there was no specific definition for 'gross', but decided it was worth a try.

Piggybacking on the breach Ourey had already performed, Joe filed an Economic Hardship request with the spaceport, logging it as having come from the captain, and adding a personal appeal for clemency. Within five minutes, a response came back that, pending an inspection, the ship would be allowed to depart.

"Holy shit!" the exec proclaimed as the captain rushed aboard, a relieved smile on his face. "I don't know what you did, but you just earned your bonus!"

"Uhhh...thanks, sir. I was trying everything I could! Glad something worked."

Joe wasn't sure if the man was lying or not, but so long as the fiction held, he was happy.

"Inspector should be here in five minutes."

"Will they come aboard?" The Krilla Industries exec appeared concerned. "You know that wouldn't be ideal."

<Oh dammit,> Ferra muttered. <Did we find the one ship that's smuggling shit? Just our luck.>

"I'll take care of it, sir," the pilot said. "The usual arrangement should work, though they might charge a bit more."

"Whatever it takes, just get it done."

<Drop some probes,> Joe ordered Ourey. <I want to know what's going on out there. I'd prefer not to be surprised.>

<Or have to do some sort of dance in the aisles if there's an inspection,> Bella added.

Ourey deployed the drones, and the team watched as an inspector wearing a station uniform approached the ship.

He talked with the captain for a moment and then nodded and walked up the ramp with the captain following after. He stepped onto the ship and moved a meter down the passage, looking everything over with a stern expression.

Joe moved out of the aisle, standing between a pair of couches, his hand ready to reach out and plant a dose of breach nano on the inspector.

But the official didn't move any further into the ship.

He looked intently at his hand for a moment, whistled a short tune, ran a finger along the back of a seat—all while ignoring the company executive sitting halfway down the main cabin—and then turned, nodded to the captain, and walked off.

<Well that was anticlimactic,> Ferra commented. <I really wanted to see you drop him, Admiral.>

<Wouldn't have helped our cause much,> Joe replied. <I do wonder what this ship is hauling, though.>

<I'll rummage around,> Ferra said from the back. <I bet Mister Impatient Pants won't have it too far from his person.>

The captain walked into the cockpit, but left the door open, and Ourey followed after her, keeping a feed running to the rest of the team as he watched over the captain's shoulder.

Preflight checks and connection to Polux's STC took ten minutes to complete, and then the ship began to lift off, pushing itself away from the deck on an a-grav column.

<Once we get ten k away from the asteroid, we blow the escape pods,> Joe instructed. <Lance and Bella, secure the aft one. I'll work on breaching the ship's safety systems so it ejects them all—six, as it turns out. Ourey, see if you can tap into their comm systems without the captain knowing. We need to signal the Falconer.>

A round of affirmatives came back, reinforcing the feeling that he'd missed being in the field, even though he'd only rarely been on this sort of mission, and when he had, it had almost always been with Tangel.

The ship continued to rise on its grav drive for another five minutes before the fusion burner came online and the craft began to boost away from Polux.

<He's boosting parallel to the rock's orbit,> Ourey said from the cockpit. <We're four minutes from being ten k out. I sent a ping for the Falconer with this tub's ident. Hopefully they got it.>

<We have to assume they did,> Joe said as he worked through the ship's safety protocols, looking for one he could trigger without it looking too suspicious.

Breaching wasn't his forte, but after having watched Tanis and Angela for decades, he'd picked up a few tricks. It didn't hurt that Orion eschewed advanced NSAI, making it easy to fool the ship's computers.

<We've tripped the pod's door, sir,> Bella reported. <Should we get in?>

<Yeah, and get snuggly. When we're ready, we won't have

*much time to file in.>*

*<Yes, sir.>*

After another minute, Joe found a command system for the manual testing of the escape pods, and discovered that there was a full-release test mode. It required the captain's tokens, but he ran through a set of manufacturer's default tokens that the ISF's intelligence division had compiled, and after another minute of searching, one matched.

*<OK, Lance, if you haven't found what they're smuggling, get back with Bella and Ferra.>*

*<Actually, Admiral, I might have,>* the private replied. *<There's a case tucked up under a seat, two spots behind our exec buddy. It's where the emergency EV skin is supposed to be. I wouldn't have noticed it, but there's a bit of EM coming off it in the UV spectrum.>*

Joe moved back to stand next to the Krilla exec. *<OK, I have our buddy covered in case it's alarmed. Pull it out nice and careful, and let's have a look.>*

*<On it, sir.>*

To his credit, the Marine removed the case without making a sound, and a moment later, he reported in.

*<OK, got it out. Using a nanoshim to open the case, and…huh…looks like some purple slime. Two small vials of it.>*

*<Markings?>* Joe asked, doing his best to keep any urgency out of his tone.

*<Just the letters RHY.>*

*<Change of plan,>* Joe announced. *<These two are coming with us, and we're blowing the ship. If there's any more of that shit aboard, we can't let it fall into the wrong hands.>*

<What is it, sir?> Bella asked.

<Best-case scenario, the same stuff Admiral Jessica is made of now. Worst-case, a weaponized variant that's capable of wiping out all Terran-based life in the galaxy.>

<Oh...so nothing serious, then,> Ferra laughed.

Joe ignored the comment. <Lance, run that back to the pod. Ferra, get to the cockpit, Bella, get up here and cover our corporate smuggler.>

<In out, in out,> Ferra chuckled, earning a reprimand from the sergeant.

A minute later, everyone was in position, and Joe disabled his stealth systems, appearing in the aisle next to the ship's lone passenger, whose name he'd finally looked up and found to be Jamey.

"OK, Jamey," he drawled. "We were just going to borrow your escape pods, but it seems you've been a bad boy, so we're going to want to have a chat with you, too."

The blood drained from Jamey's face, and he sank back into his seat. "Who are you? Are you OG Intel? I swear, I'm just couriering it for my buyer. I didn't steal it."

Joe shook his head. "No, we're much worse than Guard Intel. How much more of the Retyna do you have aboard?"

"Just the one case," the man said hurriedly.

The bioreadouts on Joe's HUD suggested that the man was being truthful, but he leant in close, his helmeted head centimeters from Jamey's. "You sure?"

"Y-yes! That was all I could get. Are you pirates?"

Straightening, Joe shrugged. "Ever heard of the

Hand?"

"Transcend?" the exec blurted out. "Here in New Sol?"

"That seems to be the case," he nodded. "We are indeed in the New Sol System. Now, are you *sure* that's the only case?"

Jamey nodded wordlessly, and Joe decided he would have to be satisfied with the response. "Bella, get him to the pod."

"You got it." The sergeant shimmered into view, and grabbed the exec by the arm, dragging him from his seat and toward the back of the craft. *<Not room for seven in one pod, Admiral.>*

*<Yeah, I figured that. You and Lance go with him. Ferra, Ourey and I will dump out with the captain. Between these two, he's much more likely to put up a fight.>*

*<Nah, he's pragmatic,>* Bella replied. *<I doubt he'll give any trouble.>*

Joe walked to the cockpit where Ourey had revealed himself and had his sidearm trained on the captain's head.

"Sorry about the trouble," Joe said. "But you're going to have to come with us."

"Come with you?" the man asked, a scowl forming on his brow. "Where?"

"To the escape pod." Joe gestured to the hatch, which opened, Ferra appearing beside it.

She waved a hand at the opening. "Hop in, buddy boy. Unless, that is, you want be on the ship when it blows."

"You're going to destroy it?" he asked, face ashen.

"Why? How?"

"Cover," Joe replied. "Chop-chop, we haven't got all day. We're already past our marker."

The captain got out of his seat after a light slap on the shoulder from Ourey, who escorted him to the opening.

<Sir, how're we going to blow it?> the corporal asked.

<I dropped some nano in the cabin back there. It's already gotten to the intermixers. This engine is only rated for fifty-percent deuterium, and it's about to get one hundred percent.>

Ourey laughed. <That'll do it. I guess we should get gone.>

<Sooner the better.>

\* \* \* \* \*

"Shoot," Tracey muttered. "Why haven't they blown the pods yet?"

The ship Joe had escaped on was fifteen thousand kilometers ahead of Polux now, but still hadn't released any pods, or showed any sign of changing course. Tracey was starting to wonder if she should bring the *Falconer* closer and send a team of Marines aboard, when comm turned and caught her eye.

"Captain, the ship's started broadcasting a mayday. Something about intermix failure, and safeties not cutting the fuel flow. It's going to go critical!"

"Shit," she muttered. *What are you up to, Joe? If you blow up out here—*

A second later, the ship's escape pods blew, and Scan tagged all six, placing them on the main holotank.

"OK, then." The captain looked them over. "Which

appears to have the most mass? That'll be our target."

"I've got two," Scan reported. "Best estimate is that there are three or four people in each."

The pods were boosting away from the ship, the two with people inside on similar trajectories, and Tracey ordered helm to move into an intercept position. It took three minutes to get close, the pilots at the helm of the stealthed cruiser managing its burn carefully, making sure not to give their position away.

At the forty-five-hundred-meter mark, the passenger ship exploded.

"Hot damn!" Scan blurted out. "That was big!"

"Too big," Tracey muttered.

Normally, a ship that size would only suffer a meltdown of its reaction chamber when it burned too much deuterium. While it was dangerous, it wasn't usually a violent failure.

"There must have been some sort of issue with an energy storage system," Scan suggested. "Crap, a piece of hull—"

The holotank focused in on one of the pods, the ship's scan systems estimating a seventy-percent chance of impact with a section of hull from the ship.

Tracey wavered on ordering a shield extension to protect the pod—doing so would give away the *Falconer*'s position. Every ship and scanning system in the area would be focusing in on the explosion, and they'd spot a large graviton emission.

Then the hull fragment hit, shoving the escape pod off course, sending it spinning into the black with a thin wisp of atmosphere escaping.

"Get us on an intercept and track that other pod! I don't want to lose either of them."

"Ma'am!" Comm called back. "Hector just signaled. He and Tim have boosted off from the refinery."

"Shit," the captain muttered. "It never rains, but it pours."

Tracey allowed herself a moment to regain her composure, and then called down to the aft shuttle bay.

<Chief Wallace, how's Jenny's bird looking?>

<Almost there, ma'am, just need to put on the final ultra-black coating and then layer on the active stealth systems on the affected panels.>

<It's going to have to do the way it is. Get Jenny in there, I want that bird in the black in five minutes. We're moving too far, too fast to track Hector and Tim much longer than that.>

<Aye, ma'am!>

The chief's response didn't contain a single note of complaint, only steely resolve, and Tracey took a second to thank the stars that even after months in the black, her people were still displaying unwavering dedication.

*Of course, we're so deep in enemy territory that it would take over a decade to get home without jump gates, and our home is a single speck of light amidst a sea of hateful stars.... We don't have any other option.*

She briefed Lieutenant Jenny, and the pilot seemed entirely nonplussed at the mission before her.

<Don't worry, Captain. I've pulled Hector's hide out of the fire so many times now that I could do it with my eyes closed.>

<Well, don't go daring yourself, Lieutenant. Just get them back in one piece.>

<Aye, ma'am.>

The captain pulled her attention back to the situation on the bridge, and saw that Helm had the ship closing in on the damaged pod with a time to intercept of six minutes. She widened the view of local space, noting with relief that rescue craft hadn't yet left Polux, and no other ships nearby had yet altered trajectory to lend aid.

<*Chief Kala,*> Tracey reached out to the *Falconer's* forward bay. <*Every eye for a hundred thousand klicks is on us. We need to kick something out that's the same size as that pod, and then blow it.*>

<*What? Really?*> Kala's tone wavered in her response, but she continued before Tracey could speak up. <*OK, yeah, I got something that might work.*>

<*It has to work,*> the captain said, watching as scan picked up two search and rescue craft passing through Polux's southern spaceport's shield. <*And when we get the second pod, if it's clean, get our people out, and then kick it back into the black on the same trajectory.*>

The bay chief didn't respond at first, but then she replied, <*OK, Captain, but I can't promise it'll be perfect. Doing all this while stealthed is something normally considered impossible, you know.*>

<*Andromeda scooped up* Sabrina *at Bollam's World, and no one was the wiser,*> Tracey said. <*I was on that bridge. We were sweating bullets, but we did it. You can do this too.*>

<*Yes, ma'am.*> The chief's voice sounded more certain. <*You're right. We've got this.*>

<*Glad to hear it.*>

The *Falconer's* crew erupted into a fury of activity over the next five minutes. Jenny's pinnace deployed on time, Kala found a piece of scrap similar in mass to the damaged pod and got it ready to send out, and Helm plotted a series of careful grav drive burns to catch the one pod and then grab the other while avoiding debris from both the ship and the scrap they were about to detonate.

The entire time, Tracey watched scan like a hawk, eyeing nearby Orion Guard patrol craft, waiting to see if any would move in to take a closer look. But somehow, each maneuver went off without a hitch.

Jenny was on an intercept to get Hector and Tim where they drifted in the black. The dock team grabbed the first pod and kicked out the decoy, then moved onto a vector to grab the second pod.

Admiral Joe wasn't in the damaged pod, but an Oggie named Jamey was, plus a case carried by Private Lance that he insisted be put in biohazard containment immediately in case it had leaked at all.

Chief Kala reported that the case wasn't even scuffed, but the corporal was uncharacteristically nervous, so they followed protocol.

Fifteen minutes later, Joe stepped out of the second pod, and Tracey addressed him via holo from the bridge.

"Glad to have you back aboard, sir," she said, giving him a sharp salute.

"Glad to *be* back aboard, Captain," he replied. "How're we looking?"

"Really good, despite you nearly giving me an aneurism with that stunt. What was it all about? The stuff in that case?"

Joe nodded. "Yeah, a little mess that I thought the Hand had cleared up long ago. As soon as we get the other listening post teams back aboard, we have to make for Cape Point and jump to Star City. Tangel is going to need to see this."

# COMING HOME

**STELLAR DATE: 01.01.8950 (Adjusted Years)**
**LOCATION: ISS *I2***
**REGION: Star City, Orion Freedom Alliance, Perseus Arm**

The *I2* hung above Star City's outer shell, near the gate array that serviced the construction of the ring emitters surrounding the dyson sphere.

Despite the joy it gave Tangel to see the mighty ship looming over Manhattan's skyline, she knew their endeavors were better served with the vessel out in space, ready to aid in the city's defense if Orion decided to attack again.

The lift chimed as it reached the bottom level of Dock A1, the *I2*'s kilometer-wide dock that ran from one side of the ship to the other. She stepped out, and the air felt thick, as though she were walking through a haze as she approached the waiting dockcar. Once aboard, it took her to the cradle where the next ship would settle down.

Still feeling strangely disconnected, Tangel stepped onto the deck and waited for the ship she knew was on final approach, having jumped in an hour before.

She and Joe had already greeted one another over the Link, talking in real-time with more than just clipped sentences over the QC network for the first time in months.

It had been strained, but not as bad as she'd worried it would be. It was clear Joe blamed himself. Tangel felt the same way, but to a lesser extent. She knew that a part of that was because of her ascension. Emotions that would have overwhelmed her in the past were unable to do so now. She still felt strongly about things—especially the plight of her daughters—but somehow, it was easier to cordon off the emotional anguish it caused.

Joe did not have that same luxury. She knew that he would be tearing himself up inside. He would also be worried that she was angry at him, but she was not...she just missed him terribly, almost as much as their daughters.

*"All personnel, clear route 3A for cradle 19."*

The announcement came over the Link as well as Dock A1's audible systems. Tangel knew what ship it was for, since she was watching it via the *I2*'s external sensors.

"Welcome home, *Falconer*," she said in a quiet voice as the cruiser eased through the shield at the starboard end of the dock and drifted down its length to the assigned cradle.

She knew that Joe would remain on the bridge until the ship settled into place, and she'd have to wait several minutes before he made his way to the lower debarkation ramp.

Waiting wouldn't be a problem, she was used to it.

Though a thousand issues demanded her attention, Tangel pushed all other concerns and considerations from her mind, and instead focused on the energy around her, the bleed-through from other dimensions where humanity barely made an imprint.

She was surprised to see a dark undercurrent running through the entire ship before her. After a moment's consideration, she realized that it shouldn't have been a surprise at all. From what she could see, it was as though the entire crew blamed themselves for the loss of their four charges.

They'd spent months in the black with little to show for it other than establishing listening posts, and that had taken its toll. Everyone aboard was in need of healing, but not the sort that could be performed in a medbay. Even if the *Perilous Dream* was found—and Cary, Saanvi, Faleena, and Priscilla were all safe and sound—it would still take the crew of the *Falconer* some time to recover from the events they'd been through.

Her melancholy musings were disrupted by the ship's forward bay door opening, revealing a dozen figures standing on the deck. First and foremost amongst those was Joe, and next to him stood a biohazard cylinder on a hoverpad.

He gave her a jaunty wave, though she could see that his eyes were haunted. The long ramp reached the bay, and he walked onto it, the hoverpad and its cargo following after.

The other crewmembers trailed behind, keeping their distance, though each one gave her a respectful nod when her gaze met their eyes.

Despite the weariness she could see suffusing his body and mind, Joe didn't slow as he reached the bottom of the ramp, a smile on his lips as he held out his arms and wrapped her in a warm embrace.

"I'm sorry," he whispered, the words barely audible over the general din of a kilometer-long cruiser settling on a cradle, and her crew embarking on a hundred different tasks.

"You don't have a thing to be sorry for," Tangel whispered. "It's I who should be sorry...I should have come to help, but...."

"But then you'd just be Mom, dragging her daughter back home to be disciplined." Joe nodded slowly. "I know she has to do this, the only way out is through, and all that. But stars, it hurts so much. And it's going to change her forever. We'll never get our daughter back."

Tangel took a step back and placed her hands on Joe's shoulders, her eyes locked on his. "No matter how this played out, she'd be changed. We're all changed. That day we defended Carthage and pulled out all the stops...for all of us, the only way out is through. And none of us are going to be the same."

"You're so uplifting." Joe gave a rueful laugh, but it faded away, and he cocked an eyebrow. "You're doing something to me, Tangel. I can feel it."

"There's a wound inside you," she replied. "It's festering."

"It's sadness," Joe countered. "And I need it. There's no other option than sorrow."

Tangel nodded. "You're right. Sorrow is natural, and shouldn't be stopped. But this is more than sorrow, this is the rut worn in your mind from a cyclical thought process that is poisoning you. I'm not going to stop you from thinking what you want to, but if you let me, I can make it less of a compulsion, break the pattern."

"Isn't that what you're already doing?" he asked sharply.

"No," Tangel shook her head, funneling every ounce of compassion she could into her voice. "I'm just stroking you gently, helping to calm you. It's just not with a corporeal hand."

"Oh," he replied, his eyes falling from hers. "I suppose that's OK."

They stood in silence, the crew of the ship and the dockhands giving the pair a respectful berth as they passed by.

"What's in the container?" she asked after a minute.

Joe cocked an eyebrow, and a bit of his old self showed through. "Oh, just a little present from RHY. Purple, glows, shouldn't exist."

"Shit," Tangel muttered. "Nadine and Nerishka shut that down, or so we thought."

"Someone must have gotten a sample out. Not sure if this is weaponized or not, but we're treating it like it is. I figured since Finaeus and Earnest are here, this was the best place to bring it."

"Actually, they're not here," Tangel replied. "Though they will be shortly, along with a new member of this star system."

"Sorry, what?"

Tangel guided Joe toward the lift bank, the hoverpad following close behind. "I hadn't sent this out over the QC network because we're keeping a really tight lid on it, but we're jumping Star City out of the galaxy."

Joe stopped short, nearly being run into by the hoverpad.

"You're what?"

Tangel proceeded to explain the plan to Joe, his eyes growing wider as she unveiled the rationale and the solutions to the problem of moving a star.

"So…all that construction out there…." Joe spoke the words slowly. "That's a stargate?"

"Yup," Tangel said with a grin and a nod. "We don't have to build a ring for a stargate, just discrete emitters. We'll move them, not the star, and then it will jump on its current trajectory."

"And because of mass balancing, you have to jump in another star at the same time?"

"The plan is to do two," Tangel said. "Grey Wolf is just a test star, though we're also going to use its drag for stellar braking before the big switcheroo."

"How long until it makes an appearance?"

"Just a few days, if everything stays on schedule."

Joe whistled. "You know…I've seen a lot of firsts since signing up on this bird, but this might be the firstiest."

"Firstiest, eh?"

"Yeah," he chuckled, and his eyes glinted for a moment. "That's the technical term."

# FINAL MOVEMENT
**STELLAR DATE: 05.04.8950 (Adjusted Years)**
**LOCATION: *Perilous Dream*, interstellar space**
**REGION: Outside New Sol, Orion Freedom Alliance**

*Four months later...*

A1 sat in the command chair of the *Perilous Dream*, her mind stretched throughout the ship, feeling its hull as her skin, the Widows within as her cells, her agents, seeing her will done and keeping her body healthy.

Though there were very few within her body now.

She looked outward around the *Perilous Dream*, at the fleet surrounding her flagship. It wasn't as big as she'd hoped, but five hundred vessels would have to do. Five hundred ships that would mask her approach to New Earth, and provide the distraction she needed to strike the blow that would end the war with Orion.

She pulled her thoughts back into her body and glanced at E12, who stood next to her chair.

"Everything is in readiness, A1," the Widow said, her voice lisping softly in the near-silence of the bridge. "H11 has just sent word that the admiralty and the praetor are all back on New Earth. Her team is in position to disable the insystem jump array. They'll not be able to escape."

"Excellent," A1 replied. "Inform her that the plan is commencing. We'll be in position in three days."

"Yes, A1," E12 replied.

A1 knew that the Widow would be loading the message and final timeline onto a shuttle. That vessel would travel the one light year through the dark layer to the edge of the New Sol System, and seed fragments of a message into the public navigation relays. H11 would be watching for the fragments and would assemble them. There was no doubt in her mind that H11 would properly execute her tasks.

When the fleet struck, the praetor and his admirals would be days away from the closest functional jump gates.

Moreover, the Widow-controlled ships had seen significant upgrades—that work consuming the majority of the seven months since she'd fled the Rega System—and when the Widow fleet struck, Orion would be powerless against them.

"New Sol will fall," she whispered.

E12 looked down at A1, her eyes wide and questioning.

"What will we do then?" the Widow asked.

A1 knew the answer, but she knew that E12—despite the compulsion she was under—still wouldn't understand.

She reached up and touched the Widow's arm. Her sister's arm. "We'll go home."

"Home." E12 breathed the word as though it were sacred to her. "I'd like that."

"Yes, I'm sure you would."

A1 didn't share the fear that was lodged inside of herself, a fear that many of the Widows would never see home again—whatever that meant for them.

But most of all, her fear was that she and her sisters would be amongst that number.

\* \* \* \* \*

"It's happening," Faleena whispered to Priscilla, the two women crouched in the small shipping container in the back of Hold 129. "She's finally making her strike."

The former avatar sat back on her heels, shaking her head slowly. "Stars, I wish you'd left me in that stasis pod. I mean…what are we going to do against her? You saw what happened to U23 last week when she questioned Cary. Your dear sister just shredded the poor thing right then and there. Took her apart atom by atom."

"I should never have agreed to leave her mind." Faleena hung her head. "None of this would have happened if I'd stayed."

"Or maybe it would have," Priscilla countered. "Maybe it would have been worse. But you need to shut down that emotional, human side of yourself for now…we need cold logic. What should we do?"

Faleena raised her eyes and met Priscilla's. "Cold logic? It's pretty clear. Based on that, we don't stop Cary, we *help* her."

"OK…" Priscilla chuckled. "Maybe a combination."

"Then we stay the course, and send out a signal when we get to New Sol. Hopefully, Dad is there waiting. He'll hear the signal and come running to help."

"And what help will that be?" Priscilla asked. "We still don't know exactly what Cary plans."

Faleena laughed, shaking her head as she did so. "Well, no matter what she has up her sleeve, Cary's going to need help. Five hundred ships won't be enough for a safe exfil, even with the upgrades she's made."

"Good point," Priscilla replied. "Then let's hope the admiral arrives in time for us all to catch a ride out."

# PART 5 – STARFIRE

## THIRD STAR
**STELLAR DATE: 05.06.8950 (Adjusted Years)**
**LOCATION: ISS *I2***
**REGION: Star City, Orion Freedom Alliance, Perseus Arm**

"Is it weird to feel sorry for a star?"

Tangel chuckled at Rachel's question, wondering for a moment if she shared the captain's view on the plight of Grey Wolf.

The two women stood in the *I2*'s forward observation lounge, watching the dim light from the distant dwarf star—and the mining operation tearing it apart—slide past the windows.

"It is a bit sad that we brought it out here just to strip it down in record time," she replied. "Though we'll not take it down beyond half a Sol, I think."

Rachel turned and regarded Tangel with a smirk playing at the corners of her mouth. "Was that an estimate, Admiral? You're not really prone to giving estimates anymore."

"I suppose it might have been," she replied, considering the lack of specificity she'd implied. "In my defense, my response was colored by the daily debates Earnest and Finaeus are having over the best method to swap out Star City with its replacements. They've still not solved how to deal with the gravitational waves hitting the second neutron star and wracking the thing with starquakes. Too many of those, and the orbital firing system will be twisted into a pretzel, and we lose our war-ending weapon."

"Will it really end the war?" Rachel asked. "I mean, to do that, you'll have to use it."

Tangel hunched her shoulders, rolling them forward and then back, carefully stretching out her muscles and relieving the tension building in them.

It was entirely possible to do the same thing with her mods, inducing relaxation via a number of methods. She could even do it extra-dimensionally, altering energy flows in her body to sooth and calm it.

But something about doing it the old-fashioned way was soothing to Tangel—especially because she possessed the ability to introspect her body on the cellular level, and could be much more specific and exacting with her movements, achieving the perfect result every time.

"I will use it," she said after a minute. "I even have my first target."

"Shit," Rachel whispered. "I figured there would be a bunch of bluster before we got that far."

"Bluster won't help until people see what we can do with this weapon."

She saw the captain's eyes tick to the right, where a special gate was being built that could jump neutronium bullets to any destination. Like the picobombs, they were a terrible weapon, but unlike pico, they had no power to create or build. Only to tear down.

"What are you going to hit?" Rachel asked, her voice

too calm, belying a nervous fear.

"I have a target in New Sol," Tangel replied. "One with minimal loss of life, but maximal impact—no pun intended."

"New Earth's moon, Luxa." The *I2*'s captain said the words with absolute certainty, and Tangel nodded.

"The listening posts that Joe left behind have not picked up any hint that Cary's fleet is insystem, but they have detected some interesting chatter. I'm all but certain that there is a DMG, probably more than one, inside Luxa."

"Like the one inside the moon in the Machete System," Rachel said. "The one Svetlana went up against."

"Exactly," Tangel replied. "I don't think that Orion possesses the ability to make mobile DMGs like Airtha could, but they do know how to tuck them into solid planets and moons. We know *that* for a fact. Plus, it makes the moon a viable military target."

"I suppose so," Rachel replied. "Kinda wish I could be there to see it hit…it will probably be quite the show."

"We'll be in New Sol soon enough, one way or another."

Rachel snorted a laugh. "Wow, Tangel, if you lower your brow and hunch your back, you could be a bit more ominous. Try it again."

Tangel looked at the captain, who was pantomiming the expression and posture, and was unable to hold back a laugh that bubbled up her throat.

"A giggle!" Rachel exclaimed. "That was a giggle! I didn't even know you *could* giggle anymore. I figured you'd ascended beyond that ability."

The smile on her friend's lips and the laughter in her voice caused Tangel to laugh all the harder, while the *I2*'s captain declared her to be the 'giggler in chief' and the 'giggle marshal'.

"Okay! Stop!" Tangel gasped out a breath, surprised at how she'd so completely lost control of her body, but finding that she'd forgotten how enjoyable the sensation could be. "I get it, I'm too serious now. I'm sorry. I'll try to giggle more."

"And eat more BLTs," Rachel added. "You've hardly eaten enough of them lately. When the BLT quotient in your blood gets too low, we all suffer."

"Noted," Tangel replied, drawing a deep breath to steady herself.

She glanced over her shoulder and saw a few other patrons in the forward lounge look away, their actions eliciting a fresh round of laughter.

"Yes! I laugh." Tangel raised her voice, letting the sound reflect off the window. "You can look. I know it's a rare occurrence and warrants a bit of gaping."

"*So* many jokes I could make right now," Rachel snickered. "Gaping is a word that just invites mockery."

Tangel was about to reply with an innuendo-laden response when Bob reached out to the two women.

<We have an update from New Sol. It's begun.>

Every iota of levity drained out of Tangel in an instant.

"Get us to the jump gate, Captain. It's time to get my daughters back."

# CLOSING

**STELLAR DATE: 05.06.8950 (Adjusted Years)**
**LOCATION: Palatine, Euros**
**REGION: Earth, New Sol, Orion Freedom Alliance**

"Those are the missing ships, alright," Admiral Myka advised Praetor Kirkland.

The pair stood deep in the Guard Command complex, not far from the Star Chamber in the admiralty's C&C. Before them was a vast holodisplay of the entire New Sol system, showing five hundred ships closing from nearly every direction.

Almost every ship was on its own, though here and there, a pair of cruisers broke the mold. They were all headed toward soft targets within the system. Stations with few defenses, and moons with little in the way of protection.

It was a maneuver that made little sense to Kirkland.

"Surely Lisa can't believe that her little fleet poses any real threat," Kirkland said, his brow lowered. "Sure, she might damage a few stations, but we have over a hundred thousand ships here. Her invasion force won't last a day."

"If that," Myka nodded. "Which means it's a feint...or something."

"What sort of something?" Kirkland turned to the admiral. "Either it's a feint or an act of desperation."

"I agree," the leader of the Guard replied. "But what appears desperate is often a feint, hiding something. The *Perilous Dream* isn't out there, which means—"

"Which means that it *is* out there, we just haven't been able to find it," Praetor Kirkland interrupted. "It's one of our ships, with our stealth tech, we *should* be able to locate it."

Myka pursed her lips, shaking her head slowly. "I don't feel the need to go over my long-standing distrust of Garza and Wrentham. But it's clear that they developed—or stole—technology that they hid from the rest of us. It's entirely possible that we won't see the *Dream* until it's right on our doorstep."

"What can one ship do?" Kirkland asked. "It has to reveal itself to strike, and we'll destroy it in an instant once it does."

Myka didn't respond, her eyes roving over the holo.

"Right?" Kirkland prompted. "We didn't spend thousands of years building this empire just to have one of our own destroy it. New Sol is one of the most heavily defended systems in the galaxy. If you think one ship can get past everything we've established, then you need to tell me how."

"That's just it," Myka replied. "I can't think of how, but clearly Lisa can. Otherwise she wouldn't be doing this."

Kirkland stared at the head of the admiralty for several long moments, then shook his head. "Well, you'd better figure it out before she shows us. How long until we engage the ships she's sent in?"

"Rails fired an hour ago, we should see initial impacts in a few minutes."

"If they don't jink out of the way," Kirkland muttered, remembering how things used to be before all the advances that nearly destroyed humanity.

Back then, jinking wasn't possible without killing everyone aboard the ship. Now it was almost impossible to fire on attacking ships.

All part and parcel of rampant technology needing better controls.

Myka focused the view of the battlespace to a ship approaching a station orbiting Dorne, one of the outer planets beyond the system's kuiper belt.

The ship was a Uke-class cruiser named the *Call of Triumph*. It was braking, firing its engines directly at the station, which was attempting to shoot directly up the engine wash, but its weapons weren't able to penetrate the ionized plasma and gamma streaming off the ship.

Thus far, the station's shields were holding, but Kirkland saw that the tactical NSAI only gave them another few minutes.

"Here they come," Myka pointed at the markers for a trio of rail slugs. A counter scrolled through numbers beside each, and then three impact tokens appeared.

Optical feeds showed flares of light, but the light was too bright, too white. When it faded, the cruiser was still there. Its engines had ceased their burn, but the hull seemed entirely unmarred.

"Fuck." Myka breathed the word in a shocked gasp. "No...."

"What is it?"

"Colonel!" the admiral barked at a man nearby. "Confirm analysis. Tell me that doesn't mean what I think it does."

The man's face was pale to begin with, but it grew

ashen as he looked up from his console and nodded. "The event matches impacts against stasis shields."

"How the hell did Lisa get stasis shields?" Kirkland's voice was a hoarse rasp. "I always thought she kept *some* tech from us, but this?"

"Stasis shields aren't impenetrable," Myka advised. "Now that we know what we're up against, we can adjust tactics. Atom beams up engine washes will do it."

"Not all of our ships can fire atom beams," Kirkland said. "We need to activate the DMGs."

"Sir." Myka shook her head. "Not yet. We need Lisa to show her hand first. We need to draw her in."

Kirkland folded his arms across his chest and glared at the display of the New Sol System. Somewhere amongst those worlds and stations was the woman he had rescued from the Tomlinsons, who he'd cared for and aided in her darkest hour.

*And now she seeks to take everything from me.* He shook his head. "Admiral Myka. The moment you lay eyes on the *Perilous Dream,* I want the DMGs to fire."

For a moment, he thought that a flicker of defiance showed in the admiral's eyes, but then she ducked her head.

"Yes, Praetor."

# FIREPOWER

**STELLAR DATE: 05.06.8950 (Adjusted Years)**
**LOCATION:** *Perilous Dream*, **approaching Dorne**
**REGION: Outer New Sol, Orion Freedom Alliance**

"They've begun firing on our ships," the Widow on scan called out. "So far, the shields are holding."

A1 nodded silently in response. She had seen the update as well, but it comforted even Widows to hear audible status calls as the plan progressed.

She was sure that the Widow made the announcement because no one was certain how well the stasis shields would actually hold up. No one except for A1.

E12 was intimately familiar with the ISF's stasis shield technology, and if one possessed both stasis technology and graviton emitters—as well as the correct implementation knowledge—it was shockingly simple to create the shields.

Which was why the ISF guarded the secret so closely.

CriEn modules, however, were much more difficult to build, and A1 had not been able to secure more than a handful in the intervening months. Only a few dozen of her five hundred ships possessed the power cores, and only those were expected to make it to New Earth.

The rest of the ships—and the Widows aboard them—would perish.

A part of A1 felt a modicum of guilt for sending those Widows to their deaths. As she sifted through the emotion, she found herself uncertain as to whether or not that came from Lisa or Cary. One cared about her Widows and the other about people in general. A1 knew that and understood their grievances. But to her, Widows were just tools to be used.

*Used up and discarded.*

She was glad for the smooth and implacable façade her helmet showed. If not for it, the Widows on the bridge would have seen the conflict on her face as she repeated the thought again and again to convince herself of its truth.

"Continue on course," she directed. "We'll brake around Dorne and then approach New Earth past its moon, Luxa."

The Widow on scan pushed an update to the main holotank. "A1, with the data we have amassed, I believe we face a high probability of being detected when we pass by Luxa. The nature of the traffic patterns creates ion trails that will tax our stealth systems."

"Then we'll rely on our stasis shields," A1 replied. "We have five CriEn modules. They will sustain us long enough to reach New Earth."

The Widow nodded and resumed her duties. "Understood."

Movement next to A1 caught her attention, and she looked at E12. The Widow had very reluctantly made the modifications to the CriEn modules that would see their mission to completion. Deep down, the Widow's leader knew her sister railed at the plan A1 had created, but she knew it had to be done.

*Kirkland will pay for what he's done to me.*

\* \* \* \* \*

Priscilla strode down a corridor on Deck 17A, headed to the CriEn chamber there. Faleena had picked up a message that all five of the ship's modules were being moved to one central chamber, and neither of the two women could think of a logical reason to do so.

For the past seven months, Priscilla had been operating under the guise of Widow Q73, an environmental specialist who had no real reason to be at the CriEn chambers, but Faleena's position as L19 currently had her on the bridge as the chief scan officer, and she couldn't get away to investigate herself.

In all honesty, Priscilla was glad that it wasn't her on the bridge. Being in close proximity to A1 day in and day out would have been too much for her. Granted, Faleena said it took a toll on her as well—especially seeing Saanvi in Cary's thrall.

The pair had debated freeing Saanvi several times, but A1 almost never separated from her sister anymore, and even over the span of seven months, no opportunities for deprograming Saanvi had presented themselves.

*Soon.*

Priscilla didn't know *what* they'd do 'soon', but she knew they'd have to do something. Things were coming to a head, and any opportunity to free Saanvi—or at least wrest her from A1's grasp—would have to be taken before long.

*But first I need to figure out what Cary's doing with the CriEns.*

Though Priscilla hated the fact that Cary was lost in the A1 person she'd become, and that she'd effectively enslaved her sister, she didn't want to see their mission fail because of some silly mistake. They'd come too far and sacrificed too much.

She turned down the passage that led to the central CriEn chamber, and was surprised to see a Widow standing at the door. Nothing on the *Perilous Dream* was guarded, theoretically because A1 fully trusted every one of her Widows.

The fact that the CriEn chamber was under watch meant that something was most certainly afoot.

Any attempt to get past the guard would trigger a visit from A1, so Priscilla walked past the door to the chamber without slowing. A careful observation of her would have picked up a casual flick of her left index finger, but she and Faleena had carefully mapped out all optical sensors in the ship, and she knew that none would have a view of her hand in that location.

She carried on without slowing, and continued down Deck 17A to the next F&W facility, taking her time in the room while waiting for the glob of nano she'd flung to work its way through the door and survey the room. It wouldn't be able to send a message back through the bulkhead, so it would need to exit the chamber and establish a point-to-point Link hookup in order to send her what it saw.

When her automated ablutions were complete, Priscilla took a roundabout route back, stopping to inspect a backup air scrubber before finally coming around past the CriEn chamber once more.

At first, there was no signal as she approached, and she feared the nano had not yet completed its task, but then she picked up the connection on a rarely used band and accepted the data packet.

Without slowing her pace, she drew up the image the nano had captured, and nearly let out an audible gasp.

Four of the modules were bundled together, and the fifth was nowhere to be seen.

But it wasn't the proximity of the modules that concerned her; it was the fact that two of them were physically inverted. From what she knew of the module's function, that inversion would cause the spacetime warping effect of vacuum energy draw to magnify.

*If our stasis shields take a beating, those modules are going to rip a hole right through the fabric of spacetime!*

Priscilla knew that there was no way Cary and Saanvi wouldn't know that, which meant it was their intention.

<When your shift ends, we need to meet,> she sent to Faleena. <A1's plan is insane.>

\* \* \* \* \*

Faleena only sent a quick affirmation to Priscilla, silently wondering what the woman had found in the CriEn chamber, but assuming the worst, based on the words chosen.

It would be another two hours before her shift on the bridge ended and she could meet to get the full details, but she began to consider worst-case scenarios. Given A1's objective of killing Kirkland and his high command, the most obvious conclusion was that she'd simply drive the ship right into the Guard's command complex.

The stasis shields would light up like a star upon hitting atmosphere. Radiation would pour down across the landscape, and the air would superheat, sending a shockwave across the continent.

But that would be the least of the damage done.

Provided the CriEn modules didn't reach a critical energy draw from breaching atmosphere—and likely taking heavy fire from defensive emplacements—things would get far worse when the ship touched the planet's surface.

The stasis shields would annihilate whatever they touched in an antimatter-like explosion, and that would cause the CriEn modules to draw an obscene amount of vacuum energy. It would be enough to destabilize the foundational layers of the universe.

*Reality will collapse.*

That was the best description Bob had ever provided for what would come to pass, should CriEn modules dig too deeply and destabilize the quantum foam. Even he wasn't sure what the result would be, but privately, he'd shared a suspicion with his Avatars that the event would create a white hole.

The opposite of a black hole, a white hole would spew out all light and energy within itself, allowing nothing from the outside universe to enter. It would pump more energy out into the physical universe in one hour than all the stars in the Milky Way released in a year.

The wave of energy would sterilize star systems for a thousand light years.

*Or it might just consume the planet and then fizzle out.*

No one knew for certain, and no one was eager to find out.

The conclusion was simple. Though she and Priscilla had supported Cary's goal—or at least, not worked to actively stop her—that had to change. A1 could not be allowed to slam a stasis-shielded ship into a planet. Under any circumstances.

Faleena was considering options for getting off the bridge before the end of her shift, when the *Perilous Dream*'s passive sensor array picked up a curious message. She would have discarded it offhand, but random segments of the message contained repeating patterns that were suspiciously similar to a code she knew.

It wasn't an ISF or TSF code, but rather one that Cary and Saanvi had once used to share messages that they thought their parents couldn't read. Their mother had told Faleena about it once, laughing that she and Joe had spotted the coded messages being passed on the household network and that Angela had cracked it, but they never read the contents.

Faleena drew in the code fragments in the message and carefully assembled them, running through decoding algorithms until one worked, and the encrypted message became clear.

Her father's voice came into her mind, and Faleena stilled her roiling thoughts at the sound of it and focused intently on his words.

*"Faleena, Orion has DMGs. Svetlana encountered one in a moon at Machete. We believe Luxa houses an array of them. If*

*they see the* Perilous Dream, *they'll fire."*

He hadn't needed to add the last sentence for her to come to the same conclusion. Scan showed that, thus far, the enemy was only using conventional weapons to attack the decoy fleet—which had only suffered one loss.

As predicted, the Orion Guard ships in the system were moving to protect the soft targets the Widow fleet was attacking. Many of their vessels were being held in reserve, but Faleena could see that it was thinning the protection along the *Dream*'s approach vector enough that the ship *should* be able to slip through.

Until they reached Luxa. Then all bets were off.

It occurred to Faleena that she could use this news to dissuade A1 from her insane plan. If the ship could never make it to New Earth, then it couldn't kill Kirkland, and there was no point in the suicide run. Aborting would be the only logical choice.

She quickly fabricated supporting data and a transmission that would point to there being a DMG in Luxa, as well as adding a report of the destruction of the DMG at Machete.

"A1," she turned in her seat to face the Widows' leader. "I've just picked up information that leads me to believe that Orion possesses weapons capable of penetrating stasis shields."

Though the Widows on the bridge appeared nonplussed by the news, Faleena was certain she felt a subtle rise in the level of tension.

"Pass it to me," A1 ordered, and Faleena complied. After a minute, she shook her head. "I suspected they might have this ability. Airtha possessed it as well. We will continue as planned."

Several Widows shifted, and Faleena saw the commands flow across the shipnet from A1 to the bridge crew, bringing them back in line with her wishes.

"No one will speak of this. If our stealth is compromised, we will take evasive action. The DMG in Luxa—if one exists—will not be able to track us at close range, and we will strike our target as planned."

Faleena wanted to shout that 'striking' the target was the last thing they wanted to do, but she knew that there was no way she could stand against Cary. Not unless she were to devise a way to take her sister unawares and kill her instantly.

She wasn't ready to go to those ends yet. It was time to call for help.

# ENGAGEMENT
**STELLAR DATE: 05.06.8950 (Adjusted Years)**
**LOCATION: ISS *I2***
**REGION: Outer New Sol, Orion Freedom Alliance**

<*I've detected a message from Faleena,*> Bob said, causing Tangel and Joe to turn from the forward display, eyes settling on the bridge's holotank, where the words appeared.

"*Moms, Dad. Cary plans to use CriEns going critical to destroy New Earth. She knows about the DMG in Luxa, but won't stop. We're going to do what we can, but I don't know how we can stand against her. Please help.*"

Tangel glanced at Joe, seeing the moisture forming in the corner of his eyes, and felt dismayed that none seemed to be seeping into hers. Instead, she felt a cold determination; the knowledge that she would need to do whatever was necessary to stop her daughter steeling her.

"Cary," she whispered.

Joe clasped her hand, his expression saying what he was unable to voice. She nodded in response and then turned to Captain Rachel.

"Captain, max speed, bring us to within fifty AU of the star and then drop a gate. We'll take the *Falconer* in."

"And should we continue insystem from there?" the captain asked.

Tangel gave a strangled laugh. "Stars, you'd better. We're going to need one hell of a rescue."

<*I don't like you leaving me behind,*> Bob said. <*We have*

*almost no intel on what other defenses Kirkland might have.>*

"It's my daughters." Her voice brooked no argument. "This is what we're doing. Besides, if she hits New Earth and it sparks a white hole fueled by vacuum energy, the repercussions will be unimaginably bad. The death toll from this war will seem like a footnote."

*<I understand. Please come see me in my node.>*

Tangel nodded, and then turned back to face Joe. "I'll meet you on the *Falconer*. We're going to jump straight to Luxa. You'll lead one team to storm the moon and disable the DMG, and I'll go to the *Perilous Dream* and stop this before it starts—if I can."

Joe swallowed and nodded. Then he squared his shoulders, eyes narrowing as the father was replaced by the admiral. "Better if we jump two ships. From the coordinates Faleena sent, they're still a ways away from the moon. Take a pinnace through the gate and get to the ship before they're too close. I'll be the fallback."

"Great plan," Rachel said as she approached, worry etched into her features. "But just how are you going to get off the moon? It's going to be crawling with enemies."

"That's where you come in," Tangel replied to the captain. "Cary was right about one thing…. The war with Orion has to end. Today. Once Luxa is out of commission, and the *I2* is above New Earth, we'll demand Kirkland's surrender."

"Do you think he'll comply?" the captain asked.

Joe nodded. "If he won't, then his second in command will. Tangel's right. Today we close the Orion Front."

Rachel cocked an eyebrow, a smirk forming on her

lips. "Well…it's getting close to the second shift, and we still have four AU to go to get to the jump point. Probably tomorrow."

Tangel gave Joe a quick embrace. "I'll see you on the dock. Don't leave without saying goodbye." Then she turned and wrapped her arms around Rachel. "Keep my girl safe while I'm gone, you smartass."

Rachel squeezed back, her voice hoarse as she said, "Always."

\* \* \* \* \*

A minute later, both Joe and Tangel were gone, and Rachel stared into the holotank, soaking in the enormity of what had just happened.

"Ma'am," the fleet coordination officer said from her station.

Rachel drew in a deep breath, praying her voice would hold. "Yes?"

"I couldn't help but overhear…. Uh…I've never heard the admiral say something like that before. Has she?"

A lump formed in Rachel's throat and she shook her head. Her voice was barely a whisper when she finally spoke.

"No…she hasn't."

\* \* \* \* \*

Tangel walked into Bob's primary node with a heavy heart, and placed her hands on the railing as she stared through the physical construct at the entity within.

"Why are you so worried? It's freaking me out."

Bob didn't reply for almost a minute. When he did, his voice carried an unfamiliar quality.

*<I promised myself that I'd never lie to you, Tangel. But that means I can't answer that question.>*

"More of you knowing the future and not wanting me to screw it up?" she asked.

*<Stars...if only it were that simple. Let's just say that you have already screwed everything up. The way forward is entirely opaque to me now, shrouded by the peril that looms on every side.>*

"Can you give me some clue?" Tangel asked. "Dammit, I feel like I might as well be at Delphi staring at animal entrails half the time I talk to you, Bob."

*<I'll take that as a compliment, though you don't mean it to be one. Regarding my fears, do you ever wonder why the core AIs sent Airtha to the Transcend, but didn't send anyone to Orion?>*

"I'd considered it," she replied. "Since we believe their goal was to deepen the distrust between Jeffrey and Kirkland, it seems that they only needed to utilize Airtha."

*<If that was in fact their goal. But what if they did send someone to Orion as well?>*

Tangel considered that information, playing out different scenarios and eventualities.

"I suppose most outcomes fall into one of two categories. Either their emissary failed and was somehow constrained by Kirkland, or they succeeded, and are in total control of Orion."

*<Neither of which is a possibility that we can take lightly.>*

"Agreed. What do you propose?"

*<I need to safeguard you, Tangel. Stopping what is about to happen is of the utmost importance, but your journey cannot end here.>*

Tangel's eyes widened as she realized what Bob was proposing.

"Do it," she said, and closed her corporeal eyes as the multinodal, ascended being's thousand limbs stretched out of the node and drifted toward her.

*<This will be uncomfortable.>*

"I imagine it will be."

* * * * *

Joe stood next to the pinnace he'd readied for Tangel. It was the fastest one in the First Fleet, with the best stealth systems and a mini CriEn that could power its stasis shield for days if needs be.

Tangel was taking longer than he'd expected, but they weren't in a huge rush. It would still be more than an hour until they reached the fifty-AU marker, where the engineers aboard the *Falconer* believed the inner perimeter of the interdictor field ended.

Then the fun would begin.

He was glad that Tangel had picked the *Falconer* to be the ship that went into New Sol. Not only did the crew know the system well, having stealthily traversed it for several months, but no one had liked the idea of leaving before their mission was complete. They were eager to see things through.

Captain Tracey had wasted no time getting her crew

back aboard and ordering them to stock additional weapons and energy cores. The ship and crew were ready for an assault unlike any other they'd ever performed.

"Joe." Tangel's voice came to him, and Joe turned to see his wife approaching, a smile on her lips. "Sorry I'm late. Bob was long-winded."

<*Sure, blame it on me,*> the AI said.

"Always." A grin was on Tangel's lips, and Joe couldn't help but feel his own mood lighten just looking at her.

"Why so jovial?" he asked. "Did Bob give you some sort of secret knowledge? We going to kick ass?"

Tangel stepped in close and planted a kiss on his lips, then pulled back. "We always kick ass."

"Well, mostly," he nodded. "So you're feeling good about this?"

"I am," Tangel nodded. "For the first time since Xavia's attack at Aldebaran, I'm feeling really good. We've got this in the bag."

"Glad you feel so optimistic," he laughed. "I have to admit, you seemed worried on the bridge."

She nodded. "Yeah, I was. Honestly, I still am, a bit. This isn't going to be a cakewalk, but seriously, they're Oggies. We got this. Before you know it, the girls will be back, and we'll have Orion surrendering."

"All in a day's work."

Tangel winked. "Or maybe two. It could take a bit to do the paperwork."

"OK, two. Then we meet back on the *I2* for drinks in the forward lounge."

"Deal," Tangel said as she turned away to face her pinnace. "OK, I'd better get aboard and do preflight."

"I already did it for you," he whispered in her ear as he embraced her from behind.

"Sure." She leant her head back against his. "But I know this vacuum jockey that would have my hide if I didn't at least do my own run-through before I took off."

Joe sighed. "I know that guy, too. He's probably right." He kissed her neck and stepped back. "Go get 'em."

"I will. I promise."

* * * * *

Tangel sat in the pinnace's cockpit and sucked in a deep breath, watching on the forward display as Joe walked up the ramp into the *Falconer*.

~*Are you sure?*~ she asked. ~*Does it have to be this way?*~

~*It does.*~ Bob's reply was laden with emotion. ~*You have to trust me. It'll work out. I promise.*~

She nodded silently, finishing her prechecks, and then initiated lift-off, easing toward the dock's exit. As she reached the grav field at the end of the dock, a message came in over the QC network from Star City. It was from Eric.

*[Barrage fired.]*

~*We're on the clock now,*~ she said to Bob.

~*We are. Good luck.*~

She snorted in response, shaking her head at the AI's poor humor. ~*I don't need luck.*~

# DESPERATION
**STELLAR DATE: 05.06.8950 (Adjusted Years)**
**LOCATION:** *Perilous Dream*
**REGION: Inner New Sol, Orion Freedom Alliance**

"So what do we do?" Priscilla asked. "Do you think they got the message?"

"I don't know," Faleena replied. "But we have to assume they didn't."

"Which means taking out the CriEn modules ourselves. No CriEns, no kaboom."

"How do you propose we 'take them out'?" Faleena asked. "The moment we breach that chamber, Cary will come, take them from us, and put them back."

Priscilla tapped a finger against her chin, staring into Faleena's eyes—or where she knew them to be behind the Widow's helmet. "We need a diversion."

"What do you have in mind?"

Ten minutes later, Priscilla and Faleena stood in a small hold near the primary stasis chambers. Within rested a single stasis pod containing a Widow, held there for the past seven months.

"You sure about this?" Faleena whispered. "She's going to be hard to control."

"That's sort of the point," Priscilla replied. "Unless you have a better idea, let's set her loose and get this underway."

"My only other idea is 'wait'," Faleena said. "Which isn't much of an idea."

Priscilla gave the AI a rueful smile, and then bent

over and keyed in the command to bring the Widow out of stasis. She and Faleena stepped back, rifles aimed at the figure as the pod's cover slid aside.

It took a moment for the Widow to stir, but when she did, it was only to say, "So, are you going to kill me?"

"Not so long as you don't give us a reason to," Faleena said. "Get out."

"Why don't you just make me?" Lisa Wrentham asked. "Maybe I've spent so long as your little sock puppet that I don't remember how to move myself."

"Figure it out," Priscilla growled. "We need your help."

The Widow in the stasis pod barked a laugh, and then sat up, swinging her legs over the side, where she stopped and regarded the pair and their rifles.

"Not a very friendly way to ask for help."

"That's because we're not friends," Priscilla countered. "We need to take control of the ship from our sister, and we figured you'd know better than anyone how to do that."

"Oh? Not happy with the new boss?" Lisa asked. "She running things into the ground?"

"In a manner of speaking," Faleena replied. "She's going to cause this ship to slam into New Earth, overloading its CriEn modules."

Lisa cocked her head to the side. "That won't work, other than as a kinetic weapon. The modules can't draw enough power on impact to—"

"She's upgraded the ship with stasis shields," Faleena interrupted. "They'll draw enough."

"Fuck." The Widows' progenitor breathed out the

word. "That'll destroy the entire star system…or—"

"Or a thousand star systems," Priscilla nodded impatiently. "We know. That's why we have to stop her. We need you to somehow get control of the ship while we steal the CriEns. If we can get two off the ship, her plan won't work."

For a moment, Lisa didn't move, but then she nodded. "OK, I know of a way I can override the engines, and even she won't be able to stop me—so long as I can get there in time."

"Trust me," Faleena chuckled. "Once we take the CriEns, all of her attention is going to be on us."

A minute later, they'd set a timetable and started a synchronized countdown.

"Don't double-cross us," Priscilla warned as she palmed the control panel to open the door. "We can still control your body."

"As can I," a voice said as the door slid open, and Priscilla turned to see A1 and E12 standing in the passageway. "I'm glad you woke Lisa Wrentham. I have need of her, and it's time for us to go."

"Go?" Faleena asked, taking a step back. "What are you talking about?"

A1 shook her head. "I have no plan to go down with the ship. We're not going to be here when the *Perilous Dream* impacts New Earth. But to make sure that happens, we need to get down to Luxa and disable that damn DMG."

"But how did you know?" Priscilla pressed.

A1 laughed, and for a moment, it sounded like Cary again. "It was Faleena. I didn't pick up on it at first, but when you share your mind with someone, you learn a lot of their verbal patterns. It took a day or two, but I eventually figured out that my scan officer was my sister. After following her for a few shifts, I discovered that you were free from stasis as well, Priscilla.

"You both seemed to be aiding my plan, so I decided to go along for a while and see where things led us."

"Which is to an impasse," Priscilla said. "We can't let you do this."

Tendrils of light snaked out from Cary and wrapped around Priscilla's and Faleena's necks.

"You're not *letting* me do anything. You're also not going to get in the way, though I still have to save you. Moms and Dad will expect to see you back."

"Car—"

Priscilla's voice cut off as Cary's ethereal limb passed through her neck and froze her vocal cords.

"Sorry, Priscilla. I don't have time for discussion right now. We have to get to a pinnace and get down to Luxa before they spot the *Dream* and fire on her." A1 turned to Lisa Wrentham. "Lisa would you be a dear and pretend to be A1 for a bit? I need you to keep the ship on course."

"Yes, A1," Lisa said, her voice trembling ever so slightly with what Priscilla could only imagine was forcibly contained rage.

"Good. Off with you."

Lisa stepped out of the hold and walked past A1 and the silent E12, disappearing from view.

"Now," A1 gestured in the other direction. "After you. We don't have much time."

# MOON LANDING
**STELLAR DATE: 05.06.8950 (Adjusted Years)**
**LOCATION: ISS _Falconer_, Luxa**
**REGION: Inner New Sol, Orion Freedom Alliance**

"Shit that's close!" Captain Tracey exclaimed as the forward display was filled with the view of Luxa.

"We're a thousand klicks up," Joe said, as he looked at the scan data. "We need to be a lot closer, as close to landing as you can get and still have maneuverability."

"On it, sir," Tracey said as she gave helm orders, while looking over the view of Luxa on the holotank. "Here." She jabbed her finger at a location in the southern hemisphere. "That looks like the best ingress point."

Joe pulled it up and saw a small spaceport on the moon's surface that was all but overflowing with small, insystem craft.

He nodded in agreement "Looks pretty suspicious."

"I'll get us there," Tracey replied. "I assume you plan to be on the assault team."

"Read my mind. I'm heading to the armory now."

The captain offered her hand "Good luck, sir."

"Thanks," Joe shook it, and his gaze swept across the _Falconer_'s bridge crew. "To all of you."

\* \* \* \* \*

Unlike the drop onto Polux, when the Marines' boots hit Luxa's regolith, there was no attempt at stealth. Beam weapons and railguns fired into the soldiers guarding the spaceport, tearing through the defenders in wave after wave as the platoons of Marines advanced in leaps and bounds.

Their target was the maglev terminal that would take them deep into the moon, where intel believed the DMG's fire controls systems lay.

<Remember, people,> Lieutenant Gallia said as the Marines secured the maglev train. <We do this by the numbers. No one's rash, no one's hasty, and we all get back in time for pastry.>

<Stars, LT, I thought you'd given up on that one,> Sergeant Bella muttered.

<Oldie but a goodie,> the lieutenant replied as she began directing the Marines into the maglev tunnel. <Watch out for tracks and rats.>

Joe moved in with Bella's squad, wondering if the lieutenant actually thought they might encounter rats in the tunnels, but not wanting to ask lest she resort to limerick again.

Hector's squad was in the lead, and three times, they encountered resistance: twice from automated drones, and the third from a group of soldiers.

<Resistance seems really light,> he commented to the lieutenant.

<It does, sir,> she replied. <Ferra's just managed to tap the network down. What do you have, Private?>

<Some sort of fighting is going on nearby,> the Marine replied a moment later. <Ah shit, they're being attacked by Widows.>

<Figures,> Joe muttered, wondering if Cary was with

them or not. <*If we see any, don't engage unless they do first, and go for non-lethal. Our people could be with them and either under a compulsion or undercover.*>

<*Yes, sir,*> Lieutenant Gallia replied before passing the order on to the platoon.

After another five minutes, they came to a platform strewn with the bodies of Orion soldiers. There weren't many scorch marks on the walls, and Joe suspected he knew why.

<*Double-time, people,*> he ordered, moving forward to join Bella's platoon as the Marines jogged down the passages, counting on the feeds from their drones to provide a view of what lay ahead.

For the most part, the view was similar to what the Marines had seen on the maglev platforms: dozens of Orion soldiers who looked as though they'd barely put up a fight before being torn apart—literally.

The further they went, the less Joe wanted to believe that he was following in Cary's wake. The carnage was extreme; many of the soldiers had been felled as they were running away, many more weren't even holding weapons.

After several more minutes, they came to a wide foyer with reinforced doors that had been torn free of the bulkhead. The ISF Marines eased through the opening and spread out, advancing on the four doors on the far side of the room.

Joe followed Bella toward her door, and when they reached it, he threaded nanofilament around the jamb, sucking in a sharp breath at the tableau within.

The room was a long, oval space, roughly eighty by

sixty meters. President Kirkland and a group of Orion brass stood at the far end on a raised platform. Four Widows stood in the center of the room, three holding rifles, and the fourth unarmed, standing a few paces ahead.

"It's over, Kirkland. You've lost," the black figure in the lead called out, and Joe knew it was Cary, though her voice hissed and lisped like a Widow's.

The praetor shook his head, a look of dismay on his features. "No, it's you who have lost. I must say, I'm glad this isn't you, Lisa. I would have been truly saddened to have you turn on me like this."

"She wouldn't be," Cary retorted. "You're right that I'm not her, but I *know* her. I know Lisa better than she even knows herself. She hates you with every fiber of her being."

"Is that so?" Kirkland asked. "Well, perhaps she and I can discuss that at some point in the future."

"Wrong," Cary shot back. "You have no fut—"

Joe started as Cary's words cut off, watching in horror as an energy field suddenly encapsulated her.

"A brane," he whispered aloud.

"Do you really think that we kept Orion pure this long without knowing how to deal with ascended beings?" Kirkland asked, taking a step forward as the other three Widows fell to the ground. "The core AIs sent one to me long ago, just as they did to Tomlinson. I let mine think it had my ear, but all the while, we worked to subdue and capture it. It took decades, but ultimately, human ingenuity won out. I learned a lot from that sad thing. I really did feel pity for it. I'm not sure I feel the same for you—Tangel, I assume?"

"You'd be so lucky," Cary said. "That is my mother. I'm A1."

"A1?" Kirkland cocked an eyebrow. "Interesting. Do you also go by 'Cary', then? There have been whispers that Tangel's daughter had ascended as well."

Cary didn't reply, and Kirkland shook his head. "I suppose it doesn't matter." Then he looked up at the doors, his gaze settling on the one Joe stood behind. "The brane that holds this person—be she Tangel or Cary—is capable of killing her in an instant. It wouldn't be the first time I've used one, so don't think it's just a bluff. Unless you want her to die, I suggest those of you in the antechamber surrender."

*<We've got Oggies in the passage on our six,>* Hector said. *<Orders?>*

*<We have to surrender,>* Joe said. *<Sergeant Hector, when we do, I need you to stealth and take a team back. We need to get word to the* Falconer, *and have them reach out to Tangel. She'll be able to stop this.>*

*<Aye, sir.>*

The ISF admiral stood and pulled off his helmet. *<The rest of you, disarm.>*

# THE REAL LISA WRENTHAM

**STELLAR DATE: 05.06.8950 (Adjusted Years)**
**LOCATION: ISF Pinnace, Luxa**
**REGION: Inner New Sol, Orion Freedom Alliance**

The stars were only gone for an instant before they snapped back into view and Tangel began to search for the *Perilous Dream*.

She knew that the pinnace's meager arrays could never pick up the Widows' ship, but that wasn't her plan. Bob had calculated its most likely trajectory, and with her extradimensional sight, she'd be able to see the CriEns' energy draw.

Her gaze roved across the stations orbiting New Earth and the ships plying the black. Most did not possess CriEn modules, but a few military vessels did. She filtered every vessel not drawing vacuum energy out of her view, and then began to tag each one the pinnace could scan as well.

A minute later, she found it. An anomalous energy draw with no visible ship.

"Gotcha," she whispered.

Careful not to give the pinnace away to any of the many eyes in the system, nor her prey, Tangel carefully guided it onto an intercept course with the *Perilous Dream*, and then programmed in a flight path to take the small craft safely out of the way afterward.

Bob's calculations had been very close to the mark, and twenty minutes later, the pinnace had matched $v$ with the *Dream*, and sat only a hundred meters off the stealthed cruiser's port bow.

"OK," Tangel said to the cockpit. "Here goes nothing."

Stretching out her non-corporeal limbs, she eased her way through the holodisplay and the bulkhead beyond, passing into space. Gathering herself on the hull of the pinnace, she fought against what could only be described as a type of vertigo as she stared out into the blinding light of New Sol's star.

*Easy does it,* she thought. *Just push off and drift over. Have to do it fast, the pinnace is going to change course in a minute.*

With the words echoing in her mind, she pushed off from the small craft, leaving its lone occupant, and crossing the gap between the ships.

Her body sank into the *Perilous Dream*'s hull, and for a moment, Tangel felt stuck, as though she'd been embedded in the ship. Then she shifted the wavelengths of her limbs, and found purchase on the ship's matter and pulled herself in, passing through hull, pipes, and conduit, to finally emerge inside a passageway.

"That was unsettling," she said softly, stretching her perception up and down the corridor, while also reaching into the ship's network, searching for the location of the bridge.

As she searched, a Widow came around the corner and stopped, frozen in her tracks for a moment before she managed to stammer, "W-what are you?"

"I'm Tangel. I'm here for my daughters. Take me to the bridge."

The Widow pulled her sidearm free and trained it on

Tangel. "I don't think so."

Without bothering with a verbal response, Tangel reached out and took the weapon apart, atom by atom, absorbing the energy released in the process.

The Widow didn't move, so Tangel moved onto the enemy's arm, dissolving it as well.

That set the black assassin screeching, and she turned to run, but Tangel touched her mind and put the tortured being to sleep.

"Don't worry, I'll find my own way."

She encountered several other Widows on the way to the ship's bridge, none providing any more trouble than the first. A few minutes later, she stood before the sealed door and shook her head.

"Cary, you may as well open it. You know a door won't stop me."

No response came from within, and Tangel made good on her promise, shredding the door and moving through onto the bridge.

Six Widows stood between her and the captain's chair. Tangel reached out, casually sweeping them aside as she moved forward, her gaze raking over the Widow the ship's systems recognized as A1.

"You're not Cary," Tangel's limbs flashed out and she took apart the helmet obscuring the Widow's face. "You're her, the real Lisa Wrentham."

"And you must be Tangel," Lisa replied. "Stars, and you wonder why we worked so hard to stop you. You're a monster."

An echoing laugh burst from Tangel as she regarded the ruined creature that had once been such a brilliant mind in the FGT. She gestured to the black-clad figures all around her.

"Seems like the kettle calling the pot black. No matter, though, where is she? You can't hide her from me."

"Hide her?" Lisa asked. "I can't do anything she doesn't order me to. However, she didn't order me not to tell you where she's gone." The Widow turned and pointed to Luxa, the view of which dominated the forward display. "She's gone there, to destroy the DMG, I imagine."

Tangel resisted a groan. She was about to render the Widow unconscious when Lisa barked a cruel laugh.

"Oh, look at that, the praetor is reaching out. Shall I put him through?"

Without replying, Tangel reached into the ship's network and configured the response to relay through several public networks so that Kirkland's people would not be able to triangulate the *Dream*'s position too quickly.

With that done, she sent a response, and Kirkland appeared on the screen.

"Ah!" his brow lifted. "Well, then, you must be Tangel, and this must be Cary. Good to have that settled."

"Glad to put your mind at ease," Tangel responded. "Let my daughter go. There's no way you can win this fight."

"No?" Kirkland asked, a smirk pulling at one side of his mouth. "Are you sure about that?"

The view changed to show a black brane holding a Widow, with a group standing to one side. Three of them were Widows—which she identified as Priscilla, Saanvi, and Faleena—and the fourth was Joe.

"Shit," she whispered. "Oh shit, no."

"Oh yes," Kirkland was grinning ear to ear. "I'm sorry, I shouldn't be so impolite, but I really never expected you to march on in here and essentially turn yourselves over to me. I guess it shouldn't be that surprising. I've been playing the long game for some time. You just came onto the field."

"What do you want?" Tangel asked.

"I want your surrender. I want you next to your daughter, and when you are, you'll order the ISF to stand down, and surrender all of your abhorrently advanced technology to Orion."

Tangel wondered if this was what Bob had seen that he didn't want to share with her. He was right that she would have altered it—she would have done anything to alter it. But it also might be that she'd already done something to change what he saw. For centuries, his schtick had been that her 'luck' messed up his vision.

*Some luck.*

Even so, she wasn't going to give in without a fight.

"There's no way," she retorted. "You'll simply kill my people. You think we're all abominations."

Kirkland stared into the optical pickup for a minute and then shook his head. "I suspected you'd need more motivations."

A rifle's retort sounded, and Priscilla's head exploded, her body staying upright for a moment before falling to the deck.

"What an ass," Lisa muttered, and it took every

remaining ounce of willpower Tangel possessed not to smash the abhorrent woman against the bulkhead.

"OK," she whispered after regaining her composure. "I'm coming down."

"You have half an hour. I know the *Dream* is at least that close."

"I'll be there," Tangel replied and killed the connection.

Lisa shook her head, her soulless eyes locked on Tangel's. "You know he'll capture you too. Going down there is a death sentence."

"We'll see about that."

Tangel reached out and touched the minds of the Widows on the bridge, dropping them all into a deep sleep before pushing off from the deck and pulling her way through the ship to where the CriEn modules were positioned. With more care than she felt she had time for, Tangel took each one off the stack and disabled it, ensuring that Cary's master plan to destroy the star system would fail.

From there, she moved through the ship and disintegrated the stasis field generators. Her last stop was the aft bay, where a stealth shuttle waited.

She adjusted her form to move in the corporeal world, and boarded the vessel, running an abbreviated pre-flight, smiling as she thought of Joe's displeasure at her haste, and then took off.

When she was a thousand kilometers from the *Perilous Dream*, she sent a command back to the ship, dropping its stealth systems.

Less than a minute later, a beam of energy streaked

out of Luxa and speared the Widows' ship, tearing it in half and sending it spinning off course.

Tangel couldn't help a rueful laugh. "Vindictive."

# ENFORCED
**STELLAR DATE: 05.06.8950 (Adjusted Years)**
**LOCATION: Luxa**
**REGION: Inner New Sol, Orion Freedom Alliance**

Tangel drifted through the moon's surface, eschewing the passages and corridors, most of which were filled with Orion soldiers.

She wondered if they had a type of slepton weapon like the ISF employed for capturing ascended beings. Though she fully expected to be captured in a brane at some point before the day was done, she didn't want it to be before she reached the DMG control chamber.

*No time to waste.*

Partway through the moon, she saw a familiar energy signature, and realized that it was a team of ISF Marines moving back toward the surface.

*~Sergeant Hector,~* she said, slowing her descent near the tunnel he was moving through. *~You need to get off Luxa.~*

*Who? What?* His thoughts were more startled than panicked.

*~This is Admiral Richards. You need to go, there's nothing more you can do here. Cary left a shuttle in the spaceport, it has a CriEn and stasis shields.~*

*How do you know that?* he blurted out. *Er…ma'am.*

*~I just do. Now go. That's an order. I'll take care of the DMG and rescue our people.~*

He seemed hesitant, and she provided a mental push.

*~Sergeant, **go**.~*

A feeling of sorrow came from the Marine, but the words *Yes, Admiral,* sounded in his mind, and she watched him get his team on their way back to the spaceport before moving on.

Three minutes before her deadline expired, Tangel fell through the ceiling of the oval chamber and landed a dozen meters from where Cary was captured. On the far side of the brane were her other daughters and Joe. Further back in the room were the Marines, out of their armor and under guard by nearly a full company of Oggies.

"You know," she turned to address Kirkland. "Even without me here, my Marines would still kick your ass. Kill my daughter, and you'll find out they don't need weapons to take down your people."

"So much bluster." Kirkland shook his head.

"It was more of an observation. I don't really have much of a filter right now—I'm kind of at the end of my rope."

The praetor pursed his lips and nodded. "I can see why. Either way, just so they don't get any ideas, they should know that this room can produce a rather powerful EMP. My people won't suffer much from a full blast, but I suspect folks with as many mods as your Marines—not to mention your daughters and husband—will not enjoy the experience."

"Don't worry," Tangel said. "They won't do anything rash. Like I said, it was just an observation."

"For all your advances, you certainly are weak." Kirkland folded his arms across his chest. "Get up here and stand next to your daughter. I have a cage waiting for you."

Tangel ignored his order and instead peered through Luxa and out into space, searching for her salvation. Now, more than ever, the timing had to be perfect. Seeing the brane that held Cary, Tangel wasn't sure that she could do what she had to if Kirkland trapped her as well.

"And if you weren't fighting us so much," she replied while still scanning the black, "we could already be in an alliance, fighting against the core AIs. They're the real enemy. Why can't you see that?"

"They're *an* enemy," Kirkland countered. "But if I helped you destroy them, *you* would simply take their place. That's not an option, so far as I'm concerned. Now get up here."

To emphasize his point, the brane surrounding Cary contracted, and she let out a muffled shriek, the N-dimensional field wrapping tightly around her body.

*~I'm sorry, Mother,~* Cary whispered. *~I screwed it all up. I really thought it would work. It should have worked.~*

*~We're going to make it through this,~* Tangel whispered into her daughter's mind. *~And when we do, you'll understand.~*

*~Understand what?~* Cary asked. *~My failure?~*

*~Look.~* Tangel gestured out into space. *~Look beyond the moon, look into the deep. Tell me, what do you see?~*

Cary didn't respond for a moment, and Kirkland began to yell that he'd shoot Faleena if Tangel didn't comply. She spotted the soldier holding the rifle on Faleena, and saw that the man was aiming for the AI's head.

She ignored Kirkland and implored her daughter.

*~What do you see?~* she pressed.

*~Lights,~* Cary replied. *~So many lights. What are they?~*

A rifle barked, the sound echoing in the enclosed chamber as Faleena fell to the ground.

*~They're our salvation,~* Tangel replied with far more calm than she felt. *~When this is over, you must be strong for me. You must forget Lisa Wrentham, scrub her from your mind, memory by memory. Come back to your father and mothers and sisters. Promise me you'll do this, Cary. Promise me.~*

*~I promise.~* Cary's voice was quiet and scared, reminding Tangel of the little girl she once was.

Tangel reached out, wishing she could penetrate the brane to touch her daughter one last time. *~That's my girl.~*

A fraction of a second later, two dozen neutronium bullets traveling at 0.7c hit Luxa and pulverized the moon.

# FALCONER

**STELLAR DATE: 05.07.8950 (Adjusted Years)**
**LOCATION: ISS *Falconer*, Luxa**
**REGION: Inner New Sol, Orion Freedom Alliance**

When Tangel ordered Tracey to move away from Luxa, the captain had strongly considered disobeying orders. She had debated closing in and landing more troops on its surface, right up until the moment the moon exploded.

A replay of scan had shown that it wasn't an explosion, but instead the result of two dozen neutronium bullets hitting Luxa.

Despite the fact that each bullet wasn't much larger than two of her fingers, the kinetic energy unleashed would have been enough to destroy an earth-sized planet.

That was nothing compared to the shock that ran through the crew of the *Falconer*.

It had taken Captain Tracey a full minute to regain the powers of speech, so she was glad that Ella had the foresight to activate the stasis shields and protect them from the relativistic spray of debris that was tearing its way through the New Sol System.

"Damage?" she asked, turning to the engineering chief.

He didn't respond, and she rose from her chair and placed a hand on his shoulder.

"We've still got a ship to fly, and we're still deep in enemy territory, mister. I need a status report."

"Yes—" The word rasped through a dry throat, and he swallowed, closed his eyes, and nodded. "Yes, ma'am."

"Message from the *I2*," the comm officer said in a breathless voice. "It's from Bob, he says 'find them'."

The two words spurred Tracey into action, and she leapt back to her chair.

"OK, people! If Bob thinks they're out there, then they're out there. Scan, I want you to map the path of all that crap and plot the most likely course. Weapons, you blast the shit out of any Orion ship that even gets close to us. No way are we letting those bastards pick up our people. Everyone else, help scan look for them. Whatever they're in, it has to be bigger than most of the gravel Luxa got pulverized into."

The bridge crew leapt into action, holos appearing over consoles showing sections of the moon's rapidly expanding debris field, teams reviewing data and deploying drones to aid in triangulation.

"We found something!" Scan called out five minutes later. "It's a pinnace, Orion make, but with stasis shields."

"Trying to raise them," Comm added. "It's Sergeant Hector! He has four Marines with him."

"And Tangel?" Tracey demanded.

"No...he says she ordered him back to the surface."

"Shit," the captain muttered. "If his ship can fly, get him in on the search, otherwise get him aboard."

The sergeant's pinnace was in good enough condition to join in, and its smaller profile made it able to move through the debris field with less disruption.

The search went on for another thirty minutes before someone on the bridge blurted out, "What the hell is that?"

An image appeared on the main holotank, and Captain Tracey rose to her feet, staring at it in wonder.

"It's a crystalline sphere," she whispered. "That must be them. Helm, get us over there."

\* \* \* \* \*

"The *Falconer* found them," the Comm officer called out, and cheers erupted across the *I2*'s bridge. "They're in some sort of sphere, but they can't figure out how to get it open, and it won't fit in any of their bays."

*<Tell them to keep it safe until we arrive,>* Bob intoned.

"Yeah," Rachel said, feeling almost breathless. "Tell them that."

"We're forty-seven minutes out," Helm added. "Going to be some hard braking."

"Deploy the fleet," Rachel ordered. "I want to make sure that we keep the Oggies at bay."

"Aye," the fleet coordination officer responded.

"So far, they seem to be keeping back," Scan said. "Plus, those other Widow ships are still advancing through the system."

*<We'll have to deal with those,>* Bob said. *<We can't have stasis tech leaking out.>*

Rachel nodded. "No rest for the weary. I'll call for help."

*<I've already done that. Krissy is bringing a fleet.>*

"Sheesh, Bob, what do you need me for?"

*<Moral support.>*

The incongruity of that statement had Rachel laughing so hard, tears were streaming down her face before she managed to get control of herself, only to find that half the bridge crew had joined in.

\* \* \* \* \*

The crystalline sphere settled onto the deck in the forward docking bay, and Rachel approached it nervously.

*<What are we going to find inside?>* she asked Bob privately, not wanting to worry the crew around her.

*<I'm not sure,>* the AI replied.

As he spoke, two sinuous tendrils of light passed though the overhead and stretched toward the sphere. They paused in front of it, and then traced a five-meter circle near the base. With a light sucking sound, the section of sphere fell out and landed on the deck.

One of the tendrils of light hovered in the entrance to the sphere and then retreated.

*<They're OK,>* Bob said.

The first person to emerge was a Widow, holding another one of her kind in her arms.

Marines lifted their weapons, a fireteam moving toward the pair.

*<That is Saanvi and Cary. Get them to medical.>*

"You heard him," Rachel barked. "Medics!"

A Marine was out next, and Rachel recognized Lieutenant Gallia.

"We've got prisoners coming out next," she hollered.

"Two 'toons of their goons and some brass. Kirkland too."

"Tangel? Joe?" Rachel asked as she approached the Marine. "What about Faleena and Priscilla?"

Gallia's eyes fell to the deck, and she stepped aside so as not to impede the flow of prisoners exiting the sphere. She heaved a deep breath and looked up at Rachel.

"Not everyone made it, ma'am."

Rachel saw the sorrow the lieutenant was trying to keep at bay, and didn't press the woman any further. A rage began to build up in the I2's captain, and she turned to glare at the prisoners as they were escorted from the sphere.

When the officers and Kirkland emerged, she directed a special detail to secure them, placing each one in stasis before moving them to the brig.

Finally the procession was finished, and she stepped into the sphere, surprised to find part of a room within. In the center, Joe crouched next to a pair of bodies, and Rachel sped to his side, gasping in horror as she realized both were headless.

"Who?" she finally managed to sputter.

"Faleena." Joe whispered the name, pointing at the body on the right. "She's OK. Saanvi has her core."

"And Priscilla?" the name rasped its way out of Rachel's throat as she fell to her knees next to Joe, staring at the remains of a woman who had been both a comrade and a good friend.

"She's gone." The words fell from Joe's lips like lead. "And so—"

His voice cut out, the words ending in a strangled

cough.

"So is Tangel?" Rachel whispered, looking around for another body. "Where...."

Joe gestured at the sphere around them. "This is her body. She did it to save us. I don't...I don't understand how, but Cary said it consumed all of Tangel to save us."

<She's right,> Bob's voice came into their minds. <Tangel has passed away. I hoped it wouldn't come to this, but—>

"Bob," Joe hissed. "Right about now, I'd like you to shut up."

The AI didn't speak further, and Rachel reached out, wrapping her arms around the man she'd long thought of as a surrogate father, as sobs began to wrack his body.

# ADRIFT

**STELLAR DATE: 05.07.8950 (Adjusted Years)**
**LOCATION: ISF Pinnace**
**REGION: Outer New Sol, Orion Freedom Alliance**

Consciousness came back to Tanis in slow, pulsing waves, almost as though her mind was reinitializing itself, coming back to life after a long dormancy.

It seemed to take forever to form a coherent thought, but when she did, it was a single word.

*<Angela?>*

*<I'm here, Tanis. Though I don't know where 'here' is.>*

*<Why can't I see? Wait…I can't feel, either. Are we dead?>*

The AI laughed, the silvery sound of mirth letting Tanis know that everything would be alright. *<If we are, then this must be hell, being stuck with you forever.>*

*<Seriously? I thought it would be heaven. You know how I light up a room.>*

*<In your own mind. OK, I've figured it out. It's our brains. They're kinda disconnected from your body. Give me a minute.>*

A thousand reasons for such an occurrence ran through Tanis's mind. She tried to remember where she'd been last, what she'd been doing. It was foggy…something about the Albany System, the planet Pyra.

*<Crash-landed! We're stuck on Pyra. I lost my arm.>*

*<Well, not anymore,>* Angela said. *<You've got both arms, so far as I can tell.>*

*<You gonna hook me up, or just leave me trapped in here?>*

289

<I'm working on it. Your delicate little brain can't take much abuse.>

<Funny, Angela—oh! Vision. That's a start.>

<The rest is coming. Looks like we're in a pinnace.>

Tanis nodded, then realized she'd actually nodded. "Oh, that feels weird. Like my head is floating…wait, no, we're just in zero-g."

<Seems like it—oh shit.>

" 'Oh shit' what?" Tanis glanced around the cockpit, noting that it was clearly an ISF design.

<We've lost time.>

"How much?"

She checked her internal chrono, gasped, and then looked at the one on the pinnace's holodisplay.

<A year.>

She let out a shuddering breath. "OK. What the hell happened on Pyra?"

## THE END

\* \* \* \* \*

### Read on for how to get a brand new Free Book.

Although the Allies have captured Kirkland and his high command, the rogue Widow ships and the hundred thousand Orion ships in New Sol still pose a serious threat.

Moreover, the I2 and First Fleet must deal with the loss

of Tangel, and what that means for the road forward. And, of course, Tanis and Angela must get back to the *I2*....

Find out what happens next in *Race Across Spacetime*, book 11 in The Orion War series.

Wait! Don't go anywhere, I have a FREE BOOK for you! (OK, I might not have it finished yet, but you'll get it as soon as it's done.)

You may have noticed that we didn't learn about the missions that both Jessica and Sera were sent on. This is because those stories got so big that they turned into their own books, and I couldn't get those parts done in time for this publication.

Because of that, I'm going to offer them to you as a *free book* as my appreciation to you for following me on this journey. Sign up on this special mailing list, and I'll let you know as soon as the book is ready (likely late summer 2019).

Email signup: http://eepurl.com/gs8Dhz

Thanks,
M. D. Cooper

# THE BOOKS OF AEON 14

Keep up to date with what is releasing in Aeon 14 with the free
Aeon 14 Reading Guide.

**The Sentience Wars: Origins** (Age of the Sentience Wars – w/James
S. Aaron)
- Books 1-3 Omnibus: Lyssa's Rise

- Book 1: Lyssa's Dream
- Book 2: Lyssa's Run
- Book 3: Lyssa's Flight
- Book 4: Lyssa's Call
- Book 5: Lyssa's Flame

**Legends of the Sentience Wars** (Age of the Sentience Wars –
w/James S. Aaron)
- Volume 1: The Proteus Bridge
- Volume 2: Vesta Burning

**The Sentience Wars: Solar War 1** (Age of the Sentience Wars –
w/James S. Aaron)
- Book 1: Eve of Destruction

**Enfield Genesis** (Age of the Sentience Wars – w/Lisa Richman)
- Book 1: Alpha Centauri
- Book 2: Proxima Centauri
- Book 3: Tau Ceti
- Book 4: Epsilon Eridani
- Book 5: Sirius

**Origins of Destiny** (The Age of Terra)
- Prequel: Storming the Norse Wind
- Prequel: Angel's Rise: The Huntress (available on Patreon)

- Book 1: <u>Tanis Richards: Shore Leave</u>
- Book 2: <u>Tanis Richards: Masquerade</u>
- Book 3: <u>Tanis Richards: Blackest Night</u>
- Book 4: <u>Tanis Richards: Kill Shot</u>

**The Intrepid Saga** (The Age of Terra)
- Book 1: <u>Outsystem</u>
- Book 2: <u>A Path in the Darkness</u>
- Book 3: <u>Building Victoria</u>

- <u>The Intrepid Saga Omnibus</u> – *Also contains Destiny Lost, book 1 of the Orion War series*

- <u>Destiny Rising</u> – *Special Author's Extended Edition comprised of both Outsystem and A Path in the Darkness with over 100 pages of new content.*

**The Warlord** (Before the Age of the Orion War)
- Books 1-3 Omnibus: <u>The Warlord of Midditerra</u>

- Book 1: <u>The Woman Without a World</u>
- Book 2: <u>The Woman Who Seized an Empire</u>
- Book 3: <u>The Woman Who Lost Everything</u>

**The Orion War**
- <u>Books 1-3 Omnibus</u> (includes Ignite the Stars anthology)

- Book 1: <u>Destiny Lost</u>
- Book 2: <u>New Canaan</u>
- Book 3: <u>Orion Rising</u>
- Book 4: <u>The Scipio Alliance</u>
- Book 5: <u>Attack on Thebes</u>
- Book 6: <u>War on a Thousand Fronts</u>
- Book 7: <u>Precipice of Darkness</u>
- Book 8: <u>Airtha Ascendancy</u>
- Book 9: <u>The Orion Front</u>
- Book 10: <u>Starfire</u>
- Book 11: <u>Race Across Spacetime</u> (2019)

- Book 12: Return to Sol (2019)

**Building New Canaan** (Age of the Orion War – w/J.J. Green)
- Book 1: Carthage
- Book 2: Tyre
- Book 3: Troy
- Book 4: Athens

**Tales of the Orion War**
- Book 1: Set the Galaxy on Fire
- Book 2: Ignite the Stars

**Perilous Alliance** (Age of the Orion War – w/Chris J. Pike)
**-** Book 1-3 Omnibus: Crisis in Silstrand

- Book 1: Close Proximity
- Book 2: Strike Vector
- Book 3: Collision Course
- Book 4: Impact Imminent
- Book 5: Critical Inertia
- Book 6: Impulse Shock

**Rika's Marauders** (Age of the Orion War)
- Book 1-3 Omnibus: Rika Activated

- Prequel: Rika Mechanized
- Book 1: Rika Outcast
- Book 2: Rika Redeemed
- Book 3: Rika Triumphant
- Book 4: Rika Commander
- Book 5: Rika Infiltrator
- Book 6: Rika Unleashed
- Book 7: Rika Conqueror

*Non-Aeon 14 Anthologies containing Rika stories*
- Bob's Bar Volume 2
- Backblast Area Clear

**The Genevian Queen** (Age of the Orion War)
- Book 1: <u>Rika Rising</u>
- Book 2: <u>Rika Coronated</u> (2019)
- Book 3: Rika Reigns (2019)

**Perseus Gate** (Age of the Orion War)
*Season 1: Orion Space*
- Episode 1: <u>The Gate at the Grey Wolf Star</u>
- Episode 2: <u>The World at the Edge of Space</u>
- Episode 3: <u>The Dance on the Moons of Serenity</u>
- Episode 4: <u>The Last Bastion of Star City</u>
- Episode 5: <u>The Toll Road Between the Stars</u>
- Episode 6: <u>The Final Stroll on Perseus's Arm</u>
- Eps 1-3 Omnibus: <u>The Trail Through the Stars</u>
- Eps 4-6 Omnibus: <u>The Path Amongst the Clouds</u>

*Season 2: Inner Stars*
- Episode 1: <u>A Meeting of Bodies and Minds</u>
- Episode 2: <u>A Deception and a Promise Kept</u>
- Episode 3: <u>A Surreptitious Rescue of Friends and Foes</u>
- Episode 4: <u>A Victory and a Crushing Defeat</u>
- Episode 5: A Trial and the Tribulations (2019)
- Episode 6: A Deal and a True Story Told (2019)
- Episode 7: A New Empire and An Old Ally (2019)
- Eps 1-3 Omnibus: <u>A Siege and a Salvation from Enemies</u>

**Hand's Assassin** (Age of the Orion War – w/T.G. Ayer)
- Book 1: <u>Death Dealer</u>
- Book 2: Death Mark (2019)

**Machete System Bounty Hunter** (Age of the Orion War – w/Zen DiPietro)
- Book 1: <u>Hired Gun</u>
- Book 2: <u>Gunning for Trouble</u>
- Book 3: <u>With Guns Blazing</u>

**Fennington Station Murder Mysteries** (Age of the Orion War)
- Book 1: <u>Whole Latte Death</u> (w/Chris J. Pike)

- Book 2: <u>Cocoa Crush</u> (w/Chris J. Pike)

**The Empire** (Age of the Orion War)
- Book 1: <u>The Empress and the Ambassador</u>
- Book 2: <u>Consort of the Scorpion Empress</u> (2019)
- Book 3: <u>By the Empress's Command</u> (2019)

**The Sol Dissolution** (The Age of Terra)
- Book 1: Venusian Uprising (2019)
- Book 2: Scattered Disk (2019)
- Book 3: Jovian Offensive (2019)
- Book 4: Fall of Terra (2019)

# ABOUT THE AUTHOR

Malorie Cooper likes to think of herself as a dreamer and a wanderer, yet her feet are firmly grounded in reality.

A twenty-year software development veteran, Malorie eventually climbed the ladder to the position of software architect and CTO, where she gained a wealth of experience managing complex systems and large groups of people.

Her experiences there translated well into the realm of science fiction, and when her novels took off, she was primed and ready to make the jump into a career as a full-time author.

A 'maker' from an early age, Malorie loves to craft things, from furniture, to cosplay costumes, to a well-spun tale, she can't help but to create new things every day.

A rare extrovert writer, she loves to hang out with readers, and people in general. If you meet her at a convention, she just might be rocking a catsuit, cosplaying one of her own characters, or maybe her latest favorite from Overwatch!

She shares her home with a brilliant young girl, her wonderful wife (who also writes), a cat that chirps at birds, a never-ending list of things she would like to build, and ideas…

Find out what's coming next at www.aeon14.com.
Follow her on Instagram at www.instagram.com/m.d.cooper.
Hang out with the fans on Facebook at
www.facebook.com/groups/aeon14fans.

43888367R00183

Made in the USA
San Bernardino, CA
16 July 2019